By MARGUERITE LABBE

Pandora

Published by DSP PUBLICATIONS
www.dsppublications.com

PANDORA

MARGUERITE LABBE

DSP PUBLICATIONS

Published by

DSP Publications

5032 Capital Circle SW, Suite 2, PMB# 279, Tallahassee, FL 32305-7886 USA
www.dsppublications.com

Pandora
© 2017 Marguerite Labbe.

Cover Art
© 2017 Reese Dante.
http://www.reesedante.com
Cover content is for illustrative purposes only and any person depicted on the cover is a model.

ISBN: 978-1-63533-353-4
Digital ISBN: 978-1-63533-354-1
Library of Congress Control Number: 2016915374
Published April 2017
v. 2.0
First Edition published as "Pandora" in the Deep Into Darkness: Aliens, Alphas and Antiheroes Anthology, October 2015.

Printed in the United States of America

This paper meets the requirements of
ANSI/NISO Z39.48-1992 (Permanence of Paper).

For Ayla, who encouraged me to write this story for years, and for Ella,
Elise, Annie, and Kim, who made me realize
it was a sci-fi story the whole time.

Chapter One

The derelict ship twisted in a slow, graceful spiral against the backdrop of a rogue moon. Signs of life remained. Lights flickered near the nose, slanted down as if poised for an endless dive. A stabilizer sputtered, altering the course of the ship's rotation by degrees. Scans had come back negative for dangerous leakage, but it didn't mean there wouldn't be surprises whenever Riff Khora led a recon for a salvage mission.

It was easy to forget how terrifyingly vast the universe was until Riff came across sights like this and was reminded that their salvage ship, though solid and enormous, was only a speck of dust in an immense sea of stars. The derelict, *Pandora*, was reported missing a year ago. All this time it had waited, losing hope in its isolation.

Riff pressed his lips together at the unwelcome pang of empathy. "Any chance of survivors?" he asked, taking a step closer to the porthole.

"Still thinking like a medic, instead of a lifer. You'd think after three years of serving time that would've been scoured away." Captain Vidal stood with his back to Riff, staring out the porthole, hands clasped behind him. His gaze bored into Riff from the reflection.

Riff kept his face expressionless, but the barb stung. Asshole.

Vidal was short, slight, and carried himself as if he were the largest dog in the pack, which he was. A dog with a vicious bite. His hair held more gray than red and was cut with military precision, as exacting as the way he ordered the rest of his life. He had the colorless pallor of a man who spent years away from the warmth of the sun. The blocky shape of his face, the round eyes that saw everything, and the thin-lipped mouth gave him the mien of a humorless, cold automaton.

"All signs indicate no survivors. No one left to argue over my salvage rights," Vidal replied with a hard note of avarice in his voice.

Riff's lip twisted in derision. Of course that was Vidal's sole concern. His rights. His property. Not one thought for the lives lost.

Riff focused on the ship again. The captain's suite was the only place on board the penal salvage scow that had sizable viewing ports. The derelict wasn't large, probably belonged to a rich corporation. A pleasure yacht that had wandered off course and found trouble. Pampered travelers often forgot the dangers of space travel. They only noticed the beauty.

Vidal turned to face him, tapping a riding crop against his leg. His neatly pressed pants, shined boots, and shirt with every tuck and fold in place made Riff very aware of his own nudity. Riff's gaze drifted to the crop and its restless tapping. He longed to feel the bite with an unrelenting hunger.

"Your attention should always be on me." The crop came up and patted Riff's cheek in a move meant to insult. Riff bit down on a hot flush of anger. He'd asked for this. Not for the degradation. He needed the pain, craved it long before he was sentenced here. Then the need took on a whole new life. At least while the whip was singing, Riff wasn't haunted by screams and long-dead faces. But the slights and humiliations from Vidal burned. "Who are you picking for your team?"

"Tuputala, Quinet, Wilt, and Jakobsen." Riff met the captain's cold gray gaze with an insolent stare in return.

Vidal's mouth pinched. His hand sank into Riff's hair and fisted hard enough to make him hiss. Riff closed his eyes, savoring the sting. *Just a little harder.* The captain's hand tightened as he shook Riff by his hair until he opened his eyes, pushing past the pleasure to focus on Vidal.

"Why Jakobsen? He's raw. What makes you think he's ready for a recon?"

"We need a fifth man," Riff replied. "He has a knack for picking apart salvage for what's usable. He has experience as a master engineering mechanic. I want to see how he judges an entire ship." And Zed Jakobsen drew Riff to him on an instinctive level. A reason Riff kept to himself as Vidal studied him.

"On your knees." The command was deceptively soft and uttered with the assurance of a man who was used to immediate obedience.

Riff hesitated, holding out until Vidal's hand tightened again, sending pinpricks of pain over his scalp. Riff caught his breath and sank to his knees. Score one for him in their ongoing battle. It was a dance. When Vidal withheld pain, Riff withheld his submission as they waited for the other to give in first. Theirs was a twisted and perverse relationship of mutual gratification. Vidal got more pleasure out of a willing victim, and Riff used that leverage as much as he could to get what he wanted in return.

"Yes, Captain?" Riff's excitement stirred. If only Vidal would give him a couple of licks before the mission, just enough to see him through until their next meeting.

Vidal used his hair as a handle to pull his head back at an uncomfortable angle. Riff swallowed against a tight throat as he met the captain's glittering gaze. "Try not to lose another crew member," Vidal taunted as he released him.

The swift and cutting unwelcome pain killed Riff's desire with ruthless ease. He looked away, his jaw tightening. It infuriated him to know Vidal got more pleasure out of that blow than any physical one. Riff had no defense against those attacks.

"I accept your reasoning for Jakobsen," Vidal said. "I expect a full report when you return."

A full report, what a cosmic joke. It was an excuse for Riff to see him again. His report would involve him being on his knees, and nothing would be said about the derelict vessel. Vidal would get his information from the detailed reports.

"Understood."

Still aching from the final barb, Riff dressed and left without another word, passing by the two guards at the entrance to Vidal's suite. Another guard, Regina Flaubert, escorted him down to the prep room. Flaubert's long face was expressionless, but Riff recognized the familiar contempt in her eyes. Contempt for a lifer. Contempt for his so-called relationship with Vidal.

"You should be grateful," Riff said in an undertone as they passed through the security separating the captain's side of the ship with the rest. The long, narrow hallway connecting the two sections thrummed from the giant engines underneath. The dim corridor had all of the soft luxury stripped away, leaving bare decking and cold, dark walls with no chance of seeing outside. The prison and workrooms on the other side were even starker. Riff actually preferred the reality to the illusion that Vidal and his crew were any better than their prisoners.

Flaubert glanced at him, the corner of her hard mouth slanting in a sneer. "Why? Because you suck the captain's dick for perks you don't deserve?"

"Because if it wasn't for me and the other prisoners' labor, you wouldn't get that fine payout of yours." Riff sneered, his voice full of scorn. The dig hit, and her eyes flashed. "And if Vidal didn't have prisoners to use and abuse, he'd turn to a guard without a moment's thought. He's god on this ship, and no one would intervene if you complained."

"Lucky for me his tastes don't run toward women," Flaubert replied. The decking clanged under their boots down the long passage toward the second guard station. They nodded her through, and to Riff's surprise she stayed with him when they reached the first of the vast, echoing salvage rooms. There was no need for an escort unless she wanted to keep him from speaking with another inmate or stopping by his cell. Or just to be a bitch and make him feel even more caged.

The salvage room hummed with activity as men and women worked on sorting and repair under the watching eyes of guards. There was always work to do. The routes between planets were littered with the remnants of ships left over from the constant wars, the depredations of pirates, and the occasional ill luck of a breakdown or accident. If they weren't working on cleaning up a mess, they were dismantling the salvageable bits to sell to the highest bidders.

"You believe you're the feudal lord to his god, but you don't have as much power as you think," Flaubert continued. "You weren't able to help Bryce, were you?"

Riff halted and turned a bitter glare on her. "The only reason I couldn't help Bryce is because you and your cronies are the worst hypocrites I've ever had the displeasure to meet. You make my old sergeant seem like Lord Vishnu. One of these days, I'm going to find out who tormented Bryce so bad he felt he had no other way out."

"And when that day comes, you won't do a damn thing about it." Flaubert punched in the access code for the recon prep room and gestured for Riff to go in. "Be a good boy. Take your place."

Riff clenched his jaw, gritting his teeth against his impotency. First the captain, now Flaubert, throwing Bryce's death at him as if he were the one responsible for his suicide. Flaubert was right. There wouldn't be a damn thing he could do about getting payback. Picking at the guards brought temporary relief but did nothing to change the situation or stop the constant bubbling anger. No amount of prayers over his *tulsi mala* eased that anger. He touched the beads around his wrist and told himself he only needed time; Bryce's death was still a raw wound, but he didn't think time would heal this one. The light of his faith sometimes had a difficult time shining through a growing tide of pessimism.

He got to work, examining each evac suit, making sure there were no rips or worn areas where dangerous substances could slip through. His thoughts returned to the problem of the derelict. It still concerned him that the ship hadn't had a chance to send out a distress signal when there was no obvious external damage.

"It's about time we had another one."

Josephina Tuputala ducked as she came through the hatch. Taller than most men, she seemed to fill the small room with broad shoulders and curves. Her jovial round face and the smile lines around her angular eyes were offset by her stoic mask and the uncompromising slant to her mouth. She shot Riff a questioning glance, and Riff jerked his chin toward the diagnostic and tool kits. Tuputala nodded and began digging through them, checking to see if they were fully equipped. She was one of the few people Riff considered a friend, and any chance he had he made sure Tuputala was at his back.

"Recon, salvage, or repair?" Tuputala asked in her quiet, melodic voice. Her long black hair was gathered in a fat braid, bristling with curls that threatened to escape.

"Recon," Riff replied. "But we'll probably need to do some repairs before we can start a full salvage. I'm about to take a look at the scans."

Marty Quinet and Cybil Wilt entered and went straight to work without a word, checking the air tanks first. Quinet sent darting glances around the room with a nervous air, like he saw things no one else did and wasn't happy about it. His lean body, sagging eyes, and the way he hunched made him seem like more of a shadow than a man. Riff found him hard to get to know, but he was a genius with computers.

Wilt tapped him on the arm, commanding Quinet's attention. She was an older woman with spiky, short gray hair, tattoos, a smattering of freckles, and a salty tongue that cut through Quinet's tension as they suited up. The pair did everything together and had been working the recon-and-salvage gig long before Riff took over as team leader. As far as he could tell, they'd never been lovers despite sharing a cell. Other prisoners and some of the guards had issues with their closeness, perceiving it as a threat, but Riff didn't care. They worked well together, and their skills complemented each other. That's all that mattered.

Quinet glanced at the ceiling and a shadow passed through Riff like skeletons dancing on his heart. Then Wilt drew Quinet's attention away with a low comment and conspiratorial nudge of her elbow. No one mentioned their missing team member, but Bryce's presence lingered ghostlike, as if his body still hung from the ceiling. Even Riff found himself looking up and wishing he'd read the signs better or gotten to the room earlier. Maybe he could've done something to save Bryce, and then none of them would be feeling the ache of his absence.

If they didn't need another mechanic Riff would've kept it to the four of them for this first mission without Bryce. He had to have a pair in the engine room, though, and his skills did not run in that direction. Flaubert was right in one regard. If it wasn't for his relationship with Vidal, he'd be stuck drudging it out in the salvage rooms with no chance of leaving the ship for missions, much less leading one. He sure as hell wasn't about to feel any shame for it.

Riff finished checking the helmets for damage and moved to study the schematics and readouts of the ship as they waited for their final team member to arrive. The rest of the crew headed to the transport bay for the preflight check and to load the tools.

The hatchway opened, and Zed Jakobsen hovered in the hallway with an uncertain expression until the guard shoved him inside. Hazel eyes flashed with anger, but Jakobsen wisely held his tongue. He wasn't the handsomest man. His face had a florid cast, and his chin was weak. Those details didn't matter. It was Jakobsen's eyes that caught Riff's attention, such an unusual green and amber. Those eyes pierced through Riff when Jakobsen looked at him. And the expression in those eyes when he'd stepped aboard with the other prisoners, the helpless anger, had called to Riff in recognition.

Riff straightened as the hatchway shut, leaving them alone. He met Jakobsen's forthright, challenging gaze with a rush of forbidden pleasure. He hadn't lied to the captain about Jakobsen's eye for usable junk or his past mechanical experience, but if Vidal knew how much Riff looked forward to another chance for a stolen conversation with Jakobsen, they'd both be in trouble.

"Good to see you again," Riff said.

"I know you didn't call me down so we can ogle each other," Jakobsen said with a pointed look. "I prefer to keep my balls, and I don't think Captain will let me if he hears of us meeting alone."

"We need another team member. I recommended you."

Jakobsen's gaze darkened. "I heard about Bryce. I'm sorry."

"Thanks," Riff replied. Jakobsen said what he meant without artifice or embellishment. As much as Jakobsen excited his senses, Riff found him soothing too, which was a fucking laugh because he'd never been attracted to that quality in a man before.

"So, your turn, Jakobsen. Tell me one thing about you."

"I've never been planetside," Jakobsen said after a moment. "I was born at the shipyards, was schooled there, did an apprenticeship on a freighter, but until now, that was the most traveling I'd ever done."

Now Jakobsen was just another lifer like Riff, and he'd never get a chance to travel. The only escape he could look forward to was missions like this.

"You?" Jakobsen asked, stepping closer.

"Grew up in Bhubaneswar, on Old Earth. Signed on with the Interstellar Marines the day I hit my majority and have never gone back." There had been too much to see, and the Marines weren't keen on letting people go once they recruited them.

"What type of a ship are we dealing with?" Tuputala asked, leading the team back into the room. Riff bit back a swear of disappointment. Another interlude with Jakobsen cut short.

"Looks to be a modified Scimitar-class ship dubbed *Pandora*. Been missing a year. Scans picked up no life signs." Riff brought up the live feed of the derelict, drifting off their portside.

"Jakobsen, you're new to the salvage part of our operation. Meet Joey Tuputala, Cybil Wilt, and Marty Quinet." Riff pointed to each of the crew in turn. Tuputala towered over Jakobsen, making him seem shorter than he was. Wilt nodded an acknowledgment while Quinet looked away, biting the inside of his cheek. "You have any questions or issues, run it by me first. If you give me any problems, you lose your chance on going out on another mission. Do we understand each other?"

"Loud and clear," Jakobsen replied in an even tone. His attention seemed to be more on the screen, which showed the ship spinning, helpless and hopeless in the vacuum. A chill touched Riff's spine. The ominous image captivated him.

"Tuputala, I want you to get the stabilizers and life support running. Jakobsen, if you're done with your look-see, I want you to help Tuputala with repairs. I also want an analysis of what you think can be salvaged out of the equipment, including fuel reserves."

Jakobsen glanced at him, his eyes narrowing, assessing, and a rush of heat went through Riff. It had been a long damn time since somebody had affected him like that. Riff maintained eye contact, and Jakobsen stared back steadily until Riff looked away. Oh yeah, the man got under his skin.

"You'd better know what you're doing," Tuputala rumbled under her breath to Jakobsen as she pulled on her evac suit.

"I've been around an engine or two," Jakobsen replied.

"Just keep up," Tuputala said, fastening the suit before stepping into her boots. "I'm not waiting for you to adjust."

Jakobsen's jaw tightened, but he made no other response as he began putting on his own equipment. He wore his ever-present thin leather gloves and kept them on as he suited up. Every time Riff saw him, he was gloved and swathed from neck to ankles in an oversized jumpsuit. A stickler for safety, Riff supposed. There were worse quirks.

"Quinet, I want you to find the captain's log and see what information you can get out of the ship's computers. Wilt, make an inventory of supplies we can scrounge from the galley. They may have some gourmet protein packs we haven't seen yet." Riff glanced at the schematics, noting the location of the ship's infirmary. He'd head there at some point. He might be able to find some medicine to help with an infection currently running through the weaker inmates. The penal wing held almost two hundred prisoners, a mix of men and women, young and old. There was always somebody who needed care, especially since Dr. Barboza was stingy when it came to doling out medicines.

"You've got it, boss man." Wilt grabbed two helmets and tossed one to Quinet.

"Good. I'm going to check out the hold and will be on hand if any of you need aid. If you run into any bodies, tag 'em and let me know immediately so I can take a look." They might give him the clues he needed to figure out what happened over there.

Jakobsen looked a little uneasy but remained silent. He'd better not get squeamish on them if they did come upon a slaughterhouse. Riff had witnessed too many battlefields and worked in too many hastily erected field hospitals for it to have that effect on him. Those sights weighed on his heart, not his stomach.

"Okay, gather around," Riff said once the team had their equipment on. He enlarged the schematics of the ship. "We'll enter here, near the hold. The more intel we have, the more we can accomplish the next round. Wilt, it's your turn to handle the explosives."

"Hot damn," Wilt replied with a grin and a gleam in her eyes. "'Bout time I get to kick in a door. Mama's coming home."

Quinet smiled and shook his head. "Then I'm on docking duty?"

"Yep." Riff caught Jakobsen's eye. "You ever manually dock a transport before?"

Jakobsen nodded and offered no embellishment as he crowded closer for a better look.

Riff pointed out the significant areas and gave his team a chance to study the layout. "Ready?"

"Ready to get off this damn ship," Tuputala grumbled, a sentiment Riff echoed. They moved fast, both with the ease of long practice, except for Jakobsen, and with the knowledge that for a few hours they'd be relatively free. They'd have to come back to their prison, there was nowhere else to go, but no one would be looking over their shoulders, breathing down their necks.

Riff took his place in the pilot's seat, Tuputala beside him. He fired up the engines and tensed as it rumbled awake. There wasn't much holding the transport together but the prayers of lifers and scavenged equipment. He'd have to swallow his pride and ask Vidal for the supplies to make some necessary repairs, or they wouldn't be making many more trips. It was only a matter of time before a critical element blew.

"What's with the new guy?" Tuputala asked as Riff made one last check to be sure nothing had shaken loose.

"We needed a new mechanic, and I've seen the tech he's managed to dig up and piece together since he's been here." Riff eased the transport out of the docking bay and set it on a course toward the derelict.

"He's short." Tuputala's large brown hands flew over the console, moving with a grace that didn't seem possible given their size.

"A Terran giraffe would be short to you," Riff retorted.

"I'm pointing out you have a type. Short and dominant. I saw that gleam in your eye. Before you think about having your fun on the side while we're off ship, please remember Captain Vidal's not one to share."

Tuputala shot him a significant look for emphasis. "I thought he was going to skin you and serve you up as the mystery meat the last time he thought you were getting a little on the side."

"Good thing I'm not looking." It hadn't been as bad as Tuputala suggested, but it had been bad enough while Vidal had tried to beat the name of the other man out of him. It might've been worth it if Riff had actually been getting some action. Vidal had taken his lack of success with ill grace and ever since regarded new men around Riff with heavy suspicion. Enough reason to stay away from Jakobsen and not act on his attraction.

Riff slowed down the transport, swinging it under the belly of the stricken ship.

"Do you know why he was sentenced?" Tuputala asked, and Riff cast her a sharp look. Tuputala's expression remained impassive. She never revealed her sources, and there were times when it had been useful, but Riff didn't like rumors. It stirred up the denizens of the prison too much. "Or did you decide you don't care because it would interfere with your hormones?"

"I don't want to know anybody's story. They're all fucked-up. I care about what they do after they arrive."

"He tried to kill the Director of the Deneb shipyards."

"At least he didn't succeed. They'd have executed him," Riff murmured, concentrating on the maneuver.

"And it's rumored he's behind his niece's—"

Riff held up a finger, cutting off Tuputala's litany. "Enough. Can you work with him? Because we need another qualified mechanic, and right now he's our best option." Tuputala grumbled under her breath with a curt nod. "Do you think his past puts us in danger?"

"Only if you let him fuck you," Tuputala retorted.

"Don't worry, I'm contemplating monkhood."

Tuputala snickered as Riff studied the derelict. He'd seen many strange phenomena since he'd been auctioned off to Vidal's ship, and this ranked high among them. Whatever crippled the occupants happened fast. Riff slowed the transport and stopped as he located the panel they wanted to blow.

"Wilt, you're up," he called back. "Quinet and Jakobsen, get ready to manually dock us once Wilt has the hatch open."

Riff listened to the team moving about as he ran another scan. Still no traces of anything unusual. A fast-acting illness could've decimated the ship. "It's an interesting puzzle."

"I don't like it," Tuputala muttered.

"Name one situation you have liked." Riff kept an eye on Wilt as she drifted out of the airlock.

"You've got me there." Tuputala rose and hauled out the diagnostic and tool kits. "Want me to see if I can find some parts for this unwieldy bitch of ours?"

"Only if you can manage to get them on board without Jakobsen seeing. Don't worry about it too much. I plan on getting Vidal to let us have what we need. I'm going to see what I can do about some medicines, but until we know we can trust Jakobsen I want to keep it quiet." Riff watched Wilt set the explosives, and moments later the hatchway dissolved.

"We've got entry," Wilt confirmed. "Looks quiet."

"Is that why you stay with Vidal? For perks like that?" Tuputala asked, giving him a penetrating look. "Doesn't seem like it's worth it."

"It's had its benefits." Riff killed the engines and heard the clang of grappling hooks latching on. The small ship shuddered, and the computer confirmed they were docked. "But it's not up to me to end it. As much as Vidal isn't one to share, he's not one to let people go either."

"True enough." Tuputala clapped his shoulder. "See you on the other side."

Riff listened to the team gather their equipment and depart. While everything he said to Tuputala was true, there was more to his relationship with the captain than that. They were trapped by their mutual needs, and he didn't see a way out of it. He supposed that made them both crazy. Despite his interest in Jakobsen, they'd both be better off if he left it unacknowledged, no matter the pull and tug he felt toward him. Fucking Vidal and the deal Riff made with him.

Chapter Two

ZED TURNED and the helmet lamp cut a swath of stark white light through the darkness, illuminating destruction. It revealed smashed equipment, pulverized into tangles of jagged metal and broken cords. Clothing and bedding, shredded and stained, littered the decking. Bloodstains spattered the walls, ceilings, and floors in thick arcs and black blotches that screamed people had died here. Violent, brutal deaths.

Zed forced himself to look closer. Khora considered all intel important. The blood was old, glittering with frost. It had dried in matted pools on the decking, smeared along the floor as if bodies had been dragged or people had tried to crawl away. Everywhere his gaze fell, there was blood. It sickened him, his stomach tight and knotted against the bile that threatened to rise. Never had he felt so far away from the clean, orderly shipyards where he grew up.

It was a small mercy the thin beam of light didn't reveal more details, but it made the rest of the surrounding darkness too dense. Nightmares hid in shadows. Nightmares also wore expensive clothes, ran high-profile shipyards, and terrorized the innocent.

Zed and Tuputala stumbled along, half-blind with only the schematics to guide them through the listing corridors. He tried telling himself they were alone on the ship but still tensed every time they peered around a corner.

"Where are the bodies?" Zed asked in a hushed voice.

"Fuck if I know. Given the slaughter, they should be here," Tuputala replied, her lamp providing more illumination. The light was too bright, too stark, outlining smashed panels and stripped wiring in heavy shadows. "Khora, you find any bodies?"

Tuputala's voice seemed unnaturally loud in this utter quiet broken only by Zed's breathing. He wanted to get to the engine room and work on a problem that made sense. Finding a stack of broken bodies was not what he'd been looking forward to when they embarked. But they had to be somewhere on the ship, and waiting to discover them scraped his nerves.

"No," Khora replied after a long, silent moment. "Evidence of violence but no people. Wilt, Quinet, how about you?"

"No," Wilt replied shortly. "How close are you to the engine room? Some motherfucking lights in this tomb would be welcome."

Zed glanced at the schematics on his helmet screen. "We still have a bit to go. We'll let you know when we arrive."

"I'm not finding any bodies either," Quinet said. "Splitting up was a bad idea. Wilt, meet me on the bridge. I'm almost there. We can worry about inventory later."

"I agree," Khora said. "I'll head toward you after I survey the hold."

Zed angled his body around a corner as the gravity shifted and pressed heavily against him, constricting his lungs and sharpening his nerves. Breathe, slow and steady, he reminded himself, slow and steady to preserve oxygen. The long moaning sound of overtaxed generators struggling to keep the ship alive sent a chill through him.

A light at the end of the corridor sputtered fitfully, casting flickering shadows, tricking the eye into thinking something lurked there. Zed pulled himself up with a grunt, cursing the slope of the decking and the screwed-up gravity field. Restoring life support and the stabilizers was a priority.

The ship had been targeted, but how a raiding party got on board without any external damage was a mystery. Subterfuge of some kind. The urge to touch the walls with his bare hand hit with a burning curiosity. He'd see the lingering psychic residue, the images and emotions that remained. It would give them clues to what happened.

Zed tightened his fist in reluctance. What had been a minor ability, nebulous and undefined when he'd been younger, had grown wild the last few years. Some of the memories he witnessed took a long time to fade from his mind. They left afterimages burned into his retinas, and those images haunted him.

No, his curiosity was not that strong. Besides, he'd learned the hard way that his crazy ability was an excuse to be ostracized. His new teammates didn't need to know what a freak he was. He couldn't take off the glove without decompressing anyway.

At least the evac suit he wore over his clothes cocooned him from the mental barrage with no danger of accidentally brushing against unwanted touches. For the first time in a long time, Zed felt like his sanity was safe. He'd have to get on more missions, anything to escape penal hell and the miserable minds pressing against him. Despite the bizarreness of this outing, the mental silence was a blessing.

"Did you say something?" Tuputala turned toward him, her gaze grim. She was a beautiful woman, though there was a hardness to her demeanor whenever she looked at him.

"No." Zed checked their location and pointed down the corridor branching off starboard. "If the schematics are right, the engine room should be down here."

Tuputala frowned and tapped the side of her helmet, muttering low. They were all on edge. The slanting corridors and half-turned-upside-down rooms warped his vision and unsettled him. He wasn't the only one struggling with bouts of vertigo, judging from the whispered curses he heard from Wilt.

Zed wasn't one for conversation, but the eeriness of the ship made him long for the sound of voices. "I'm surprised the captain didn't send guards with us." Zed grabbed the bar running along the corridor and hauled himself up as the climb steepened. The light continued to flicker as Zed kept a wary eye on a stack of broken junk. A boot broke free and tumbled past them.

"Where would we go?" Tuputala replied, pulling herself up behind Zed. "The suits only have enough air for six hours. The transport isn't capable of long-distance voyages. If we tried to escape, the captain would blow us to hell. The offensive capability of his ship isn't a myth."

That made sense. Why waste manpower on convicts who had nowhere to go? Zed hauled himself through the first of several hatchways. He turned and offered his hand to Tuputala, who ignored him and heaved herself up. The look she shot Zed made his stomach sour. The last woman to look at him with such dislike was his sister. He should've gotten used to being glared at like he was the sludge that gunked up the engine, but it continued to ache.

He quelled the quick flare of temper. Here was a chance to get off the ship and lay his hands on an engine as classy and streamlined as *Pandora*'s. He might never have another opportunity if he screwed this up. All he ever saw in the hold were the leavings after a salvage crew scuttled a ship. He was determined to make a good impression so he'd be assigned to another recon mission. To do that he'd have to win Tuputala's good graces. He'd been on board long enough to know that she and Khora were a team. He'd need their approval to be included again.

Missions would give him peace from the constant bombardment of his mind. The space station had been quiet with little to disturb him. Then he began getting impressions from people too. The memory of his niece still made his gut churn. But coming here, trapped in a cell that had contained violent men and women… there was no escape. He had to find some shield, something to keep him grounded, or he wouldn't last long.

Zed thought about confronting Tuputala and seeing what her problem was, before deciding against it. The last thing he wanted was to draw attention. He was learning that when it came to the other denizens of the prison, actions spoke louder than words. He'd prove to Tuputala he was an asset on the recon team. Still, it rankled to be judged and damned before he'd said more than a dozen words to her.

The guards treated him the same way. That's how they got to everybody. Break them down, make them feel helpless and less than human, then give them a taste of normalcy just to see how much they beg for that again. With a grim smile, Zed turned away. Not him. He wasn't going to play that game. First viable chance he had, he was out of there.

The hatchway to the engine room was half-closed and frozen in place. Zed peered inside, his eyes widening as he realized the extent of the damage. Console stations had been smashed, some barely recognizable after the damage. Pipes had been hacked, pierced, and fluids leaked. Panels had been torn off and wires ripped out, left to dangle against the walls. It was too quiet. An engine room should hum with life and activity. This one barely held on.

"It's bad." Zed heaved himself into the engine room. "We're going to have to erect a normal gravity field before we can work." A bloody handprint stood out on the wall, and the hatchway was marred with claw marks as if someone had tried to scratch their way out.

Zed winced and looked away with a shiver. It would take time to run a comprehensive diagnostic. The casings surrounding the most vital systems appeared to be intact—not for lack of trying, from the evidence of dents and more hack marks. Getting life support online looked more plausible now.

"Attack of the fucking crazies, that's what happened here." Tuputala pushed past him and labored her way toward a console station that was more intact than the rest. "Good idea on the gravity field. Get on that. I'll see if anything is working."

Zed's gaze swept the jumbled surrounding mess, searching for a likely spot that would keep Tuputala within his line of sight. Just in case functions went wonky as they fiddled with systems or a madman jumped out of the lingering shadows. Zed sighed and moved deeper into the engine room. His imagination was all over the place, and for this job he'd need his concentration.

"Do you hear drumming?" Quinet asked over the comm, his voice tense.

Zed strained to listen, but the giant engines were silent except for the faintest hum of energy. The only pounding he heard was his heart. "Quiet on my end," he responded as he knelt down and pulled tools from the kit. He glanced at Tuputala to see her reaction. She shook her head as she made a slow survey of the room.

"We made it to the engine room," Tuputala said into the comm, her voice heavy with suspicion and unease. "It's a friggin' mess. It's been sabotaged, but not by anybody who knows what they're doing. No precision or delicacy of target. Just a furious fit, like a drunk, pissed-off psychotic went supernova with a sledgehammer and an ax."

That fit Zed's assessment. This was destruction for the sake of destruction, just to see how many pieces a thing could be broken into. This ship could've been a huge payload for the captain with little work required beyond towing this beauty back to a port and auctioning it off. Even scuttling it and taking the best parts away would've been easier. Then the captain wouldn't have to share proceeds with any living relatives of the occupants. However, sorting through the dross and mess for decent salvage would be a tedious pain in the ass.

"See what you can do," Khora responded. "Get life support online first. I'm sick of having to half crawl everywhere."

"We'll try, but don't hold your breath," Tuputala replied.

There was a pause and a spatter of static. "I hear the drums too," Khora said. "Must be something in this section of the ship. I'll see what the scans bring up."

Zed frowned, mulling that over as he constructed the gravity field. If Khora was investigating the hold, then he shouldn't be anywhere near Quinet.

A flicker of motion caught his eye. Zed turned his head to catch sight of a lean, long figure slipping around the pipes, heading toward the exit. His heart froze, and his mouth went dry. He seemed almost familiar, but Dray Heller couldn't possibly be on this ship. Zed frowned, pulling himself to his feet.

"Did you see that?" he asked Tuputala, making sure the comm was open just between the two of them. Quinet sounded on edge enough.

"See what?" Tuputala asked, moving into his line of sight with a curious expression.

Zed worked his way through the higher gravity to the hatchway and looked down the empty corridor. He squelched a nervous laugh, trying to banish the sensation of unseen watchers.

"Nothing…. Thought I saw someone slip out of here, moving toward you."

"Reality check, Jakobsen, nobody is moving with any ease in this gravity."

The comment made him feel like a paranoid idiot. Tuputala had a point. There was no sign of life. He wouldn't lay odds on someone surviving by themselves in these conditions for a year. The figure wore no evac suit either, which meant they couldn't breathe. He was letting the evidence of violence and destruction screw with his head.

"Yeah, sorry. You're right."

Zed mulled it over, trying to picture what he'd seen. It wasn't like the visions he received when he touched an object or person. The punch of emotion he got from a sending was missing. This was more like a hallucination.

"Let me help," Tuputala offered, cutting into his thoughts. The unease in her voice echoed Zed's feelings. "The faster we normalize the gravity, the faster we'll feel better. This whole situation is fucked."

It didn't take long to set the field up, and once the pressure eased off his body, some of Zed's tension bled away. "Let's get started on life support," Zed suggested.

"I'll work on that. You run a diagnostic of the engines and other systems. We need to see how much work we'll have to do there." Tuputala's mouth twisted with an expression of distaste, and the moment of camaraderie vanished.

"What's your problem?" Zed demanded, determined to discover the root of her derision. "You're no better than me."

"I don't like kid killers." Tuputala's gaze hardened. "You may know your shit, and Khora might be taken by your pretty eyes, but I'm not. Keep to yourself, Jakobsen."

Zed clenched his jaw on a hot rush of anger to keep from protesting his innocence. The fact that the authorities thought his niece, Hannah, was dead was his best chance at keeping her safe. He'd already been tried and condemned, and his only regret was that he hadn't succeeded in killing Heller.

The members of this team were all violent criminals, a fact he'd have to remember. Though Tuputala didn't have a reputation for causing trouble, she was here for a reason too. They wouldn't believe one word about his lack of guilt.

"You need to get your shit straight," Zed replied in a low, tight voice. "I was charged with attempted murder and kidnapping, not child murder."

"We all know what happens to young girls who disappear, so don't try that shit with me." Tuputala shoved him aside.

"Go fuck yourself, Tuputala," Zed snarled as she walked away. The thought of people judging him because of Heller's sick actions infuriated him. He tried to remember the hell he was going through was for the best reasons. It gave him some pleasure to know that Hannah's stepfather was enraged by Zed's silence. They might have trumped up his charges and given him a shit excuse for a lawyer, but Heller would never be able to touch Hannah again.

Zed turned his thoughts from those painful memories and focused on Tuputala's comment about Khora as he worked. Relationships had been scarce after he discovered his abilities had expanded to include people. Touching had become uncomfortable except for with those who he knew the best. And most wouldn't desire his touch if they knew what he could sense. It had wreaked havoc with his sex life.

He had to admit Khora stuck out in his mind with his fierce and sensual appearance. His shaggy black hair and heavy brows deepened the dark brown of his eyes. He had a slashing scar above his prominent nose, his skin had a rich golden tone. The intelligence in his gaze intrigued Zed the most, along with his cool public demeanor that clashed with the flashes of warm camaraderie that Zed witnessed with the other team members. He'd caught moments of that when they were alone together and shared tidbits of their past.

Despite the attraction, he needed to keep a distance. Khora managed to remain the captain's favorite fuck for years and, as a result, wielded a considerable amount of power in the penal wing. Khora was not a man to cross. Zed had to consider the captain too. He'd never met the man, and from the rumors he didn't want to.

Zed focused on the diagnostic. It didn't take him long to realize that most of the destruction was surface. The shield around the engine core was intact, which explained the lack of leakage. He didn't think they'd have a chance of getting it back online soon, though. Whoever did all this damage had probably been hoping for a breach that would lead to a meltdown, but they didn't get far enough.

He sent the diagnostic to the rest of the team, then went to investigate the backup generators. He drummed his fingers on the wall as he examined them. One was dead with a broken spar driven into the center. The second was fine, probably could do with a tune-up, but for the moment it was working. The third struggled, the casing shaking as the motor moaned and a rhythmic knocking started up.

Zed frowned and crouched for a closer look. "Tuputala, I'm going to shut down one of the generators for a look-see. Sounds like it might need some parts swapped out. If I can get it fixed, that should give you the juice you need to get life support online."

"Keep the comm open," Tuputala responded. "There's something screwed up going on here."

"Roger that." Zed cut the power and got to work. A couple of parts had burnt out, but he was able to strip the broken generator for new ones. As he began to replace them, the generator started knocking again, the sound escalating to a deep, booming drum. Zed fell back with a startled shout, and as quick as it came, the sound disappeared, leaving his heart beating rapidly.

"What's wrong?" Tuputala called.

"Didn't you hear that?" Zed replied, crouching in front of the generator. As far as he could tell, the parts were bolted down tight. Nothing should have made that sound.

"All I heard was you screaming like a bitch."

Zed's jaw tightened. "Kiss my ass."

"Do I need to separate you two?" Khora cut in. "What the hell happened?"

"Nothing," Zed replied shortly as he tightened the replacement capacitor in place. "I thought I heard the drumming too. But it's not possible, especially if Tuputala didn't hear it. I'm fine." Last thing he needed was Khora thinking he couldn't hold his shit together.

"I'll run another scan to see if there's anything evident that might cause hallucinations." Khora sounded doubtful, not that Zed blamed him. He didn't know of any substance that could seep through their suits so quickly to cause symptoms like that. But there had to be an explanation. Uneasiness stirred as Zed locked the casing back over the generator. What if they'd all been exposed? "How close are you two to getting life support online?"

Zed turned the generator back on, and it hummed gently. "You've got power, Tuputala."

"Give me a moment," Tuputala muttered as Zed gathered his tools. "Let's see if this works. Hold on to something, boys and girls."

A light tremor went through the small ship, and the generators next to Zed whined. He eyed them warily until they settled into a normal rumble. "Fuck me," Wilt replied happily. "We've got gravity, and I can hear the air ventilators coming on."

"Pressure's normal throughout the ship," Tuputala said. "How are the generators holding?"

"Good for now." Zed grabbed his tool kit. "I'll check on the engines."

"What was that?"

Zed jerked his head up at the alarm in Tuputala's voice. He scanned the long row of pipes and conduits, but other than the broken materials and tools scattered on the ground, nothing was amiss. He moved closer until Tuputala came into view. She was studying the engine room, her stance tense. Zed looked around as well, not sure if he'd rather see someone and justify his earlier sighting or not, because it made the sense of being watched even stronger.

"Was it a lean figure?"

"No." The word was drawn out uncertainly, confused and saddened. Tuputala shook her head and turned back to what she was doing. "It's another impossibility. We're all seeing and hearing things," Tuputala said, her voice gaining confidence. "If we keep this up, we're all going to be jumping at every shadow and machine knock."

Zed wanted to believe her, but the weight of all those missing souls on the ship got under his skin. He tried telling himself it didn't matter how they died. The captain was only concerned about salvage. He tried to tell himself he didn't give one damn about any rich corporate types. They sure as hell hadn't shown him or his niece any consideration.

Telling himself didn't help for jack shit. They'd been people who left behind loved ones. Even if he couldn't pass along any messages, at least he might have an idea of their fate. It should be safe now with life support on. Zed turned his back on Tuputala and gently worked the gloves off his left hand. A broken pipe, old blood and hair matting one end, lay nearby. Zed crouched, hesitated, and then brushed his fingertips over the clean end.

Rage. Hate. Violence. Lust. Fear. Emotions slammed into Zed, stealing breath and sight. He fell back with a cry, shaking and nauseous as he curled his hand tightly against his body. He tried to grab a hold of the fleeting images that came with the emotions, but they slipped away tenuous and undefined.

"Fuck, Jakobsen. What the hell?" Tuputala said. "What happened this time?"

Zed shook his head, reaching for his gloves, his heart pounding a frenzied tattoo. His shaking made it difficult to get the gloves back on, much to his intense frustration and dismay. Images began to seep through the shock of emotion. Swinging the pipe. Hitting again and again into a body long dead. Pummeling almost like a need for sexual release.

Kill. Kill. Kill.

His stomach lurched, and Zed squeezed his eyes tight. He fumbled, searching for the talisman he wore under his suit that he used to ground himself. He pressed the threaded bolt into his skin and used the discomfort to shove the images and emotions away. Shoving it deep into that box in his mind and latching it tight. The coping mechanism didn't take away the memory, but it took away the bite and immediacy.

"I'm okay," Zed rasped around a tight throat as he finally got the gloves on. He needed to sink into a puzzle, tinker with the engineering problem so he could forget how fucked-up humanity was. "I just need to get back to work."

"If you weren't working, then what the fuck were you doing?"

"Checking out something." Zed left it at that. There wasn't any way he could explain without making himself sound crazier. To his relief, Tuputala left it alone. Zed turned to the engine core, but his heart still pounded like a drum, the sound sinking rhythmically into his blood, jarring him. And the images, God help him, the images still burned in his mind.

"We've got a body." The tense surprise in Khora's voice jerked Zed out of his trance. "Some kind of hibernation unit. Holy fuck, he's still alive. I need everyone in the infirmary now. This has become a rescue mission."

Zed straightened in shock. "I thought there were no life signs," he said to Tuputala.

"Hiber units don't always get picked up. Vitals are suppressed. And if there's only one person in hibernation, as opposed to the whole crew, that would make it even harder." Tuputala pushed away from a console, slipping a gyroscope component into her kit. "Damn Khora's rescue complex. Captain's not going to like this if it doesn't get him paid or he has to split the profits."

"You've got to be fucking with me," Wilt replied. "Is that a good idea?"

"You let me worry about Vidal," Khora retorted. "Just get your asses down here. I'm going to need help getting this bitch on board, considering the state the ship's in."

"Come on," Tuputala said gruffly. "Might as well go see what Khora's dug up."

Zed stared at Tuputala's kit, trying to get another glimpse of what she'd stolen. It would be hard to fix systems as it was without members of his team yanking intact parts. He was sure the captain expected to sell every piece scrounged. Zed doubted the part Tuputala slipped into her kit was going to wind up in the salvage hold. And it didn't explain what Khora was doing in the infirmary when he said he'd be elsewhere. If he'd landed in the middle of some black-market ring, his ass was on the line. Zed cursed inwardly but followed Tuputala without a word.

All of that was easier to contemplate than what had happened on the derelict. One thing was certain: he'd have to watch his step. First chance he got, he'd get a reading on everyone with him, his conscience be damned. Survival didn't work for the squeamish.

Chapter Three

RIFF PUSHED the hiber unit into the infirmary with Jakobsen's help. The guards, useless fucks that they were, loitered near the entrance and did nothing. Riff had left the rest of the team behind to take care of getting the transport settled and seeing what they could do for repairs. He hoped Tuputala had time to find parts they could use that they wouldn't have to beg Vidal for. He wouldn't be feeling generous, given the condition of the derelict. He'd been looking forward to the possibility of a whole ship to sell, not what they could salvage.

Dr. Barboza was absent. Typical, considering Riff had sent him a message. He checked the vital signs on the hiber unit and noted they were still strong, so there was a good chance they'd get some answers when their sleeper awoke. Riff would have to glean those answers from the captain, but that wouldn't take much effort. Vidal loved to talk once he got started.

"Everybody seems to think you're going to get in trouble for rescuing him," Jakobsen said.

Riff glanced up to meet that piercing gaze, savoring the rush of heat and want. Yeah, it was definitely the eyes that got to him and gave Jakobsen a rare kind of beauty. The demand in that gaze that wouldn't accept his unspoken question being ignored made Riff's knees weak. He couldn't give in to the desire, but it was damn nice to feel a genuine tug toward another man again.

"Probably not. That yacht was rich. Captain Vidal will make sure we strip what we can. Plus we'll get a reward for picking our sleeper up. Somebody will be willing to pay good money for his rescue." Riff glanced to see if the guards were looking, then tweaked the machine, steadying the oxygen level. "This is an expensive personal hibernation unit. The occupant is either the captain or the one who owns *Pandora*."

Riff straightened from the hiber unit and turned his attention to Jakobsen. Enough odd things happened over there that he wanted a feel for the whole picture before he made his report to the guards.

"So this person you thought you saw on *Pandora*, what did they look like?"

"Tuputala told you about that?" Jakobsen narrowed his eyes. "Did she also tell you she saw something too?"

"Of course, I like to know everything that happens when I run a mission," Riff replied, crossing his arms. Not only did Tuputala admit to it, but Wilt swore she heard the drumming, and Quinet wouldn't talk at all. He kept gnawing his knuckle and muttering under his breath.

"It's nothing. Like she said, there's no chance it could've been anybody. I guess I was jumping at shadows. It was eerie over there." The way Jakobsen's eyes slid away made Riff think he was holding back. "Don't we have to report in somewhere?"

"You don't strike me as the imaginative type, and you're not new to being off planet. So you're not likely to get jumpy on a ship despite what Tuputala said about your screaming. Humor me." Riff cast a quick glance at the hiber unit again as the vitals fluctuated. Looked like someone would be waking up soon all on their own. The unit must've been programmed to reactivate if it was moved. Riff was reluctant to leave it behind unattended. So much could go wrong at this stage.

"Nothing much, just got a quick glimpse of a lean man. But it was just an impression. Doesn't matter because nobody but a ghost was going to move fast in that gravity. The engine section had twice the normal amount." Jakobsen peeled off his ever-present gloves and stuck them in the pocket of his jumpsuit, looking uncertain.

It seemed like Jakobsen might've gotten the clearest image. Riff had seen things too, flickers out of the corner of his sight, but when he turned, they were gone. He'd heard the drums, though that seemed to be more in his head. It had been faint… almost a whisper of sound. He'd only commented on it to calm Quinet down. If they hadn't had the suits on, he would've thought it was something in the air that affected them all in varying ways, but every single test he ran, every air sample he took came up negative.

"Have you seen or heard anything unusual since we returned?" Riff asked.

Before Jakobsen could respond, Dr. Barboza entered the infirmary with an expression of perpetual disgruntlement. He was an older man with sparse mousy hair and deep lines etched into his skin. His bulbous nose bore a map of broken capillaries, his complexion was sallow, and there were other signs of a lifetime of dissipation on his face.

"What are you doing with my patient?"

"We just brought him in here." Riff refrained from mentioning the occupant's vitals or the condition of the hiber unit. Barboza wouldn't appreciate any comment from him. At best he'd have to endure another lecture about his natural state and where he belonged. At worst, well, Barboza could be a real prick.

Barboza shot him a suspicious look and shoved him away from the hiber unit. "Get out of here. You know I don't like you in my infirmary."

"Fine, I'm leaving." Riff held up his hands and backed off. He caught Jakobsen's eye and motioned toward the hatchway with a jerk of his head. No sense in both of them being targeted by Barboza's bias against lifers. "Try not to send him into a seizure as you wake him. A little sobriety might help."

Riff made it to the entrance with the uneasy sensation of Barboza's gaze on him. It had been months since he'd last given Barboza a reason to take a swipe at him. Riff should've waited outside the infirmary for him to arrive. Territorial did not even begin to describe the doctor, and if he was in a mood, he'd make up trouble.

"Wait. Guards!"

Riff swore under his breath, and Jakobsen froze. "What the fuck is going on?" Jakobsen asked out of the side of his mouth with a hard look in Riff's direction.

"A personal vendetta. Nothing that concerns you." Riff held up his hands as the guards abandoned their indolent pose and bracketed him. "I thought you wanted me to go," he said, raising his voice and glaring at the doctor over his shoulder. "Did you confuse yourself? Brains still addled from your last binge?"

"Search him for contraband," Barboza ordered. Riff sneered. He wasn't that much of a fucking moron. He'd never bring it in the infirmary. Then he remembered how the doctor brushed up against him a moment ago and a chill went through him. He might've had a chance to slip something in his pockets. Riff wouldn't put it past him, and there was no way to check.

"We kept an eye on him. He didn't pocket anything, but he did hover over the hiber unit," one of the guards replied as they searched him.

"Take him to the captain and tell him the prisoner was endangering my patient by messing with equipment he doesn't have the faculties for. And make sure he didn't swipe anything during his recon. Check his cell."

Jakobsen opened his mouth, and Riff shot him a savage look. He didn't need or want his help. If he was going to go down because Barboza wanted to start some shit, then he was going to go down swinging and get in a few licks while he could. Barboza would not be the one to dictate when Riff received a punishment. Riff determined that, and it wouldn't be because Barboza felt peevish and threatened. Riff would earn this beating.

The guards patted him down, one of them searched Riff's pockets without success. That, at least, was one small relief. The other one took liberties Vidal wouldn't tolerate if he'd seen.

"A little to the left like you mean it," Riff said, and the guard's eyes flashed in warning.

Jakobsen grabbed the guard's arm and shoved him away, angling his body in front of Riff. "Why don't you go back to diddling yourself in the morgue, you sick fuck." The guard blanched as if there was truth behind Jakobsen's barb.

"You know, Barboza, you're the biggest dickless fraud I've ever seen. You wouldn't know medicine if it crawled up your colon and spawned babies." Watching Barboza's eyes bulge brought immense satisfaction. "You're no damned doctor. You flunked out of school. At least I know what the fuck I'm doing. You know what they say about you behind your back?"

A stern hand clamped over his mouth, and Riff stared in shock at Jakobsen, who gave him a grim look in return. Well, that took balls. Riff had to give him that. He quieted at the unspoken command, promising himself he'd take it up with Jakobsen later even as a fresh rush of heat hit him hard and fast. Jakobsen's eyes widened, then narrowed, an answering heat warming them.

The guards seized him, though to Riff's cynical amusement they were careful not to deal out damage. Oh no, had to leave that pleasure to the captain. "You want to try that again, Jakobsen? Maybe when they're not holding me down?" Riff called with a laugh as he was wrestled back and dragged away.

He kept his gaze on Jakobsen, who watched him go with a puzzled expression. Riff still felt the pressure of his fingers over his mouth, and it made his blood hot and savage. He would love to get him alone to see if that had been a protective move or if there was a dominant side under his quiet reserve. He itched to know what he'd find if he started peeling back his layers.

Vidal was on the bridge, so the guards handed him off to Flaubert. She shoved him toward Vidal's favorite room with its manacles and floggers, the hard benches and stocks. "Strip and clean yourself up. You stink, Khora."

"Sorry honest work offends your nose." Riff shucked out of his jumpsuit. He slipped the *tulsi mala* off his wrist and tucked it inside his jumpsuit. Depending on Vidal's mood he might take it from him as a further punishment, and Riff didn't want to risk that even though his wrist felt bare.

Since Vidal wasn't there, he was given a bucket with a small amount of very cold water and a rag. Riff wiped the sweat off his body, already anticipating the encounter with Vidal. He was sure to punish him for mouthing off the way he had, and Riff made no attempt to disguise his aroused state.

"I didn't realize spreading your legs was considered honest work."

"It sure as hell isn't illegal." Riff shot her a grin as he tossed the rag back in the bucket. "You should try it sometime. Maybe you wouldn't be so uptight."

Flaubert's mouth hardened into a thin line, and she grabbed the bucket as Riff found a comfortable spot to wait against the wall. "I expect he'll be a while," Flaubert said with pleasure in her eyes as she shut the hatchway. Riff heard the locks engage, and then the room was plunged into darkness.

Panic seized his throat, and Riff pressed his fist against his mouth to keep from making a sound. She was listening, waiting for him to beg for the lights to be turned back on. He closed his eyes, breathing slowly in and out, trying to quell the bubbling, boiling fear. It didn't help. It never helped. When the darkness pressed on him, he could hear the screams. Screams that made him want to weep. Screams that made him remember a savage pleasure even as he was sickened.

Riff tried to move, tried to crawl his way toward his clothes so he could get to his prayer beads, but his limbs were as frozen as the mantras to Vishnu were on his lips. The ghosts came back in the dark, roaring their fury and pain in his mind. Riff thumped the back of his head against the padded wall in an even rhythm to drown out the memories. The steady beat reminded him of the drums he'd heard earlier. Only there was nothing steady about that sound—it had been wild and seductive, abandoned and sexual. Riff sank into the memory of that sound and let it drown out the screaming.

Thump. Thump. Thump.

Riff's hands joined in, beating out a rapid, wild pattern on his knees. It reminded him of the hard rhythm of fucking, the harder rhythm of beating a man to death, knowing the best place to land punches for maximum pain and damage. Riff jerked himself out of the ensnaring thoughts, his heart racing, his mouth dry, and his body aching with unfulfilled need.

What the fuck was wrong with him?

Lights flicked on, and Riff flinched, raising his hands in front of his face. "Ahhh, Riff, you were doing so well. I thought you learned your lesson the last time," Captain Vidal said.

Riff squinted at him, and his heart froze. A different man stood in the hatchway, a big man with lank brown hair and flat, vicious eyes.

"You're dead." Riff shook his head, trying to dispel the image.

The man stopped his approach, uncertainty flickering in his eyes, before he smiled. "No," he replied in the wrong voice. "But when I'm done with you, you're going to wish you were."

Rage exploded, and Riff leapt to his feet. "You're dead!" He rushed the man, hands outstretched to throttle. He'd make sure of the job this time. Better the man was left as a ghost to haunt him instead of alive and unpunished for his crime.

"Guards!" the man shouted as Riff grabbed him. He closed his hands around the man's throat and squeezed with a jolt of sick pleasure that made some corner of his mind scream in denial. A hard blow caught Riff's jaw, snapping his head back, and then another hit him between his shoulder blades. As darkness fell over him, the man's face wavered, then became Vidal's again, staring at Riff in shock and fury. "Strap him down...."

Riff woke to the splash of cold water on his naked body. He cried out in shock, lifting his head, trying to shake off the disorientation. His arms were stretched above him and back. The straps shortened so he had to scramble on his toes to relieve the aching in his shoulders.

"Now that you're awake, we can get started," Vidal said in an inhumanly wintry voice.

Riff tensed, and a cold sweat broke out on his skin. He'd attacked Vidal. What the hell had he been thinking? He never let himself lose control around the man, no matter how much he was provoked. He wasn't sure how long he'd been trapped alone in the dark. Long enough for memories to surface, though he didn't know how he could've mistaken Vidal for a dead man.

He looked over his shoulder to be sure he wasn't losing his damned mind. There was Captain Vidal in all of his short, prissy glory, though a little mussed with his hair awry and the collar of his uniform ripped open. Two bright spots of color stained his pale cheeks. The relief Riff felt to see Vidal, instead of a dead man's face, weakened his knees. He sagged against his bonds, his shoulders burning from the contorted position. His jaw throbbed, the air was cold against his wet and naked skin, but at least those sensations were familiar.

"Who am I?" Vidal circled around him as Riff steadied himself as best he could on sore toes.

"The captain," Riff replied shortly.

The blunt handle of a flogger lifted his chin. "No, I'm *your* captain."

Riff stared into eyes as cold and merciless as the vacuum of space. Riff hated him, needed him… needed that demand in the captain's gaze. Only it was so wrong because Vidal wasn't the right kind of man. He fulfilled only a small part of what Riff ached to have. He tried to gauge how much groveling and pain it was going to take to appease him and decided he didn't give a fuck anymore. The faint echo of those drums still sang in his blood, spurring him to act on how he really felt instead of playing out this tired game.

He moved his chin away, and Vidal's eyes flashed at his defiance. The heavy flogger flicked Riff's thighs, hard enough to make his breath hiss out. "And what are you?" Vidal asked in a softer voice.

"A man," Riff replied, trying to figure out Vidal's new angle.

"No, you're not a man." The lashes struck his ass this time, harder, leaving bright burning lines of pain on his skin. Riff jerked, pulling on his arms, awakening twin fires between his shoulder blades. "Try again."

"A lifer," Riff said shortly. "You think that's supposed to bother me?" Riff wasn't sure if the captain was trying to get him to admit he belonged to Vidal, but if that was the case, he'd have to beat it out of him.

"You're a killer." Vidal moved back into his line of sight. "You murdered your lover." There it was, the stab and twist that cut so deep the bleeding never stopped. Vidal knew where to hurt him. The other men he'd killed didn't matter to him, they didn't weigh on his soul, just the one. Didier Laurent.

Riff steadied his expression, determined Vidal wouldn't see he'd gotten the blow in, but from the slow smile that crossed the man's face, Riff knew he hadn't succeeded. "Now that we understand each other, let's discuss your attitude with the good doctor." Vidal lifted the flogger.

Riff clenched his jaw, and pain lanced through it. This was going to be a long damn night if Vidal started with his peeves. Trying to speak in his own defense would do no good, so Riff kept silent. Pointing out that he'd found a possible payload for Vidal wouldn't work until he was ready to hear it. Riff just had to ride it out and not show his fear. It was one thing to anticipate the lash, it was another to know he'd gone too far, and now Vidal was free to do the same.

"Then we'll discuss you daring to lay hands on me," Vidal said, his voice going deadly soft. He went to the cabinet and selected his most vicious whip, one that would flay Riff's skin open with each strike. Riff bit the inside of his cheek to keep from making a sound, but it didn't stop the fear from clawing at him. Vidal laid the whip on a table in front of him, so he'd constantly be reminded of what was coming, and picked up the flogger again.

The first blow caught him across his back, hard enough to twist Riff to the side and knock him off-balance. Riff grunted and pressed his lips together, his hands tightening around the straps on a rush of pain. He focused on the sensation, let the burning fill him, and savored the pleasure that came with it. In the beginning, he'd hung on to his memories of Didier, the sound of his voice, the sureness of his touch, the warm and stern way he'd look at Riff. Those memories had faded over the years, and the only thing that Riff could remember clearly was the sound of his screams.

The next strikes caught around his hip and ribs, laying new lines of fire, cutting through Riff's memories. He groaned, the pain and heat bringing to mind a newer memory of a hard hand over his mouth and intense hazel eyes demanding silence. Desire sparked. Would Jakobsen be ruthless when he wielded the whip like Vidal, or would he be different, catering to Riff's soul as much as his body?

Want and need filled him with every strike until he was hard and aching. The blows stopped, and Riff turned his face into his arm with a groan. He hurt from his jaw down to his toes. His heart hurt from the emptiness inside. Still, desire made his head swim, his blood beat rhythmically until he longed to be filled. He didn't even care if it was Vidal.

"What is this?" Vidal tapped Riff's hard cock, making him flinch. "Who are you thinking of to get so excited this early in the evening?"

"You," Riff replied, meeting his gaze, willing Vidal to believe him.

"Liar." Vidal wrapped his hands around Riff's throat, constricting slowly, cutting off his air. Riff gasped, trying to pull back with no leverage to help him. Fear filled all the empty places. Vidal was still enraged about the attack, looking for any excuse he could find to break Riff. This was the last time. Vidal was done with him. Riff was going to die tonight.

Vidal's grip tightened. The need to breathe overrode every other thought. His lungs screamed. Black spots flickered over his vision, and then the pressure was gone.

"Who is it?" Vidal snapped through the haze. He lashed out with the flogger, scoring Riff's chest and thighs in several fast, flickering strikes.

Riff dragged in painful, gulping breaths. "It was you," he rasped. "Knowing how much trouble I was in. Not knowing if you'd stop. It excited me." He hung his head as if in shame. Please let Vidal think he was that fucked-up.

"This will determine if you're telling the truth." Vidal picked up the whip he'd left on the table, and Riff's breath strangled in his bruised throat.

"I swear I am. I belong to you," Riff choked out. He tried to inch back, but there was no room with his limbs already strained. The ache had spread from his arms and shoulders down his back and up from his feet to seize his calves. "Please, don't."

"We still need to discuss how sorry you are for attacking me. Believe me, you will be very, very sorry." Vidal dragged the whip along Riff's back, and he turned his face into his arm again. Vidal was going to kill him. Despite everything, Riff wasn't ready to die yet.

The first blow bit into his skin and caused Riff to lose his balance on his toes. He clenched his jaw against a scream. The painful bleeding burn of the mark made the other ones seem like itches in comparison, but it wasn't as bad as what was going to come. Riff braced himself for another crack. He wouldn't scream. He wouldn't…. Though it was a losing battle before it started. Vidal would rip those screams from him.

"Captain Vidal, please excuse the interruption." The nonpadded wall flickered, a screen coming to life as Riff found his perch again on trembling, cramping toes. He lifted his head and stared at Barboza's smirking face.

"Dr. Barboza, we were just discussing you," Vidal said with a sharp flick of his wrist. Riff pressed his lips together as the whip scored a fine line on his thigh. "This had better be good."

Riff permitted himself a small smile as Barboza's smirk faltered under that silky, menacing tone. If there was one thing Vidal hated, it was to be bothered when he was alone with Riff. Barboza's fear was a little pleasure, but one Riff hung on to nonetheless. He had nothing else to sustain him to face the hours ahead.

"My patient is awake." Barboza's gaze flicked to Riff. "He wanted to meet you."

A person stepped into view, pale and lean from long-term hibernation, with deep-set features and platinum-blond hair swept up and away from his face. The wide brow and cheekbones contrasted sharply with the narrow chin and full lips, giving him an androgynous look. The way he looked at Riff with a hunter's gaze made him shiver.

"Captain Vidal, I'm Noyes," he said in a deep velvety baritone, turning his gaze from Riff to the captain. He looked pretty hale for someone who just awoke from hibernation, without the usual signs of disorientation or dehydration. "I appreciate all the assistance I've been offered." He focused on Riff again, making him acutely aware of his nudity. "This is the man who rescued me?"

"He's one of the team that did," Vidal responded.

"I hope he's not in trouble for that," Noyes said in a smooth and sensual voice.

"Not at all. Riff has trouble controlling himself, and I'm teaching him restraint." Vidal patted his flank, and Riff clenched his teeth against the sudden wave of hate. "He can be a stubborn one."

"I would like to sit down and discuss recompense with you," Noyes continued.

Vidal loved their sessions together, but he loved a payday more. Riff prayed for a respite that he didn't think would come. The pressure of Vidal's fingers still bruised his throat. His hand settled on the nape of Riff's neck, squeezing until Riff whimpered.

"I'd be happy to meet with you. This can wait for another time." Captain Vidal rubbed the top of Riff's head like he was a dog. Riff closed his eyes as relief outweighed humiliation. "Let him down and bring Noyes to my dining room," he ordered the guards.

Riff groaned and fell to his knees as the straps were loosened. He lowered his arms, the muscles burning and his back stinging as sweat trickled into the lash marks and scores. "Riff, do try to stay out of trouble? And make yourself available to me first thing in the morning."

Riff pressed his face against Vidal's hard thigh, trying to get a hold of his conflicting emotions. Vidal was letting him go? That defied belief. Of course, it only meant he had longer to stew in his own outrage and paranoia, unless the reward from Noyes put him in a better mood.

"I'm sorry," he said in a low voice, and Vidal squeezed his shoulder—whether in acknowledgment or threat, Riff didn't know.

"You'd better pray to your gods that what you brought me makes up for the stunt you tried to pull," Vidal whispered back. "If I'm not a significantly richer man...."

His whole body aching, Riff pushed himself to his feet and grabbed his jumpsuit with one last glance at Noyes. Strange. Why hadn't there been a distress beacon? Noyes had enough time to get to his hiber unit, but not enough time to send out a basic call? The unanswered questions gave him something to think about other than his appointment with Vidal in the morning.

The mystery of the derelict didn't make sense. Riff wanted answers, and he wanted to hear them firsthand. But trying to finagle a way to stay behind tonight would be sheer idiocy. An intelligent man would get out of there and hope the captain's ire cooled. Despite the curiosity nagging at him, Riff got dressed and left before Vidal changed his mind.

Chapter Four

Zed stared at the ceiling of his cell and contemplated his current situation. Quinet, Tuputala, and Wilt booted him out of their little conference after he'd reported what happened to Khora. He hadn't even had a chance to touch one of them and get a reading, which was probably just as well. What he'd received from Khora had been enough. He'd never be able to think of the man the same way again.

Zed couldn't get that expression in Khora's eyes out of his head, that absolute lack of fear as he was dragged away. The man was crazy. He had to know there would be trouble with the way he'd talked to the doctor. What Zed had received when he'd touched Khora had been frustration and scorn toward Barboza and hot anticipation for the beating to come. The flickers of memory told him that it hadn't been Khora's first confrontation with the doctor or punishment from the captain.

It wasn't just the lack of fear that Zed couldn't forget. It was the heat and promise in those near-black eyes. When that gaze had focused on him, eyes wide with shock over Zed's action, frustration had collapsed under a blast of sexual hunger so strong Zed's body had immediately reacted, tightening with a deep, aching desire. If there was ever a man who needed a keeper, it was Riff Khora.

Even now, the memory hit him on a visceral level. It had been a long damn time since he'd had any pleasure beyond that of his own hand. Khora gave Zed something to think about other than the nightmare of the last year. Khora intrigued him on an elemental level. He was also as forbidden as they came. You didn't mess with the captain's man, no matter how much he'd managed to dig himself into Zed's thoughts. Khora better make it through the night with his skin intact.

Henrick whimpered in his sleep on the bottom bunk, the sound of a cornered and trapped child. A sound that evoked memories Zed never wanted to think of again.

He kicked the bunk. "Cut it the fuck out."

The whimpering ceased for a few minutes of blessed quiet. Then Henrick began drumming his heels against the bulkhead. Zed rolled off his bunk, driven by the need to do something other than obsess over Khora in his thoughts and to escape his cellmate's unquiet distress. He glanced at Henrick as he pulled his gloves out of his pocket. The man's eyes were wide open, pupils dilated impossibly wide as he continued to kick in a pounding rhythm.

A chill touched Zed. He couldn't see Dr. Barboza making cell calls if Henrick was sick. He slid the gloves on and shook his cellmate. "Henrick. Snap out of it."

Henrick grabbed his arm, his grip painful and his gaze unfocused. "Where's my stepdaughter, Zed? Where's Hannah?"

Zed jerked his arm free, breathing hard, his heart racing. "What the fuck did you say to me?"

An image flickered out of the corner of his eye, but when Zed turned to look, it was gone. He glanced back at the bunk only to find Henrick fast asleep. Zed groped for the threaded bolt he wore on a thong around his neck and gripped it in his fist. The guards had confiscated it many times, but it was easy to find bolts and bits of leather to make a new one once he'd attuned it to himself. It gave him something to focus on when he felt like he was drowning.

He was losing his goddamned mind. Too many visions of other people in his head, too many minds in an enclosed space.

Zed needed to wash up and relax. By this time the steam rooms should be quiet, just the way he preferred it. His boots rang on the metal deck as he made his way through the honeycombed, claustrophobic section of the penal wing where they slept and lived. Most of the denizens had their cell hatches open and were lingering in one of the common areas before lockdown. He'd been harassed when he first arrived, but after a couple of fights and the leverage he'd gotten from learning secrets when they touched him, the majority had backed off.

No sounds came from the steam room, much to Zed's relief. There were fewer chances he'd brush up against anyone. The memories from the floor and walls were bad enough. He stripped, bracing himself before he put his bare foot on the floor. Crisscrossing impressions of myriad men and women washed over him, too many to sort through and nothing strong enough to stand out. Zed grabbed the bolt again, squeezed it in his palm as he ignored the onslaught.

The flood eased back, the whispers quieted to a soft ever-present hum. He tossed his jumpsuit in the bin and grabbed several threadbare towels. Quick flashes of the man in the laundry room hit him, a familiar face with quiet, dull thoughts. The impression of him was everywhere. On the jumpsuits, the bedding. He tended to whistle to himself while he worked, catchy tunes that Zed found himself mimicking at odd times.

He quickly washed in the basin provided, wincing at the shocking cold of the little water he was given. Then he went to the small, often-forgotten chamber in the back corner, wrapped one of the towels around his waist, and stepped into the billowing steam.

Khora was stretched out on his stomach on one of the benches, his head pillowed on his arms, his eyes closed. The shock of meeting him after dwelling on their last encounter brought with it remembered heat. He was all tight, wiry muscle from his stocky shoulders down to taut calves, with one of the most spectacular asses Zed had the pleasure of seeing naked in a long time. Whip marks old and new marred Khora's back, thighs, and side. Zed pressed his lips together and his jaw tightened, but there was nothing he could do about Khora's relationship with the captain.

"You going to stand and stare or take a seat and relax?" Khora asked.

"Good to see you're still alive." Zed draped a few more towels on the floor and bench opposite him before sitting down. Familiar images of the laundryman going about his routine hit him and then faded. "You had me worried."

"Not as good as it feels to be lying here still alive."

Khora opened one eye, then shifted, making no effort to hide his slow perusal of Zed's body. Zed draped a towel over his shoulders and leaned back against the wall, heat settling into his bones that had little to do with the steam rolling over him. He studied Khora in return. He liked the look of the whipcord-hard body with so much pride in every line of him.

Zed couldn't figure Khora out. He was a stern leader, had a tongue on him that flayed a man's ego, and a sensual side that begged to be challenged. He would've thought Khora was too intelligent for the deliberate goading Zed had witnessed earlier. And there was no doubt in his mind that it had been deliberate and not done because of a temper.

Zed figured his initial impression of sensual and fierce was dead-on, only cubed. Attracted or not, Zed wasn't sure Khora was the kind of man he wanted to pursue even if he was unattached. He'd be a handful, but oh, the temptation. Zed had touched him once, had a glimpse of his mind and heart, and he'd never been so enticed to take a second touch ever since his abilities had expanded.

"A ball gag would do wonders for your life expectancy," Zed said. And maybe some rope. Khora would look exceptional bound and made to wait for what he wanted. The thought of those eyes on him in expectation hit Zed with a punch of lust. He could only imagine the torrent of words that would escape Khora's lips once he let him talk again.

Khora's gaze darkened as an amused smile crossed his lips. "You think you can gag me?"

Zed's pulse jumped and his breath quickened at the challenge in his voice. This was pure insanity. Khora was off-limits in every way. "I think you're looking for someone to try," Zed taunted back, and Khora glanced away. "But I'm not interested in games."

"I'm not looking for a game either, just a fuck," Khora said with a rebellious quirk of his lips.

Damned if Zed's cock didn't react by jumping to full, aching attention. Khora's gaze dropped lower, and those sensual lips parted. It was enough to make a man's brain short-circuit.

"I thought you would've gotten your fill with the captain," Zed replied.

Khora belonged to Vidal. The man's marks were all over him, and fuck these new protective, possessive instincts toward Khora.

Khora's features tightened, and he gave Zed an insolent look as he shrugged. "We were interrupted. Probably for the best. He's going to kill me the next time he sees me."

Zed couldn't tell if Khora was joking or not. The offhanded way he said it implied a joke, but the thin line of his mouth was far grimmer.

"For rescuing the frozen man or for mouthing off to the doctor?" Zed asked. "Seems a little extreme to me."

"No… no…." Khora looked away, lost in thought, his face drawing into worry lines. He rubbed his brow. "You did well on the ship, kept your head with all that weird shit going on. Despite what Tuputala said about your screaming. We all were jumpy."

"So does that mean I'll be allowed back on the team?" That was a relief. From the way the others looked at him, he had worried he'd be left out of the next recon. If anybody had the final say, it would Khora. Even if they'd been exploring a haunted tomb, it had been such a weight off him to escape for a short while, to get his brain engaged on familiar problems instead of rehashing why he was in prison or fighting off the echoes of other minds.

"Any reason why you shouldn't be?" Khora asked with a pointed glance, and Zed wondered what Tuputala had told him.

"No," Zed replied honestly. "Unless I'm only there because you want me as your plaything when the captain's not around."

"You're on the team because I like your instincts," Khora retorted. "Having you around to tease is just a bonus."

Khora was a tease all right. "Unlike you, I don't have a death wish," Zed replied.

Khora's gaze turned serious. "We're all going to die sometime. I want to live in the time I have left."

Zed mulled that intriguing comment over. "Is that why you go to the captain? To feel alive?"

"Among other things."

Zed looked over the marks on Khora's body. It had been such a long time since anybody tempted him as much as Khora did. But this was ground he'd never crossed. It was one thing to have thoughts of bondage and control and something else entirely to handle a man like Khora.

"I don't know a damn thing about domination or dealing out pain, if that's what you want."

"You strike me as a fast learner."

"Sorry, Khora, not interested."

Khora's eyes narrowed and he shrugged. "Your loss." He stretched out on his back on the bench and half closed his eyes. He was semiaroused, his cock lifting up slightly from between hard thighs. Zed knew he should stop looking, but he was having a hard time pulling his eyes away. There were older whip marks on his chest, stomach, and thighs.

"Why?" Zed asked, gesturing to Khora's body.

"Because it feels good." Khora slid his hands down his lean stomach, his body damp from the steam.

Zed was pretty sure there was more to it than that, but Khora didn't seem inclined to provide more explanation. What would it be like to dominate a man like Khora, proud and complicated with so much hidden beneath the surface? Mysteries he'd had a brief taste of. Zed thought of him with the captain, wondered if Khora ever fully submitted to him, and experienced a rush of jealousy.

Zed lay down on the other bench and closed his eyes to get the naked view of Khora out of his head. His balls ached, making it hard to do. From the sounds of Khora shifting, he was finding it difficult to settle down too, despite the comfort of the damp heat. The steam rooms were one of the few pleasures the prisoners were given.

"Have you seen anything strange since you came back from the ship?" Khora asked, his voice thoughtful.

Zed's hands curled into loose fists. One too many times he'd turned to see a flicker of motion out of the corner of his eye, the slipping away of a familiar form—sometimes his sister, more often Hannah skipping away with a light laugh. Then there was that strange episode with Henrick.

"Maybe," he admitted after a long, tense moment. "Why?"

"I did too, but I wasn't sure if it was a side effect of being locked in the dark," Khora said softly. "I heard things too. Drums. Have you heard the drums?"

"Can't say that I have. Not since the ship." Zed glanced over to find Khora watching him with a restless, hungry look in his eyes, and the desire that had started to wane returned full force. He remembered how it felt to have his hand over Khora's mouth with him looking at Zed with such heat. He vividly recalled the hot punch of Khora's emotions washing over him. "What do they sound like?"

"Sexy… sensual…." Khora's hands slid down to his thighs. "It throbs in your blood."

As if Khora's words conjured them, Zed caught a fragment of sound, a wild, heady rush that burned through him. He shook his head, banishing the music. It wasn't like a vision, it came from within him. "What did you see?"

Khora shifted, a slight circling of his hips, so erotic Zed found it suddenly difficult to think. "Right now I'm seeing you pinning me to the steam room wall and fucking me senseless," Khora breathed.

Zed could picture it, too, his hands locked around Khora's wrists, his body blocking Khora from escape as he pounded into him. He'd bet Khora was as vocal during sex as he was any other time. Bossy, sassy mouth. His gaze lingered on Khora's lips.

Zed frowned and shook his head again. It helped clear his thoughts, though it did nothing to stop the unfulfilled ache. He brushed his fingers over the bolt around his neck and shifted to make sure he was still on the towels and wasn't inadvertently touching the bench itself. He was sure the room had been used more than once for trysts.

But the emotions came from him, pure desire and want, not at all influenced by the imprints left by other men. The way Khora looked at him with those hot dark eyes didn't make it easy to think rationally. If Khora wanted to risk the captain's wrath, who was Zed to argue against it? Even as he had the thought, it felt wrong, and Zed stopped himself from going over to him.

Khora didn't seem to have the same restraint. Zed sat up as Khora rose and came toward him. "Khora, wait a sec."

"Why?" Khora asked as he straddled Zed's half-naked thighs. "The only people we owe anything to is ourselves." He hovered over Zed, not touching him yet, and that was almost more potent than the actual physicality because it made Zed crave it more. He braced himself for the dual sensation of Khora's physical and mental touch. "You want me." Khora's fingers danced along Zed's shaft, making him gasp. "And I definitely want you."

Zed's heart pounded as he stared up at Khora. The touch had been electric and carried impressions of other sexual encounters, too fast to read, but all had been hot and willing. "Yeah, I want you," Zed admitted, trying to get his brain to work. "But not like this. I don't share well."

A quick, sad smile crossed Khora's lips. "You have the most incredible eyes," Khora murmured, lowering his mouth so that it barely brushed Zed's. "I want to get lost in them."

Zed slid his hand around the nape of Khora's neck and gave in to temptation. Khora's lips were hard and firm, and they parted eagerly for him. Zed straightened from his slouch against the wall and slid his other arm around Khora's waist, hauling him closer, kissing him deeper. The urge to take him, to make him forget about the captain, overrode his thoughts. Their tongues tangled, and Khora moaned, a hard shudder raking through his body as he melted against Zed.

Impressions came hard and fast. Surprisingly most were memories of Zed, working at the salvage tables, his expression intent. Zed coming aboard the penal ship, furious and bitter. Zed with his hand on Khora's mouth. Khora remembered that moment very clearly, and it fired him up.

"Yeah, just like that." Khora smiled against Zed's lips and nipped the lower one hard enough for it to sting. "I knew you had it in you."

Zed stared up at him, his senses reeling, his body aching for release. The steam rooms were in the farthest corner of the ship, everybody was occupied, nobody would know if he bent Khora over this bench and gave him exactly what he was begging for with those blazing greedy eyes and roaming hands that teased him into full-on need.

He kissed Khora again, claiming, taking, and Khora's mouth softened as he lowered himself to perch on Zed's thighs. He stroked Zed's cock, hard tugs that had him burning to feel Khora's lips there, to feel him suck him dry as he thrust into his mouth. More impressions came, the taste of Khora's intelligent, quick mind, the depth of his empathy… so much more that Zed let flow over him unexamined. With Khora it didn't feel intrusive, more like a quiet kinship that fit into place, allowing him to focus on the physical.

Zed gripped Khora's ass, felt the raw welts against his skin as Khora arched and rubbed against him with a hiss. "Yes," Khora panted, tearing his mouth away. "Please, make it hurt good."

Zed pulled back with a jerk, sucking in a deep breath of steam-laden air as common sense returned. This wasn't the kind of ship where anybody could hide a secret for long. Especially if they went at it with mindless rutting.

"Khora, hold up."

"Why?" Khora dragged his smooth cheek along Zed's stubble. "Got someone else who'll get jealous?"

"No, you do," Zed replied and was cut off as Khora kissed him again. Fuck, the man could kiss like a demon possessed. He pressed Khora back and turned his head to evade his mouth. Khora was covered in another man's marks, from bruised wrists and throat to fresh whip marks. The captain had started something and not finished it, and Khora didn't seem to be in any kind of a state to think clearly. They'd both pay the price if they got caught. That, at least, was one clear reading from Khora. The man might not care if he got the hide flayed off him, but Zed sure as hell did. And he refused to be the cause of Vidal tearing into Khora more.

"Khora, I'm not playing this game."

"You were playing it fine just a moment ago." Dark eyes glittered with frustration. "You started messing with me right back."

"Well, now I'm stopping it," Zed replied, tightening his hands on Khora's hips.

Khora squeezed Zed's cock, making him gasp as pleasure hit him with stunning force. "Seems to me your body is saying something else. You don't want to fuck me, fine, doesn't mean we can't take our pleasure other ways."

Khora slithered off his body and knelt between Zed's thighs, his gaze wicked and full of promise. Zed had never been so tempted by an unspoken promise in his life. He stood up and moved away before Khora could touch him again. He couldn't deny he wanted Khora. That was obvious. But when he made the decision to have him, if he made that decision, he wanted to be thinking clearly.

He turned his back on Khora and walked a few steps away, trying to calm the heat racing through his body, but it was damned difficult when the image of Khora on his knees was playing in his mind. Instead, Zed focused on the other images that flickered at him. Men relaxing in the steam. Men arguing. Men doing exactly what he longed to do with Khora at that moment.

"Zed." A hand touched his shoulder, a slow, sensuous slide down his arm. At that moment, Zed understood him. He could read him clearly. Khora would tempt and tease and push until he got exactly what he wanted or until someone made him stop. Zed turned around and shot Khora a look that only made those tempting lips curve more. Heavy black lashes lowered in a totally false expression of meekness. He took a step closer. "Kiss me again."

Zed grabbed Khora's biceps and pushed him back against the wall with hard hands. "No," he said firmly. "It's not happening tonight."

Khora's eyes widened a fraction as he tensed. Zed sensed incredulity, stung pride, and underneath deeper emotions that Zed didn't get a chance to examine before Khora wrapped pride around him like a shield that rebuffed any attempts to read him deeper.

Khora studied Zed for a long moment and then relaxed. "Okay."

Zed searched his face to see if Khora was fucking with his head again, but the heat was gone, replaced with Khora's usual cool control.

"Let go of me, please."

Zed released Khora's arms and took a step back. "Another time," Zed said. "When our heads aren't so screwed up. When we can be sure we're safe."

A quick bitter smile crossed Khora's lips as he grabbed his sodden towel off the bench and wrapped it around his hips. He shot Zed a look, weighing, measuring. "Yeah, sure, see you around."

He slipped out of the door as Zed sat back down on his bench, trying to will himself to calm down. His body ached with unfulfilled need. He wanted Khora, wanted him bad. And what intrigued him more was that moment of Khora's obedience.... What would it be like to have him like that... to be worthy of mastering him?

He'd had thoughts like that before, though never explored them even if he'd always been dominant in bed. But he'd never met a man like Khora before either. His hand slipped between his thighs, touched his aching cock, and then he stopped himself. He wanted it to be Khora's touch when he came, and if Khora didn't get any ease, then Zed wasn't going to either. He couldn't believe he was contemplating fucking the captain's man. That had to be sheer insanity.

Zed lay back, trying to decipher that look in Khora's eyes. *Yeah, sure, see you around*.... The words echoed in his head. What if Khora hadn't been joking when he said the captain was going to kill him? Zed hadn't taken it seriously because bidding for a lifer like them was expensive, and Khora worked hard for the captain above whatever he did for him when they were alone. He couldn't see the captain killing Khora for mouthing off to the doctor, but there had been a certainty in Khora's eyes that worried him. Khora didn't seem like the kind of man to blow things out of proportion.

He sifted through the memories and impressions he'd received from Khora. There were few beyond surface thoughts. Some people had stronger natural shields than others. There was one of Captain Vidal.... Zed had only seen him once, and it was interesting to view him through Khora's eyes.

Khora was cold, wet, and naked, stretched out in a painful position, and the furious expression in Vidal's eyes as he stared at him made Zed shudder. He felt the hand close around Khora's throat.

"Wait, Khora," Zed called out after him and opened the steam room door. The cooler air in the rest of the chamber slapped against his skin. The room was empty; Khora had already changed and left. Zed heard a commotion out in the hallways, the sound of shouts and fighting. "Khora?"

Zed grabbed a fresh towel and wrapped it around his hips as the noise of a brawl intensified. A man screamed in agony. What the fuck? He padded toward the hatchway on quiet feet, sensing the echo of Khora passing before him.

The sound of drums struck, a brutal pounding inside his head. His brain exploded with pain. Zed cried out and stumbled against the wall as his towel dropped to the floor. Images assailed him as a man fell into the room, a scarlet slash across his throat, his eyes wide with panic.

He froze, staring in horrified fascination at the blood. This was real. This wasn't a memory he'd picked up. Zed was watching a man die in front of him.

His thoughts flashed back to Hannah's stepfather. Everything would go back to normal if Dray Heller died. That thought overrode everything else. Zed stepped into the corridor, searching the fighting, clawing men and women's faces for a familiar one. A barrage of ugly emotion slammed into him. Rage. Hate. Bloodlust. Zed clutched his head.

No… he was supposed to be looking for someone. For a fleeting second, dark eyes filled with pain banished the fever that had taken hold of him.

Then a man stepped into view at the end of the hallway. He was a lean man, with platinum hair, alien features, and laughing eyes…. The drums returned. Everywhere Zed looked, Hannah's stepfather laughed at him.

"Once you're out of the way, you can't protect her anymore," Dray mocked.

Rage flashed through Zed. He reached for the first Dray with throttling hands.

CHAPTER FIVE

SANITY RETURNED in dribbles of half-lucid thoughts. Those brief flickers of consciousness brought the scent of dried blood and bloating flesh rotting in the stale air. They awoke the pain that stabbed through Riff's body. The temptation to sink back into madness, to let the sounds of distant drums, wild music, and piercing screams take over, to become part of the chaos again and its dancing obscene figures, won more times than Riff could count.

But the sanity always returned, and finally, with a start, Riff came to full clarity in a silent cell. The memory of hazel eyes hard with irritation first in his thoughts. It was never quiet in the penal wing, not even in the middle of the night. Snores came from the cell beside him, grunts and distressed whimpers from farther down the corridor, the continuous hum of the ship's engines. Never a silence this pregnant with foreboding.

Riff smelled the carnage around him, and it made him reluctant to open his eyes. He didn't want to see it as well. Seeing it would make it real, and fear was a living creature inside him, screaming to get out. Sharp pains stabbed his wrists, and his body ached with numerous bruises.

He had vague memories of a strange man with short near-white hair and bottomless eyes. They'd found him in a hiber unit on the derelict. The only sign of life on the entire yacht. Riff's salvage team had rescued him and taken him aboard. Noyes. Yes, that was the name.

The memories afterward were even hazier. A confrontation with Vidal. Another with Jakobsen. Rioting. Quick flashes of violence and lust, of hurting and being hurt, taking and being taken, all mixed in with that insane music. Even now he could hear the drums in the rapid beating of his heart, hear the reedy instruments in the whistle of his breath through a broken nose.

What happened to them, to the ship… or was he just hallucinating and Vidal had gone too far with his sadistic pleasures? He'd been ready to kill the last time Riff had seen him.

Riff forced himself to draw a deep breath despite the stench. This wasn't him. He didn't let fear rule him. He had to assess the situation, calculate how bad it was, then make a plan. Otherwise he'd be trapped here, a broken, terrified mess, and he'd deserve whatever punishment came his way.

He opened gummy eyes, wet cracked lips, and lifted his head. The mattress tilted crazily off the narrow bunk, and his hands were lashed to the metal frame. His wrists were lacerated and swollen from fighting the bindings. Dried blood caked his arms. The remains of his jumpsuit hung off his body in shredded rags. His skin was marked with bruises and scratches. Though his nose pulsed with pain and his wrists were raw, he didn't seem to have any other broken bones or serious injuries.

Riff twisted around on the listing bed. Nausea rose in his throat as he saw what was left of another prisoner slumped over on the floor, his face bashed in. A body in a guard's uniform had fallen across the hatchway entrance, his head and shoulders keeping it from closing. *Tulsi mala* beads were scattered across the cell, some stuck in drying blood or mixed in with other broken belongings. *Oh fuck.... What happened?*

He lay back down to block out the image and struggled to draw another calming breath. Racking his brain didn't help. It only awoke fragmented memories that gave more nightmares than answers. He strained to hear anything else in the silence, but it remained quiet. At least life support was still online in this section of the ship. That was the only positive, but it was one that Riff clung to for strength.

He gritted his teeth against calling out for help. No telling who or what might answer. His skin crawled at the thought of being in here any longer, trapped with the dead. Riff wrapped his hands around the leather thong that bound them to keep it from biting into his wrists even more. He pulled with all of his strength as he twisted his body and kicked at the bent frame at the same time. He must've been doing this in his delirium because the bar his hands were tied to was already loose.

The rhythmic kicks echoed and clanged through the emptiness, and Riff cringed with each loud bang. Until he got his hands free, he was helpless, and judging from his torn clothing and aching body, he had not been successful in staving off other attacks. He listened for any indication he'd piqued someone's interest with his struggle. Hooting laughter echoed down the corridor just as the twisted bar came free with a shriek of metal and ping from a bolt zinging across the cell to bounce off the hatchway.

Riff lowered his aching arms to his chest and panted through a dry mouth. He was free. The relief made him weak until urgency spurred him on again. Free maybe, but his hands were still hampered, and he'd alerted something out there. The laughter hadn't lessened, but it hadn't come any nearer either.

Riff rose, ignoring telltale aches in his body, and limped over to the guard. Bile burned in his throat as a pallid eye stared up at him. Riff fell to his knees and fumbled at the guard's belt for the knife that most of them carried. He'd take every little blessing he could find in this nightmare. He fumbled with the knife, almost cutting himself before he managed to slice through the tightened knots. Riff examined his wrists, probing the edges of the ridged flesh. The lacerations were deep in some places, though the worst of the bleeding had stopped. He'd have to make his way to the infirmary first and see to wrapping them and setting his nose.

Memories flitted through his head, half-formed and confused. Violent thoughts, and Riff clutched his head as he got sick in the corner, dry heaving as nothing came up from an empty stomach. He wasn't insane. He was lucid, not hallucinating. Maybe for a brief time he had been, but he wasn't now. Whatever chaos had infected their system, it was gone.

Riff couldn't do anything about those memories. He was too damn afraid that if he examined them closer he'd go crazy again. Whatever evil deeds he'd committed during that time of madness, he would pay for them in his next life. Right now he was more concerned with survival.

He wiped his mouth on his sleeve and, after a moment of debate, grabbed the guard's gun, still clipped in its holster. It looked as if the poor sod hadn't even tried to defend himself. Riff checked the other body and identified Pitzen by the crazy overgrown mole on his hand. Well, that was hardly a loss, and Riff didn't want to contemplate what he'd been doing in his cell.

Once again the prison filled with silence, broken only by his harsh breathing that seemed too loud. There had to be somebody else alive. He couldn't be the only one. At this point he'd even welcome seeing Vidal. Panic clawed at him, and ruthlessly Riff shoved it away. He refused to believe he was alone.

Riff's skin crawled as he stripped out of the ragged remains of his jumpsuit and pulled on the dead guard's uniform. It strained across his shoulders and exposed a good inch of his ankles. Not the best fit, but at least it was mostly whole, and he felt more human clothed.

His gaze fell on the scattered fragments of his prayer beads, and his heart twisted. He knelt, pulse skittering as he counted and gathered, combing his cell until he found every last one. He counted them again and closed his eyes with a heartfelt prayer of relief. *Om Namo Bhagavate Vasudevaya. I bow to the Lord who lives in the hearts of all.* He poured them into a pouch he made out of the remnants of his jumpsuit, tied it closed, and shoved it deep into his pocket. He'd find a way to string them together again once he found a safe place.

Riff slipped out of the cell, the gun nestled in his palm. The ground was littered with the remains of mattresses, clothes, and smashed personal items, signs of the madness that had infected the ship. He averted his eyes from the gruesome scenes of cracked furniture and broken corpses in the cells near him as he passed. All he found were bodies of the dead or those who were whimpering out their last breaths with a mad gleam in their eyes. Too many faces he knew. People he'd cared for. People he'd tried to shelter in this hellhole.

The laughter started again as Riff came across one of the small common areas. He froze in the entryway, his insides gripping on a fresh wave of fear. A guard crouched near the remains of a table, swaying side to side on his heels as he laughed. He was covered in bite marks and scratches. Laughter ceased as the man's head snapped around, and he pinned Riff with a glare. His eyes were glinting, crazed. A patchy beard had grown in. Several days must've passed, because Vidal was too prissy to allow that. Riff touched his own face and found it rough and itchy. How long had they been under the influence of the madness?

"I know you," the guard crooned. He lifted his hands, dirty fingers stiffened into claws. "Captain's whipping boy. I'll flay the skin right off your bones."

"That's okay. I think he's first in line for that honor." Riff raised his gun as the guard straightened. If he backtracked to the last corridor, he might—

With a shriek that raised the fine hairs on Riff's skin, the man rushed him, hands raking and clawing. Riff attempted to dodge out of the way, but the guard moved impossibly fast and slammed into him.

They went down in a tangle of limbs as the crazed man tried to bite Riff like he could chew through him. Desperately, Riff squeezed the trigger, the guard jerked to the muffled pops, and the howls stopped. Breathing hard, Riff shoved the body off him. He yanked the gun from the guard's belt, trying not to consider the thought he might be the only sane man on the ship.

Tuputala, Wilt, Quinet… Jakobsen. What happened to their team? None of them were in their cells, and he hadn't found any evidence of them among the bodies. Riff forced himself to move along with growing urgency. He couldn't help without supplies and more information. The longer he lingered in the prison, the more dread weighed him down.

The hatchway between the penal wing and the rest of the ship was wide open. The dread didn't abate as Riff made his way to the infirmary in the dead silence. There were fewer signs of violence on this side of the ship, but there weren't as many people packed into a confined space either. Possessions littered the floors in a jumbled mess, torn apart, pissed on, and bloodied in a twisted reminder of the derelict. Bodies left behind had been destroyed to the point Riff couldn't identify most of them.

He wished he couldn't imagine doing that to another human being, but the fragments of his past continued to haunt him, along with the very real recent memory of being so enraged, so wounded the only release was to pummel the object of his fury until they couldn't torment him any longer. Riff closed his eyes as bile rose up again. He recited a mantra under his breath, fingering the pouched beads in his pocket, until the horror receded from his mind.

The sound of panicked struggles came before Riff reached the infirmary. He drew the guns and listened intently until he was sure it was only one person making the noise. Still, he didn't put away the weapons as he edged closer. He had yet to find someone both alive and sane. The amount of carnage on the ship didn't leave him hopeful.

The sound ceased as the hatchway hissed open. Riff froze, heart pounding as he waited to see whether he'd spooked the person or if he'd alerted a crazy predator. His hands on the guns tightened, his fingers hovering over the triggers as sweat popped out on his brow. It was all he could do to control his breathing.

The infirmary was in shambles. Medicines, needles, and bandages mixed with blood and worse on the floor. Diagnostic machines had been destroyed, bashed beyond any chance of repair. Riff scanned the mess, seeking out what could be fixed or salvaged. They might need the equipment.

No one lurked in the immediate environs, waiting to spring. Riff nudged a body on the floor without a response. He looked like he'd been slashed to death. Riff thought he recognized him as the galley supervisor. Someone else had been making all that noise. Someone with enough wits left to them to be wary of anyone wandering around. If Riff had still been tied to the bunk, he would've gone quiet too at the sound of someone approaching. He could only hope that the sudden lack of sound implied sanity and not the wiliness of a monster sensing prey coming close.

"Who's there? Do you need help?" Riff couldn't stop himself from calling out in a soft, urgent voice. Waiting predator or not, he was desperate to find somebody, anybody, still alive, still sane.

This time the sounds that erupted were filled with pleading, with relief, the familiar muffled, wordless sounds of a gagged man. Riff moved toward the curtained area where the noise came from, the guns held steady in his hands as he kept them raised.

"It's okay, I'm coming. Keep it down. We don't want anyone else to hear."

The muffled cries subsided into whimpers, then to quick breaths as he struggled to contain his panic. Riff stepped around the curtain, his eyes widening at the sight of a man strapped down, naked on one of the exam tables. A bloody swath of bandages covered his head, leaving just his nose free.

Zed Jakobsen. He'd know that naked body anywhere. Those sick bastards. Riff tightened his hands into hard fists as he rushed over to his side.

"Jakobsen, it's me, Khora. I'm going to uncover your mouth first. Don't start screaming. We need to keep quiet." Relief made Riff's hands shake as he holstered his guns. To talk to someone again, after who knew how long…. It had started to feel like he was the only one left in the world. He found a pair of bandage scissors hanging out of a spilled-open drawer, then paused before he cut the wrappings. "You're not in any pain, are you? These aren't on for a reason?"

Jakobsen shook his head and made another small pleading sound in the back of his throat. Riff patted his shoulder. "I hear you, just give me a minute." He cut one end and gently unwound the strips of bandages.

Jakobsen's mouth was revealed first, and Riff's breath rushed out in an angry hiss at the sight of his lips sewn shut with crude stitches.

Jakobsen tried to open his mouth to talk and began making panicked sounds again, straining against the straps holding him down. Riff was grateful he hadn't freed him first.

"Calm down, or you're going to hurt yourself," Riff said, amazed at the steadiness of his own voice. "Looks like a real sick bastard got a hold of you, but there's no sign of infection. I can get these off. Just keep still, can you do that? Nod if you understand."

Jakobsen nodded his head jerkily, and Riff looked around for the supplies he'd need. He returned with what he'd gleaned out of the mess and, miraculously, a clean blanket to cover Jakobsen's hips. Contusions purpled his fair skin, but he didn't seem to have any other immediate injury.

"This may sting, but it shouldn't be too bad."

Jakobsen didn't make a sound of protest as Riff snipped and tugged. When the last stitch was cut, he made a choked sound. "Oh thank God," he said with fervent, heartfelt relief in a voice rusty from screams locked in his throat. "My eyes, please Khora, my eyes."

"Let me take a look at them. Stay still," Riff soothed, though his heart sank. He didn't want to see what the insane sadists had done to this man's eyes. "You know, I'd been fantasizing about you naked, but not quite like this," he said in an attempt to make Jakobsen think of something else. Not that he wanted to remember the humiliating incident in the steam rooms, but they didn't have a lot of interaction to go on. Strange to have such a normal thought amongst all the chaos. Strange and a relief.

"I'll bet," Jakobsen rasped. "I'm pretty sure your fantasies involved you strapped down instead of me."

Riff thought of how he'd woken up, trapped and helpless, with a shudder. "Not anytime soon." Jakobsen quieted as Riff spread a thin layer of antibiotic ointment over lips that appeared stung, emphasized by the reddish stubble. "You're lucky there isn't an infection," Riff replied. "Do you know how long you've been like this?"

"I have no idea," Jakobsen replied. "I don't know anything. What day it is. How this happened. I can only remember snatches and pain."

"Same with me." Riff unwrapped the rest of the gauze, and his mouth set in a grim line. Jakobsen's eyes had also been sewn shut. Not as bad as he feared, considering the other things he'd seen, but bad enough. There was evidence he'd been bleeding from his nose and ears, but it looked like that had stopped a while ago. He'd have to find a working scanner to be sure there was no internal bleeding or injuries to his brain.

"What's wrong? Why can't I see?" Jakobsen asked with a raw edge to his voice.

"Wait, don't try to open your eyes. You'll just hurt yourself. I can help. Be still. Trust me." Riff frowned as he leaned in to look at the crude stitches. The skin around the eyes was so delicate, it wouldn't take much for Jakobsen to tear it and cause permanent damage. It made him sick to see it.

"Stop hedging. If you want me to trust you, then tell me what the fuck is going on," Jakobsen demanded.

"Same thing as your mouth. Your eyes have been stitched shut," Riff said, keeping his voice calm. "It doesn't look like there's been any actual damage. I was once a field medic, so I know what I'm doing." Riff waited until Jakobsen calmed down and his own hands had steadied before he picked up his tools again. "So please, trust me."

"I don't really have much of a choice now, do I?" Jakobsen said with a rough laugh, though it didn't quite disguise the thread of unease in his voice. He took a deep breath and then stilled. "I'm sorry. Okay, ready whenever you are."

"I'll free you as soon as I get these stitches off. Try to stay as still as possible." Riff snipped the first thread, then gently pulled it free, holding his breath. The skin was even more reddened and irritated than around his mouth, but once again there wasn't any infection.

As soon as he tugged out the last stitch, Jakobsen's eyes popped open. Those stunning, intense hazel eyes were even more beautiful because they were totally rational.

Jakobsen blinked rapidly, relief flooding through his expression. "Oh thank God. I thought I was blind. I thought I was stuck here forever until I went stark fucking mad."

"There's enough of that going around. I'd rather you didn't." Riff peered closer at his eyes. They looked as good as they could be, considering how he'd found Jakobsen. He hadn't realized how young Jakobsen was—he couldn't be older than his early twenties. His lips were swollen, covered in pinpricks, and there were deep shadows and more angry pricks around his startling eyes. "How do you feel?"

"Like I've been through fucking hell and back." Jakobsen tugged on the restraints and gave Riff a significant look. "I don't suppose you'd care to let me go now."

The words were mild. The tone and the expression in the man's eyes was anything but. Riff hesitated, wary all over again as he searched for signs of insanity. Until he remembered what it had been like to wake up bound and helpless. He couldn't leave Jakobsen behind to try to tear at the bindings like a trapped and wild animal.

As soon as Riff reached for the first strap, Jakobsen relaxed, taking deep, even breaths. When his hands were free, he sat up to tear at the straps around his ankles.

He shook, convulsively rubbing his wrists and ankles as he shuddered. "Oh God. I thought I'd never be free. Fuck. Thank you. It's not enough, but thank you."

"Don't start hyperventilating on me. Deep breaths again. You were doing well a minute ago. Don't freak out on me now."

"I'm not going to freak out," Jakobsen snapped. He clutched his head, then began grabbing things, holding on to them for a second before releasing them. "There's something wrong with me. It's quiet."

"What do you mean it's quiet?" Riff didn't like the frenzied way Jakobsen kept touching things, almost like he was blind.

"In my head. It's quiet in my head." Jakobsen clutched Riff's shirt, his eyes squeezed shut like he was trying to listen.

Riff frowned. Maybe there was damage to his ear drums, or he could be talking about the silent engines. A mechanical engineer would pick up on that, especially one who had grown up on a space station. Or maybe he meant the drums. Then Jakobsen began to laugh, and Riff's concern increased. What if he'd been wrong and Jakobsen was as crazy as everyone else?

But then his gaze met Riff's, and all Riff saw was a profound relief. "It's quiet. For the first time in so long, it's quiet."

He didn't offer any more details, and Riff decided answers for that mystery could wait until they were safe. He scrounged for something to clean around Jakobsen's eyes, nose, and ears. As he stopped in front of him, Jakobsen's gaze softened.

He touched Riff's chin, gently tilted his head to the side. "We need to see about your nose."

"I will in a minute," Riff replied, moving his head away. As attractive as he found Jakobsen, after the humiliating way he'd gone after him in the showers only to be shot down cold, he had zero interest in trying again. He didn't know what the hell had gotten into him. "After I see to you."

Jakobsen's gaze darkened when Riff lifted his hand to daub at his eyes. He grabbed Riff's arm to look at the bruises and lacerations around his wrists. Their gazes met, and Riff's pulse jumped at the anger that matched his own when he saw Jakobsen strapped down.

"It looks like you had as rough of a time at it as me."

"Don't really remember anything before waking up, and I'm glad for it," Riff replied. "Close your eyes."

Jakobsen obeyed, and Riff made quick work of cleaning his eyes. The sight of those pinpricks, the thought of how easily he could've been maimed made bile burn his throat. If he discovered who had inflicted this cruelty on Jakobsen, he'd make them rue every stitch.

Jakobsen's eyes popped open again, and for a moment they stared at each other. Jakobsen's hand slipped around his neck, and before Riff could say it was a bad idea, Jakobsen kissed him. Riff tensed. Flashes of memory hit him… pain and coupling and death… like something remembered from a fever dream. But not Jakobsen. Jakobsen wasn't in any of those half memories of madness.

Riff stepped closer and kissed Jakobsen back, slow and sweet, a soothing balm after the horror of the day. Jakobsen eased away and brushed his thumb over Riff's lower lip. "You okay?"

"As okay as either of us." Riff gave him a rueful smile and gestured around them. "Considering, I think we're truly fucked."

"Yeah, I think you're right."

Riff continued to examine him, cleaning his ears and nose, asking Jakobsen about any pain he was experiencing. A quick search of the room showed no working scanners, and since Jakobsen didn't seem to be in any pain or distress, he reluctantly let the matter go for now, promising himself he'd keep an eye on him.

His gaze skimmed the room until he found a bag amongst the debris. They would need to go through this ship, every sector to try to find other survivors, and he wanted at least a basic kit to take with him in case they ran into others who needed medical attention. Now that he wasn't alone, and Jakobsen wasn't the kind of man likely to start trouble, Riff began making plans.

"What the fuck happened?" Jakobsen asked.

"I wish I knew. The whole place went insane. It wasn't like any riot I'd seen before." Riff began sorting through the supplies and medicines that remained unscathed. "We need to find you clothes and shoes. I hope you're not squeamish about where we get them."

"What are you doing?"

Riff glanced over to see Jakobsen watching him with narrowed eyes. "What do you think? This ship was full of prisoners and guards. Some of those guards had their families with them. That's a whole lot of people who might need these. I'm not about to let another madman destroy them. We can't stay here and hide. I'm going to see who else may have recovered."

"Don't you think help is coming?"

The bewilderment in Jakobsen's voice had Riff pausing to look at him again. "Look, if it was, it would already be here. It's been days at least. Captain Vidal's not popular, and if he put out a distress call, it's more likely people are going to raid what we have left instead of help. Considering the situation, we have to stick together if we want to survive. Right now we have the chance to take action, take charge before someone does it for us. There's no way in hell I'm going to let them shove me in a box again after what happened." Riff gathered what he'd been able to find and set it out on the spot he'd cleaned on the counter. "So are you coming with me, or are you staying?"

"That's a dumbass question. Of course I'm sticking by you." Jakobsen swung his legs over the side of the gurney, and Riff caught his arm.

"Wait. There's broken glass all over the floor." Riff handed Jakobsen one of his guns. "I'll be right back with something for you."

CHAPTER SIX

THE SENSE of purpose faded before Khora disappeared around the curtain. Zed rubbed his arms, unable to scrub the sensation of being strapped down off his skin. He was acutely aware of his nakedness and the vast silence in his head. Zed had prayed for that silence, until that part of him was amputated. Reaching for an impression had only caused pain to arc between his temples, so he'd left it alone. Even now, his brain felt stuffy and swollen.

After all the nightmares of the last year, this new horror was almost enough to make him believe he'd woken up in hell. Only he hadn't done a damn thing wrong to deserve it.

This, though, this was different. Nobody's imagination could've come up with this. Shivering with disbelief, Zed's fingertips traced over the painful tenderness of his mouth and eyes. Khora's bleak gaze had confirmed he wished he could unsee the things he'd witnessed. Zed wasn't sure he wanted to discover what waited for him on the other side of the examination curtain.

The short hairs on his neck stirred. The sensation like eyes traveling over his skin. The utter stillness suffocated him. Zed shifted, trying to peer through the gap in the curtain. "Hello?"

The room appeared empty, but the watching gaze remained. Dread skittered along his skin. Zed reached for the gun Khora left him. Hefted its unfamiliar weight. The quiet was immense and terrifying in its strangeness. The engines should throb. The hull groan and creak. Zed whistled a little tune, trying to stave off the quiet. The sound did nothing to fill the silence. It only emphasized his isolation. Zed thought of the man who did the laundry with a flash of concern. Maybe he'd found a place to hide.

Zed tried to remember what happened. How he'd gotten there. He'd been searching for something…. Zed closed his eyes, struggling to recall the terrible, violent intent that had come over him, but the memory was overwhelmed by searing helplessness and pain and the gut feeling that whoever had been experimenting on him had just gotten started.

The hatchway hissed open, and Zed tensed, raising the gun, bare fingers squeezing. The dead numbness in his brain cut him again with loss.

"Jakobsen, you still there?" Khora called, his voice wary.

The warm rush of relief washed through him. "Yeah," Zed replied.

Khora slipped around the curtain carrying a bundle under one arm and a guard's baton in his hand. Zed caught the bundle as it was tossed to him and stole a surreptitious glance at Khora. One look at his grim gaze was enough to remind him of the situation they were in. What had happened to Khora during the crazy time? Bruises marked his face, and his nose slanted at a painful angle. Had he found himself as helpless as Zed had been?

A whole ship going insane at the same time…. Zed shuddered. He didn't understand how it could happen. Zed knew mechanics, his people skills had never been the best. But if the madness was anything like the fever rage that had taken hold of him, he was surprised the ship had any integrity left.

Zed dressed, his skin cringing away from the wetness around the collar and along the ribs, very grateful he couldn't sense the owner's last moments. He still felt immeasurably better just to be clothed.

He glanced over as he rolled up pants legs that were too long for him. "Did you see anyone else? Quinet, Wilt, Tuputala, Henrick?" Henrick wasn't much of a bunkmate, but he hadn't been terrible either.

Khora pressed his lips together and shook his head, his brow wrinkling. "It's quiet, too quiet. None of them were in their cells. Everybody I've run into is either dead, dying, or crazy as fuck."

Zed studied him a long moment. Black and gray stubble covered Khora's face, and his eyes were deep, dark hollows that drew Zed in.

An anguished, blood-curdling scream rent the air. Zed froze, then straightened with a jerk as a man in a nurse's uniform barreled through the curtain. With another scream, the nurse slashed and beat at Khora with a broken-off end of a metal bar. Khora fell back with a startled yell, bringing up his baton to block the frenzied attack.

Zed flinched. His heart tripped as a fragment of memory pierced his brain…. The doctor looming over him with archaic needle and thread in hand. He shuddered. If Khora hadn't released Zed when he had….

He shook off the paralyzing memory and leapt to Khora's defense, slamming the butt of the gun down on the man's neck. The blow didn't faze him. If Zed shot him, he could hit Khora. Desperately, Zed struck him again.

"He's Dr. Barboza's patient," the man shouted, spittle flying from his lips. "He told you! He told you what he would do if you touched his patient again!"

The nurse stabbed the pipe at Khora, but Khora dodged back. Zed caught the crazed man in a choke hold from behind.

"Drop it," Zed snapped, terrified of the rabid light in the man's eyes and the strength in his tightly coiled body.

The man shrieked and flailed. He lashed out indiscriminately with the pipe and a clawed hand. Zed jerked back as he tried to rake his eyes, and the man wrenched away. He spun around, pipe raised. Shots rang out, and the man jerked. The mad light faded from his eyes. For a split second, sanity returned before that fled, too, as Khora shot him again.

Zed stared at Khora in numb shock as the body slumped to the floor. He was as stunned by the suddenness of the attack as he was by the faint, fleeting regret in Khora's gaze.

"He wouldn't go down," Khora said with an indifferent shrug that made Zed question the remorse he'd just seen. Zed couldn't deny that. The nurse wasn't going to stop until they were dead. But that moment of sanity in the man's eyes would haunt him.

"What did he mean about you messing with Dr. Barboza's patients?" Zed asked out of a need to fill the quiet. "The doctor was pretty pissed at you before everything went nuts."

"As I said, I used to be a field medic." Khora looked in a mirror and probed his nose. He grasped it and, to Zed's sick fascination, reset it with a jerk and fervent curse.

"You okay?"

"Yeah. Fuck that hurt." Khora gently touched his nose again and straightened. "Barboza didn't like the thought of me volunteering to help here. I was a lifer. And he suspected I was running some illegal underground clinic for the other prisoners. I don't know when he'd think I'd have the damn time."

"Let me see your wrists." Zed didn't believe Khora's dissembling for one minute. He remembered how Khora found that man on *Pandora*, being in the infirmary instead of the hold. And Khora's defensiveness when the doctor wanted him searched for contraband. He was pretty sure Khora was guilty on all counts, but he left it alone as he helped Khora clean and bandage the lacerations on his wrists.

Zed debated telling Khora about the dead, quiet part of his brain. He had no way of knowing if it was an injury he'd recover from or the symptom of something more serious. As much as he wanted to pretend it wasn't a potential problem, he wanted to survive and get off this ship more. He could ignore it and wind up having an aneurysm and keeling over. Khora had been a medic. He might have insight. At least then Zed would know how serious it was, instead of wondering, worrying.

"How does your head feel?" Khora tipped Zed's jaw up to examine his eyes.

"Like my brain's trying to explode through my skull," Zed admitted.

Khora's frown deepened. "Dizziness, nausea, blurry vision? You don't seem confused or disoriented."

"No, none of those," Zed replied after a quick, internal survey. "But there is one thing that's different." There weren't many psychics like him, but it was well documented, so at least he wouldn't have to convince Khora of the possibility. "I used to be able to get impressions from objects when I touched them, mostly emotion, sometimes flickers of scenes if it was intense. But I get nothing now, only pain when I try."

"Then don't try." Khora ran gentle fingers over Zed's skull. "There's no depressions or bleeding. I don't think you hit your head. Would it help you not to reach if you had gloves again?"

There was no condemnation, no looking at Zed like he was a freak, just concern and the thoughtfulness of a man working through an interesting problem. At that moment Zed wished he could read him. He wanted another taste of that fascinating mind, wanted to know if deep down Khora was repelled by him or not.

"I don't know. It's worth a shot. I might just hold on to them, though. It feels good to be unencumbered for once, to not have to rely on them." Zed flexed his bare fingers. He'd worn gloves so much his own hands seemed like strangers to him.

"Just don't keep poking at it like a sore. Give your brain a chance to heal and rest. Otherwise there's not much else I can do. The equipment I need to scan your brain is damaged. I can keep an eye on you, and I can trust you'd tell me if anything changes, good or bad."

"What do you think happened?" Zed asked as Khora checked his ears again.

Khora blew out a breath. "My best educated guess, considering I'm not a specialist and I don't know a damn thing about psychics... I think you were running around naked in the middle of a violent prison riot. I think you were experimented on. I think the part of your brain that controls whatever it is you do shut down to protect itself like an overstimulated nerve."

"Then there's a chance I could get it back." Though it had caused too much disruption in his life and Zed had seen things he never wanted to see, without that ability, Hannah would still be trapped in a nightmare with no one knowing her pain.

"I just don't know. We're stepping into new territory for me." Khora spread his hands helplessly. "If I had the right equipment and the time to research.... But we don't, not in this situation. All I can do is observe and try to anticipate. Right now, other than an understandable headache, you don't seem to have any other symptoms of brain trauma. The bleeding has stopped, and you seem alert. You might get it back or you might not, and it could be stronger or weaker than it was before. We just don't have any way of knowing without more information. I'm sorry."

Zed nodded and tried to push it from his mind. "What now? Find survivors, lock up crazies? Just the two of us? Isn't that by its own definition insane? We should find a way off this ship."

"And abandon anyone like us who might be trapped and helpless?" Khora asked with a sharp look. "I have friends on this ship. Even if I were so inclined, escaping isn't going to be easy. We need to figure out where we are. Where the closest planet is. The transport we use for recon missions is barely holding together for short trips. We need intel, options, and time. So our first priority is to find a safe place to hole up and get that intel. Then we need to decide what to do."

"Point made. We look for survivors." Zed might not give a fuck about the majority of them, and he might be looking for an escape, but after waking up the way he had, he couldn't leave anybody else to that horror. "And where can we do all that?"

"Captain's suite." Khora fished two palm lights out of his pocket, handed one to Zed with the baton, and tucked the purloined medical supplies under his arm. "If we can get the system up, we can see every

inch of the ship from there. It has its own small galley and life support.
It's shielded and secure."

Zed supposed Khora wanted to check on his lover too, and there
was wisdom in his choice of a hidey-hole. He couldn't figure Khora
out. The man was an enigma, even after the reading Zed received from
him. From what he'd seen, he was a mix of tough and compassionate,
ruthless and intelligent. He couldn't see what it was about the captain
that fascinated Khora. He remembered Khora's absolute certainty that
Vidal was going to kill him. He remembered the gleam in Vidal's eyes as
he choked Khora. Yet Khora was seeking him out.

"What if the captain's there?" Zed asked, meeting Khora's gaze.

"We take him prisoner. He'd be the perfect leverage," Khora replied
with a shrug, and the knot in Zed's gut loosened. Well, no love lost there.
It did make him wonder if Khora would dismiss Zed so easily.

"What if he has guards?"

"Not likely, there aren't many of us that I've seen who are alive
and sane."

Zed didn't like the idea of cutting through a section of the ship he
didn't know, even though Khora did. Everybody they were likely to run
into would be against them because they were lifers. There were only the
two of them.

"How thoroughly did you search the prison?"

"I didn't really, just checked to see if you and others were in your
cells." Khora shot him a curious look. "Why?"

"I think we should be sure there's no one there we could use to
back us up. I think we should look for allies first, then hit up the captain's
den. I don't think it's a coincidence we woke up approximately at the
same time. There's going to be others. Let's check the prison. We know
that area well, so it shouldn't take long."

Khora frowned. "There's only one entryway, and once we get past
the salvage and work rooms, it's a maze of corridors. If I was the captain
or one of the guards, the first thing I'd do when I woke up would be to
secure that hatchway."

"Trust me. If I can get my tools, then I can jam it open both
electrically and manually long enough for us to be in and out. I can
also set up a proximity-warning device that will let us know if anyone
approaches. It'll take the captain, or anybody else, time to get organized,
to realize we're there before locking us in. We just have to make a

decision and move fast. Trapped is trapped, Khora. We can get just as stuck in the captain's quarters if there aren't enough of us."

Khora's frown deepened, but after a long hesitation, he nodded. "Okay. The salvage rooms aren't too deep into the prisoner's territory. We'll grab you a tool kit there."

Zed stiffened in shock as he came around the curtain. The infirmary had been ripped apart, equipment smashed, implements and valuable medicines scattered. The similarity to the derelict struck him again with another punch.

He exchanged glances with Khora and saw the same recognition in his gaze—and also what? Guilt? Zed tilted his head, trying to understand that reaction. "What is it?" Zed asked, and Khora hesitated, that same emotion weighing down his expression. "Come on, tell me."

Khora gestured around the infirmary with a helpless look. "What if the survivor we rescued had been carrying whatever it was that made us all crazy? And I brought it back here. I never even considered it could've been an illness that killed off the people on the derelict, and I should've. I had a chance to see Noyes when he requested to meet the captain to discuss a reward. He didn't look sick, but I wasn't in a position to judge either."

Zed caught Khora's hand and squeezed it until the other man looked at him. "An illness wouldn't explain the lack of bodies. We were doing our jobs. Rescuing the survivor was a nonquestion. We couldn't leave him over there." Though Noyes would've been better off left on the derelict the way things turned out.

Khora didn't look convinced, but he sighed and squeezed Zed's hand back before pulling away. "If Barboza isn't a complete idiot, he would've isolated him and ran some tests before he let Noyes out of the infirmary."

"Come on, speculating is getting us nowhere," Zed said gruffly. "Let's get moving." He'd talk to Khora when they had an opportunity and convince him he'd acted on his conscience and there was no shame in that.

The salvage rooms were cast in deep shadows. The sickening sweet odor of blood and decay flowed out as they opened the hatchway. Zed and Khora exchanged grim glances before Khora eased inside. Zed tightened his grip on the gun and followed. Silence surrounded them with only the sound of their breaths to break it. Zed's eyes swept over the broken, brutalized bodies, his throat tightening convulsively. He didn't want to see the people he'd known and worked with. He couldn't help but notice.

He stepped over a woman with a bloody hammer clenched in her fist. Zed's skin crawled at the thought of touching it. The light in his hand illuminated the carnage in the immediate vicinity. It only made the surrounding shadows darker. Zed picked his way through the bodies, his body rigid with tension. Khora followed, pausing to check each one.

"What are you doing?" Zed asked in a bare whisper as Khora turned over a man with his face bashed in. "They're all dead."

"Looking for my team," Khora replied, his mouth pinched with anxiety.

Zed didn't know what good it would do to find them. These people had torn each other apart. He didn't want to put faces and names to the bodies. Tools were scattered around. Buried in bodies. Lying in filth. It would take time to cobble together a usable kit. Time he wasn't sure they had.

"Let's check the transport," Khora suggested. "It has its own kits and very few have access to it. We should be able to find something there."

"That's better than scrounging in this tomb," Zed agreed. He felt unclean and wished desperately for his gloves. He shuddered. If his ability came back now, he'd lose his fucking mind. Zed swept his light over the room as they turned toward the transport bay. Khora had said there were others still alive and crazy. Anything could be hiding in the shadows. Zed strained to hear movement and hunched his shoulders against an attack.

The hatchway to the transport bay was sealed shut. Bloody fist prints covered the entry, and several bodies were crumpled beside it. Zed averted his gaze, but the deep, raking gouges stuck in his brain. It was like they'd tried to claw themselves to pieces. A bolt lay on the ground in the corner, unmarked by blood. Zed scooped it up and cleaned it on his shirt to be sure. He clenched his fingers around it as Khora checked each corpse. The ridges digging into his flesh brought slim comfort.

Khora shook his head with a grim look. "They've all been battered, blunt force trauma and more than was needed to kill."

Zed looked away with a wince. He remembered looking for someone… someone he wanted to hurt…. Heller. Is that what happened, everybody seeing an enemy's face on each other? Somebody they hated so much they wanted to tear them apart with their bare hands?

"Khora, have you seen anything weird since you came to?" Zed hadn't, but he was pretty sure he'd be second-guessing every glimpse out of the corner of his eye for a long time. "I mean anything that couldn't possibly be there?"

Khora shook his head. "No, but if we did, I don't think we'd be in a good enough mental state to self-diagnose either. I'd like to think it's over, but I don't know. I seem to be saying that a lot."

Zed peered through the smear of dried blood on the hatchway porthole. The transport bay looked quiet, but something struck him. He nudged Khora and pointed at the porthole. "The blood's on the inside."

"Let me get the hatchway unlocked. Keep your wits about you." Khora entered the code into the lock pad, and the hatchway hissed open.

Zed stepped through, gun in hand, nerves tense. Compared to other parts of the ship, the transport bay seemed eerily normal. Equipment had been ransacked, but it seemed more methodical than helter-skelter.

"Take one more step, Jakobsen, and I'll blow your skull all over the floor." The grim threat in that implacable voice was palpable.

Zed froze, lifting his hands. "Tuputala, is that you? I'm not here to hurt you."

Tuputala stepped out from the deep shadows around the transport. Her hair had come loose from its bindings and hung in a wild black cloud around her face. She held a spar in one hand and a gun in the other and looked more than ready to use them both. With the ripped jumpsuit, blood-smeared skin, and ancient-style tattoos, she looked like an Amazon emerging from the distant past.

She glared at Zed with heavy suspicion. "Are you the one who locked me in here?" She raised the gun as Zed took a hasty step back. "Where's Khora? If you've hurt him…."

"Joey, I'm right here," Khora said, coming through the hatchway. "Please don't shoot Jakobsen. I've just finished tending to him."

A huge smile broke out over Tuputala's face. "I should've known you would emerge unscathed, you crazy bastard." The two caught each other in a rough hug, and Tuputala pulled back with a cry of pain.

"How bad are you hurt?" Khora asked, stepping back to look her over. Cuts, bite marks, and bruises marked every inch of her hands, and her eyes looked pained.

"Somebody tried to lay me open." Tuputala's expression darkened. "I don't remember how or why. It's not bleeding too much anymore."

"Let me see," Khora demanded, and Tuputala turned, revealing a broad, muscled back and a gruesome gash on her shoulder that narrowed to a point halfway down her back. "How's the transport? Any chance we could use it to get out of here and make it to a planet?"

"Not anytime soon. I was only able to get one part we needed off the derelict. Even if we had all the pieces, it would still take time, and she wouldn't be fast. Too much and she could shake apart. Not to mention that some fucknut got on board and began ripping out shit."

Khora frowned, gently probing Tuputala's back and muttering to himself. "Okay, we'll go with our original plan and take the captain's transport. Any idea where Quinet and Wilt might be?"

"Last I saw them, we were all in the mess hall." Tuputala shot Zed a hard look. "What the hell is going on?"

"Like I fucking know," Zed replied, glaring back at her. "But we're all in this together. You might want to remember that."

"I wish I knew, and I intend on finding out," Khora replied. "But not until we're safe."

Zed left them to their conversation and boarded the transport. Tuputala wasn't kidding. The inside looked as if somebody had tried dismantling the ship. Considering the condition of her hands, she was probably the culprit. Though that wouldn't explain the bites unless she gnawed herself.

By some miracle Zed managed to find their tool kits unscathed. He grabbed all of them and headed back to Tuputala and Khora. "Got 'em," he said, interrupting their conversation that, judging from their sideways glances, concerned him. "Let's get moving before more people wake up who aren't on our side."

CHAPTER SEVEN

As they approached the captain's suite, carrying the unconscious Wilt and Quinet, Riff's skin crawled. The exposed position left them vulnerable to attack from three different directions. They propped their teammates against the wall and Jakobsen knelt in front of the hatchway, busy with his tools while Tuputala and Riff covered them. They had found Wilt and Quinet holed up in the guardroom, battered but whole. Riff's relief at having his team together again was buried under the dread that something bad would happen to balance the scales.

Every instinct screamed in warning. That his whole team remained relatively unscathed when everybody else they'd seen had been butchered or was still crazed strained credulity. But how someone could've planned this chaos, he didn't know.

"Got it," Jakobsen said as the hatchway hissed open.

"Let me go first." Riff stepped through the darkened hatchway, listening for any sound. He activated the lights and scanned the empty main meeting room. The wide portholes showed glittering stars in a beautiful, cold panorama. Unlike the rest of the ship, nothing here had been touched. The cleanliness and order seemed almost abnormal. Riff did a quick search of the private adjoining rooms and found them empty as well.

"Hurry up. The longer we're out here, the more nervous I get," Tuputala said in a tense voice. "Wilt and Quinet are vulnerable."

"It's quiet," Riff replied. "Let's get them in and seal the hatchway."

They laid their teammates on the table while Jakobsen worked on reinforcing the hatchway lock. Riff hoped Jakobsen was as good as he claimed because he wouldn't put it past Vidal to have a few surprises he could wage against them if he survived.

Riff pointed toward the first hatchway on his left. "There are the sleeping quarters and a bathroom." He swept his hand toward the right. "First room's the galley, next to it is the access corridor to the captain's personal transport. We should be able to control everything not broken from here and see the rest of the ship. Main controls are behind the panel next to the table."

"I'm on it." Tuputala moved to the controls. "See to Quinet and Wilt first. I'm not bleeding anymore."

Riff checked their pulses: Wilt's was strong and steady, but Quinet's raced like he was still in the grip of some great fear. He whimpered and twitched until he curled up next to Wilt. Riff hoped they'd wake up normal. He prepared a tranquilizer just in case and made sure their bonds were secure.

"We should be good for now." Jakobsen stepped away from the hatchway. "I'd like to tinker with it more when we get some time and make certain there aren't any more back doors coded." He looked around curiously and moved toward the room next to the sleeping quarters that Riff didn't name. Riff tensed.

"That room's off-limits," he snapped, harsher than he meant, and both Tuputala and Jakobsen looked at him in surprise. Understanding dawned in Tuputala's gaze, and she turned back to work. Jakobsen studied him a long moment, his hazel eyes calm, then moved away without a word of protest.

"Would you like me to seal that room too?" Jakobsen asked in a low voice, and Riff shook his head as he looked away. It was just a room; it had no power over him. For a man who possibly had brain damage, Jakobsen seemed remarkably perceptive. Riff wondered if Jakobsen's psychic ability was limited to objects or if it had extended to people, and if so, had Jakobsen managed to pick up anything from him? He wasn't sure how he felt about that.

"No need. Take over for Tuputala while I bandage her. Then we can check on the transport's condition. First, I want a scan of this ship. We can't be the only ones awake and sane."

"I'm fine. You don't need to tend to me." Tuputala didn't budge from the console where her giant hands flew over the delicate controls.

"Please allow me to feel useful next to you tech geniuses," Riff said dryly. Tuputala might not like Jakobsen, but they didn't need this division now. He'd seen it in other units during the war. If they didn't work together, they all were going to get killed. "It's bad. There's dead tissue. If you get an infection, it could hurt us all. We need you healthy."

"Just a few minutes." The screens along the wall flickered to show Riff's cell first, then moved out on a loop through the rest of the prison. Riff's jaw tightened and he clenched his teeth. He should've known he never was free of Vidal. The bastard enjoyed his position over them all too much.

The view was grisly. The few dying men that Riff had seen had passed on. The ones who were still crazy in the penal wing all looked to be trapped and hurting themselves in their effort to get out. "There we go," Tuputala said. "We have picture at least."

"I don't know if I could handle sound too," Jakobsen said in a soft voice as he looked at the screen with sad, sick eyes. Tuputala and Riff exchanged glances, and he wondered what Tuputala saw when she looked at Jakobsen that set her off so. Riff saw a young man, completely out of his depth, but maybe he was deluding himself into thinking he might be attracted to a man who had a gentle side too. That hadn't been the case in a long time.

"Sit," Riff ordered Tuputala. He cleaned his hands and the worktable as best as he could before putting on gloves and laying out the medical supplies he'd gleaned. He'd have to drain and debride the wound before he could see if he could stitch it up and make damn sure there was no infection. "This is going to hurt like a motherfucker. I can give you something to take the edge off and save some more for your naptime."

"Pain's not really my thing," Tuputala rumbled. "But not too much. I need to be able to think."

Riff nodded and prepared a cocktail for her, praying it wouldn't take too long to clean and stitch the wound. Tuputala had been through enough of an ordeal. Riff was still worried about Jakobsen, though he seemed to be suffering no ill effects. It was possible he'd misdiagnosed him. The lack of working equipment made him long to punch a wall.

Jakobsen went to the computer, frowning as he worked. "Engines are off-line. External communications are down. And it looks like the ship was moved. We're nowhere close to any planets or *Pandora*. Looks like someone launched us blindly when everything went nuts."

"Try to figure out where we are," Riff said.

Jakobsen shot him a helpless look. "I may be an engineering genius, but I don't know a damn thing about navigation or star charts. The ship's main computer would be able to help, but it's going to take a while to get it going. We'd need to track down the problem before we can fix it."

Riff swore under his breath. Wilt and Quinet needed to wake up fast and in control of themselves. They would be able to track it down faster. Riff had some experience, and given time or a working computer, he could figure it out, but he didn't think they had that time. At least the computer on the transport should be working.

"Don't ask," Tuputala grunted as Riff probed her shoulder. "I wouldn't know where to begin."

Movement flashed on the screen, and Riff straightened. "Wait, go back to the engine room. I thought I saw something." The picture flicked back to the long, dark room, lit on one end with an ominous orange-red glow. The great engines were silent and cold, and if the fire-suppression system didn't start working, the blaze might spread. Riff tacked that onto his list of worries that superseded his fear. There was too much to do. "Leave that up on one of the screens and keep looking. This is a big ship." The room seemed empty, but there were a thousand places to hide.

"Are you sure you don't want me to give you something stronger for the pain?" Riff asked Tuputala in a low voice.

"No. You need us all to have our wits, especially considering the mixed company." Tuputala pulled her hair over her undamaged shoulder and twisted it into a rope. She didn't mention her suspicions about Jakobsen again, but Riff had gotten an earful earlier. They all were guilty of something. That's why they'd been imprisoned. He didn't want to know Jakobsen's story any more than he felt like telling his own. This was a fresh start. He'd judge Jakobsen on what he did from now on.

Riff worked the makeshift bandage off and fresh blood oozed out, thankfully looking clean. Riff went to work as quickly as he could. He cut away the dead tissue and worked out the debris in the wound. He kept an eye on Tuputala, watching for signs of shock and occasionally glancing at Jakobsen to make sure his condition remained unchanged. Tuputala stared straight ahead, answering Riff's questions with a grunt or short comments, her golden-brown complexion paler than normal as he began to stitch.

Quinet groaned, shifting on the other end of the table, and Jakobsen moved to check on him, putting his body between the waking man and where Riff worked on Tuputala. Quinet sat up with a scream that tore through the room and sent a chill through Riff's bones.

"For fuck's sake," Jakobsen swore, jumping back. Quinet looked around wildly, trying to scramble away, tearing at the bindings around his wrists. Riff shot him a measuring look, weighing the fear in his gaze with the madness he'd seen in the others.

"Slap him," Riff ordered.

"What?" Jakobsen looked at him with wide eyes.

Riff stripped the bloodied gloves from his hands, stepped around Jakobsen, and smacked Quinet hard. The hysterical screaming stopped, and Riff grabbed Quinet's ashen face in his hands.

"Hey, it's me, Khora. You're safe. Understand?"

Quinet's eyes darted around the room before settling on Riff as sense returned. "Khora?"

"Yeah, it's me," Riff soothed.

"You sure?" Quinet's voice trembled. "I saw things."

"I know. We all did. But they're gone now," Riff assured him and prayed he was right. He lightened his grip on Quinet, guiding his head so he could see everybody else. "You're with the team."

Quinet looked around at each one of them as Wilt stirred. "Shut your damn trap, Quinet, and let a body sleep."

Riff's knees weakened in relief. They were all okay. He gently shook Wilt's ankle. "Wake up, Wilt. We need you to figure out where the hell we are. Untie them, Jakobsen."

"Untie me?" Wilt struggled to sit up, her face flushed in annoyance. "What the flying fuck kind of kinky-assed shit is this?"

"Jakobsen will give you the rundown." Riff patted Quinet's cheek, grabbing his attention. "It's going to be okay if we stick together."

Riff returned to tending to Tuputala, feeling more in control than he had since he'd woken up. He'd been running salvage missions with the three of them for years. The loss of Bryce had hit them all hard, and he hadn't realized how hard until they were all threatened. He didn't want to lose another one.

Jakobsen untied them, then distracted Quinet from what Riff was doing by directing him to the computers. Riff shot him a smile of gratitude. Quinet could be twitchy on a good day, and Tuputala's wound looked more gruesome than it was. Riff expected it to heal without complications.

By the time Riff got her cleaned and rebandaged, Wilt had a fix on their location, Quinet had bolstered their security, and Jakobsen had several more screens running. The three of them discussed their progress in low voices, and the normalcy of the activity gradually eased away some of Riff's tension.

Riff cleaned up the mess he'd made patching Tuputala together and shoved it all in the incinerator, giving Tuputala a chance to steady herself after the ordeal. They'd all been through hell. Time for a few perks that some of them hadn't seen in years. Riff raided the galley and found fresh food as he'd hoped, instead of the protein bars and gunk they were served in the mess. He hid the alcohol, saving it for a celebration later. They had too much to do to get blitzed. He put a tray together and brought it out into the workroom.

Tuputala's eyes lit up as she caught sight of it, and some color returned to her face. "Is that real bread?"

"It is, a little stale, but still good. There's also some fresh fruit and cheese." Riff set the tray on the table as everyone gathered around with greedy reaching hands. The scene gave him the first rush of pleasure he'd had in a while.

"Is there more of this?" Quinet asked, breaking open a citrus fruit. He closed his eyes, breathing in the scent.

"There is, not a terrible lot, but enough for a few indulgences. Vidal has an emergency store of the usual shit, though probably better quality in case he needed to use this place as a panic room. There's also some real food and a rehydration unit. I'm going to see what I can cobble together for a hot meal from that. We'll save the protein packs for last."

If anything, having real food would raise morale as much as having a safer place to sleep and the promise of escape on the horizon.

The console beeped, and Jakobsen moved over to investigate. "Internal communications just came online," Jakobsen said in a perplexed voice. "I didn't do that."

"Could be kicking online as we get things up and running," Wilt replied.

Tuputala pulled herself to her feet and steadied herself against the table. "Let me take a look," she said. Riff watched her but refrained from saying anything as she made her way over to the console. Tuputala needed to rest, but it was useless to try to order her to.

"Let me." Wilt superseded her body in front of Tuputala.

"I'm fine. If you treat me like an invalid, I'll pound your face in," Tuputala threatened, without her usual edge.

"Please, bitch. Quinet could take you now. You can try to pound my face tomorrow." Wilt flashed her a smile. "It'll be faster if I do. I don't fuck with your engines, you stay off my computers." Wilt frowned as she worked, tracking down the code. "No…. This is someone else's work. We're definitely not alone."

A chill swept through Riff. "Pull up images of the transports. I want eyes on them at all times. Come up with ways to block access. Get on it." He bolted for the corridor, toward Vidal's private bay. Before he arrived he saw the utter darkness of space through the porthole and began cursing, venting his fury and fear. The bay doors shouldn't be open.

Riff ran to the porthole and looked out onto the empty bay. "Fuck!" He slammed his palm against the hatchway. More curses followed, each punctuated by another slap as his mind raced. Time for another plan. They had to get the other transport operational for long-distance trips. He was so far out of his depth. He'd been a field medic, not a damn tech specialist. At least he had a team that knew what they were doing, because when it came to that, Riff was as useless as balls on a monk.

Riff returned to the meeting room, and from the expressions on the others' faces, they already knew the bad news.

One of the screens flickered, and Captain Vidal appeared, sitting on the bridge with his smug smile and cruel eyes. "Good to see you looking so fit and fired up, Riff."

"Did you ever think you might need that fucking transport of yours?" Riff asked, settling his hands on his hips.

"You didn't think I was going to let you leave? You and your friends need to be punished. It's my duty to make sure you remain and carry out your sentences."

Rage pierced through Riff in a white-hot spike. "You mean it's your pleasure."

"It's all one and the same." Vidal leaned forward in his chair, his expression hardening. "I'm going to make you a one-time offer. Surrender, and there will be no repercussions for your escape attempt."

"I've got my team with me, Captain. You're alone. I'll take my chances and say no."

"Alone, am I? Are you sure?" Vidal said with a razor edge to his voice.

Riff searched Vidal's face to see if he was bluffing. He had the uneasy suspicion he wasn't. He signaled for Tuputala to kill the feed, and the screen went dark. "Lock him out. I want to be dead sure he can't see or hear us."

Wilt nodded, her narrow features drawn into a fierce frown as she worked. Everyone waited in tense silence until she pushed away from the console, her expression relaxing. "Done."

"Good. Now it's time to get our asses in gear. Jakobsen, you do whatever you can do to make sure everybody else is locked out of the controls in this room. I want to see what's happening on that bridge, even better if we can hear. He's not alone, you can bet on that."

Jakobsen's expression settled into grim lines. "Will do."

"Wilt, work on isolating the controls for the captain's bay. We're moving the other transport there, so I want to make sure it can't be jettisoned as well. We need time to repair it, but I don't want us split up between here and the prison bay. Quinet, make sure external communications stays down. I don't want Vidal calling for backup. Tuputala, you're with me. We're fetching the other transport and bringing it around."

"Wait, hold up, what's to keep you from chasing down the other transport and stranding us here?" Quinet demanded, his eyes glinting with suspicion. He'd always been a little paranoid, but he'd never looked at Riff like that before.

"Khora," Jakobsen cut in quietly. "If you run into trouble, you're going to need somebody to watch your back. Tuputala's hurt, and she's lost a lot of blood."

"I'm fine," Tuputala snapped, glaring at Jakobsen.

Riff took one look at Tuputala's haggard face and knew Jakobsen was right. He had to be doubly prepared for an altercation, and he wasn't going to get Tuputala killed because of her stubbornness.

"I'll leave her here." He held up his hand as Tuputala started to protest. "Quinet, you can't possibly think I'd go anywhere without her. Tuputala, you need rest. I need you whole."

"Who's going to watch your back?" Tuputala demanded.

Riff glanced between the others. Taking Wilt would only set off Quinet more. She steadied Quinet when his paranoia got hold of him.

"Jakobsen, you're with me," Riff ordered. "Wilt, when you're done isolating the controls, see if you can scan for the other transport." From the look on Tuputala's face, she didn't agree, but she didn't argue either.

"You're in charge," Riff said to Tuputala. "Keep an eye on us through the cameras, but try not to use the comm unless absolutely necessary. I don't want Vidal to overhear. Try to find out if he has anybody else with him."

Riff checked his weapons and followed Jakobsen out the hatchway. The hallways were echoingly quiet, but it didn't stop Riff from feeling like he was being watched. He sought out the cameras and tried telling himself that his team was keeping an eye on them. It didn't help much.

The emergency lighting in the corridor remained steady, and the low light shrouded the passageway in shadows. Riff paused when they reached a corner and peered around it cautiously. They needed to come up with a plan to neutralize those still crazy. There were bound to be some wandering about.

Silence followed them, and the quiet frayed Riff's nerves. Movement flickered, sound skittered. Riff tensed and flashed his light around the next corner. A rat peered out from underneath a body and bolted away. Riff's breath rushed as the tension in his body broke for a blessed moment.

"I know Tuputala doesn't like me because of my past," Jakobsen said in a tight voice, his eyes wary as he kept a constant lookout. "I'm new, so my word doesn't mean much, but I'm not going to jeopardize us. I want out of here just as much as you."

Riff tore his gaze away from the crumpled body. Jakobsen's expression was earnest, and the warmth there was so different from Vidal's cold cruelty that Riff had to look away, disconcerted.

"I believe you," he replied.

The salvage rooms looked unchanged. Riff didn't pause to explore, he just raced to the bay. Their boots clanged on the decking. The sound echoed hollowly in the large connecting rooms. Riff flinched and prayed they wouldn't attract attention. He slammed the hatchway to the bay shut and engaged the lock. The pounding of his heart eased once that solid barrier was between them and the rest of the ship.

Jakobsen shot him a measuring look before sweeping his gaze over the bay. "Looks quiet."

Maybe. Riff still expected some kind of last-second clusterfuck. There were a dozen places where someone could hide, including the long line of shelves that once held equipment. Riff tried to keep an eye on it all as they made their way to the transport. Jakobsen activated the ramp, and Riff walked backward up into it. He couldn't wait to hear the familiar rumble of the transport coming to life, even if the rumble meant repairs were long overdue. At least it would be normal.

As the ramp closed, Riff turned to survey the damage. "What the fuck happened in here?" he asked, his dismay growing as he noted compartments broken open, extra supplies and tools strewn about. Panels had been ripped off, wires torn loose.

"Don't worry. It's all surface. She'll still run long enough for us to get to the other bay," Jakobsen promised as he slid into the copilot's seat. "I had a good look earlier. Comm is down, but we can still send a message to the team. The stabilizers are wonky, so it'll be a rough ride, but we're not going far. Oh, and you'll need to manually steer us."

"Why didn't you say something?" Riff started the engine, letting it warm up system by system so it wouldn't overload.

"We had enough on our minds, and you were planning on using the captain's transport." Jakobsen tapped out a sequence on the console. "Sending a message to Tuputala. She's going to have to bypass and open these bay doors. It's locked from the transport."

Riff frowned as he started going through the warm-up checklist, and the transport shuddered. "Are you sure she's going to make the trip? Stabilizers are more than shaky."

Jakobsen pulled a wall panel off its dangling hinges and went to work with pliers and duct tape. The intense expression of concentration on his face reminded Riff of how he'd looked at him a few times. He glanced away before he could linger on the wish for more contact like that.

A few minutes later, the shaking evened out. "You sure it will hold?" Riff asked.

"It'll be fine. Trust me," Jakobsen said, taking his seat again. "I used to build ships like this."

Back before Jakobsen had committed his crime and landed here. He didn't seem like a killer, but Riff knew that it was only a matter of the right provocation. They all had it in them. Had it really only been days ago when he'd picked Jakobsen for the team partially because he was attracted to him? Seemed like forever.

Riff stole a glance at Jakobsen. His gaze lingered on the turn of his mouth, the long lashes around his eyes. He wanted Jakobsen to look at him again the way he did and feel that zing.

"Tuputala says to give her a minute." Jakobsen swiveled in his seat and turned to face Riff.

There it came, the quick, breathless punch of need. A need that was now more than desire and included the wish for genuine human contact, basic and clean. A minute was long enough to steal a kiss. As quick as the thought came, Riff pushed it away.

"Explain something to me," Jakobsen continued. "You seem to be a take-charge kind of guy, yet you want someone to dominate you in bed."

A flash of memory came to him of intense hazel eyes, silently demanding he obey, and Riff's pulse jumped with remembered heat.

"You want to bring this up now? Don't we have enough going on?"

"I want to think of something that doesn't remind me of how fucking terrified I am. And I want to understand you." Jakobsen's gaze slid over him, as potent as a touch. "Because you seem like one giant contradiction to me."

"What? You couldn't figure that out when you touched me, or does it only work on dead things?" Riff asked.

Jakobsen flinched, and Riff had to look away. It made Riff feel strange, a weird combination of shame and comfort, to think of Jakobsen rummaging around in his mind. He had demons in his head. Memories of the horrible things he'd done. Maybe Jakobsen hadn't delved that deep, because he didn't act as if he wanted to run away screaming.

"I get emotion mostly, and from you it was a whole hot mess of want. Made it damn difficult to think clearly. But I also got that you were in some deep shit with the captain, and I didn't want to be the cause of making it worse." Jakobsen searched Riff's face. "I'm sorry. It's not something I could control. Most of the time, I let the images and emotions wash over me. A person carries around too much history for me to make any sense of it unless I concentrate or it's an intense moment that happened recently."

Riff supposed he couldn't blame Jakobsen too much. It wasn't like he'd given Jakobsen much of an opportunity to discuss it in the steam rooms, and Jakobsen had tried to stop it. If he could let Riff in on that secret, then he supposed he could offer something in return.

"It feels good to let go and not be in charge, to let someone else take control and make the decisions," Riff admitted, turning his attention back to the controls.

"And the pain? Pleasure or punishment?" Jakobsen asked in a low voice.

Probably more than a little of both, but it was nothing he cared to get into with Jakobsen. "Look, what happened in the steam rooms, I wasn't myself, and you didn't seem interested, so let's let it go at that."

"I wasn't interested because you didn't seem like yourself. I wasn't about to be the cause of Vidal beating you senseless." Jakobsen caught his chin, and Riff was snared by his eyes, damn him. They hit him with a jolt of electricity. "He's not a part of the equation anymore. Believe me, I'm more than interested. If we ever find another moment alone when there's not so much riding on the line, I'll show you how interested I am."

CHAPTER EIGHT

"Good to have you back, Khora," Tuputala said as Khora and Zed returned to the captain's suite. "How's she running?"

"Laboring badly," Zed replied. Tuputala was just going to have to deal with him being a part of the team. "She's going to need a lot of work if we're going to trust her to get us anywhere."

"But that's a worry for later," Khora cut in. "Give me the rundown, and then I want you and Quinet to get some sleep. We're going to have to work all hours to get it fixed, and we're all still recovering from whatever illness hit us. I don't want a relapse because we're paranoid from exhaustion. So six hours at least, while three of us work on getting the transport in decent shape."

"I was able to get a visual of the bridge," Wilt replied with a grim look. "Captain's not alone. He has as many people as we do, maybe more. I saw at least five. Some of them are our favorites, Flaubert, Barboza, and D, that Big Daddy Dick of a helmsman."

Zed's hands tensed into fists, and he shook off the chill that rippled down his spine. Best not to think about his memories of the doctor. It was over, and he wasn't going to give Dr. Barboza another chance to get his hands on him.

"Oh joy," Khora muttered, his brows drawn together in thought.

"We were able to lock out the controls for the bay," Tuputala added. "Captain shouldn't be able to jettison this transport. I'm not sure what he's going to use for food and water. Cook's running around the galley julienning anybody who walks in. Someone's tearing apart the engine room. There are a couple others still alive, but not in any position to do anyone harm."

"What about survivors who might need help?" Khora asked as he moved to the screens to study them. Zed didn't know how he had the stomach for it.

"No." Wilt shot Khora a stern look. "We haven't seen anyone, but even if we did, we're not in the business of rescuing every stray. We know there's no other lifers left. Let the captain worry about his own damn crew."

"What about kids?" Zed cut in. Everybody but Quinet looked at him, Wilt surprised, Tuputala livid with rage, and Khora thoughtful. "You said some of the captain's crew had families with them, wouldn't that mean kids?"

"Nobody in their right mind would bring a kid aboard Vidal's ship." Wilt shook her head in disbelief as Tuputala's eyes narrowed dangerously.

"You'd like that, wouldn't you?" Tuputala said in a hard, menacing voice. "Add another kid to your kill list."

Zed's heart pounded with the wild rhythm of his sudden rage. His hands tightened into fists with the urge to lash out. The alien thought came as a shock. Tuputala was injured. He'd never struck a woman in his life. She was hitting where it hurt the most, but punching her back was a terrible idea. Knowing that did nothing to quell the fury pounding in him. He stepped forward into Tuputala's space, craning his head to meet her glare for glare.

"I never touched Hannah, and I don't care how crazy I got when we were sick and tearing this place apart. I've never hurt a kid, you sick fuck."

"Enough," Khora snapped as he and Wilt got between them. Wilt pushed Zed back, and he fought the wild, reckless feeling the drums aroused in him. The sound faded, but Zed sensed they weren't completely gone, just waiting for more provocation. Khora was right. They weren't entirely healthy yet. Not if he could still hear the drums.

Zed glared at Wilt, but the gray-haired computer tech only stared back at him impassively. "Concentrate on the machines, Jakobsen. Not her baiting."

"They're all dead," Quinet murmured.

"Is the captain's bed comfortable?" Tuputala asked, and Zed looked away, clenching his jaw.

She'd said that just to dig under his skin. He longed to just say fuck it and cut her out completely, but that would weaken them as a whole and Khora would never go for it. They didn't need suspicion tearing them apart. There were enough people gunning for them, and the sound of the drums had rattled him. He'd hoped that part was over. So for now he'd just stay in his own space and she'd better stay in hers.

"Comfortable enough. More important, it'll fit your oversized self with room to spare, so get out of my sight and get some rest before I get testy," Khora replied.

Zed watched them go, Tuputala leading Quinet, who gnawed on his knuckle, sending darting glances in Zed's direction.

Fuck, it couldn't happen again. Zed rubbed his arms, remembering the sensation of being strapped down. They could all lose their minds and go after each other. The thought of tearing into his teammates sickened him, and the image of those bloodied, broken bodies throughout the ship calmed the simmering anger. He needed to tell Khora he heard the drums, no matter how softly.

As soon as the hatchway shut on Tuputala and Quinet, Wilt turned to them. "Khora, we've got a problem. The ship's got offensive capabilities, both a tractor beam and enough weaponry to annihilate the transport. We've been locked out of any kind of access to them. If I can get onto the bridge, I can figure how to shut them down from there."

Khora swore and paced as he rubbed his chin, his dark eyes thoughtful. Khora had earned Zed's respect for his ability to think fast and take command of a situation. He was sure he'd come up with a solution for this too.

"Okay, let me think about it. We have a few days of repairs before we can take off anyway. Let's get to work."

"I'm worried about Quinet too," Wilt said, her delicate brows drawing together. "He's not batshit violent, but he didn't come back all there either. I don't think he can take this upside-down craziness we are dealing with. It's too much."

Khora nodded and walked away to look outside the large porthole that stretched the length of the meeting room wall. "Rest might help, that's why I sent him first. Otherwise, I think working on computer problems might steady him. That's work he's used to. We're going to have to shelter him as much as we can."

"Probably a good idea," Wilt replied and headed toward the transport bay.

Zed caught Khora's arm. "I heard the drums again a moment ago when Tuputala and I got into each other's faces. It was soft, but it was there. Did you?"

Khora shook his head, searching Zed's face. "Could be an echo considering tensions were high. Let me know if you see or hear anything else. What about when you touch things? Is that returning? No, don't reach," he said sharply as Zed brushed his fingers over the console, seeking the flash of imprinted emotions. A lightning shot of pain ricocheted through his skull.

"Fuck, no, still hurts."

Khora gave him an exasperated look. "You're resting next. Got it?"

"Only if you're resting with me." Zed traced his fingertips along Khora's jaw, savoring the warmth of touching someone without the barrier of his gloves. Heat warmed the bleakness in Khora's eyes. "And as much as I'd like to imply otherwise, I mean resting."

Khora's gaze raked over him, and his mouth quirked in a wicked smile. "Such a shame that a man with eyes and a body like yours is so damned practical."

Zed laughed. It felt good to laugh, strange in this situation but such a needed release. "I'll work on that."

"See that you do."

Zed double-checked to make sure his security measures were in place, then transferred the live feed of the ship to play in the bay and transport. There weren't that many of them holed up in the captain's suite, so he didn't know what they could do to hold them off if the captain and his crew tried to remove them. Khora shot him a grateful look, then got started sorting out the mess inside the transport while Zed and Wilt came up with a list of repairs.

As he worked he considered the obstacles they faced. The repairs were one thing and sadly the easiest problem of all, just one that would take time. The hardest part would be keeping her safe if the captain found out they had her. As for the weapons, Zed couldn't see being able to get Wilt on the bridge. It seemed to him it would be stupid to abandon. It was as much of a strategic spot as the captain's quarters. Zed didn't think the captain would be foolish enough to leave it unguarded for any lure. There had to be another way.

"You're right, Wilt. Looks like Captain managed to find a couple of guards in addition to the doctor. I was hoping you were wrong about Flaubert. She's a first-rate asshole." Khora's dispassionate tone didn't match the fury in his eyes as he stared at the screen. "The helmsman's probably the one who jettisoned the transport. D could program it back if we captured him."

"What if he doesn't want to talk?" Zed asked, not sure if he wanted the answer.

"Let me alone with D," Wilt responded. "I guarantee he'll talk."

"He'll talk. A man like him is a coward at heart. It wouldn't take much convincing at all. Even the threat of persuasion would be enough." Khora handed Wilt a length of rubber tubing and went back to rummaging and organizing.

Then there was the problem of Khora himself, Zed thought as he went back to his musing. Now was not the time to be attracted to anyone, much less start to fall for them. Zed had tried telling himself Khora was a killer, along with everyone else on the team. They'd been sentenced to the ship for a reason. But since all this happened, it didn't seem to matter anymore. Hell, if the circumstances had worked out the way Zed wanted them to, he'd be a killer. Heller deserved it, and one day that man would get what was coming to him.

He wondered what Khora knew about the helmsman that made him so sure he'd be an easy mark. There was history there, Zed heard it in his voice. Zed thought he'd known secrets because of his abilities, but Khora probably knew more about everybody on the ship and their quirks and weaknesses than anyone else. All that knowledge, locked in that brain of his, just waiting for the right time to be used.

"Hold up," Khora said with surprise, "looks like Noyes managed to survive. I wouldn't have placed odds on that. Not fresh out of a hiber unit."

Zed looked at the monitor, curious to get a glimpse of the person they rescued. The lean white-blond-haired man was bending near the captain's ear, whispering as the captain listened with a tense expression. Then he glanced up, looking right at the camera, and Zed sat up with a gasp as memory hit him.

"He was there."

"What do you mean?" Khora glanced at him with a frown. "Where was he?"

"The night...." Zed touched his temple, struggling to remember. "The night the riot started. I thought I saw him. In the penal wing...." He trailed off as the memory fragmented. He'd thought he'd seen other people that night. People who had no chance of being there.

Khora's frown deepened, and he turned to Wilt. "Did you see that man at all?"

Wilt wiggled out from under the bulkhead and studied the screen for a minute before she shook her head. "I don't know. Maybe. Who knows what happened after everything got fucked sideways."

Zed tried to think of any other incidents, but he had the bone-chilling sensation that examining those memories too much might lead to insanity again. "I heard the drums before the madness hit," he said, his voice soft, but Khora shot him a sharp look. "Just before I left the steam rooms, I think."

"Oh yeah, those drums, like a motherfucking orgy in my head," Wilt muttered, going back to work. "You think you'd get a headache from it."

That was true. There was nothing painful about the drums… more like a driving force. Zed shook his head and forced the memory away before it grabbed hold of him. He had too much to do to get distracted.

"So we all had audio or visual hallucinations before leaving the derelict," Khora said in a thoughtful voice, tapping a bundled cord of stripped wiring against his palm. "Definitely had them afterward before the riot." He glanced at Zed, his eyes narrowed. "Acting out of character, taking risks. Or was that just me? Did you experience anything like that?"

"I didn't say no right away in the steam room, and I knew what the dangers were. My rational side was not happy with me," Zed admitted.

"I tried picking a fight with Tuputala. Fuck if I even remember why, but I pissed her off pretty good. Quinet broke into his secret stash of liquor. Looked like he planned on drinking himself into a coma." Wilt peered out from underneath the bulkhead. "Are you saying we brought some kind of mutant virus back with us?"

"Contagions aren't my specialty," Khora admitted. "This isn't like anything I've seen before. It's a mass paranoia, more of a mental meltdown than a sickness, and it hit pretty damn quick, so it didn't have a long incubation period. I'm more inclined to think some kind of airborne chemical or drug lingered in the air on the ship."

Watching Khora work his way through a problem was almost as fascinating as tinkering with a broken-down engine. He could almost see the thoughts tumbling through Khora's head as he gnawed on his lip. Zed wondered what he'd see if he touched Khora, then remembered he couldn't see anything anymore. Khora made him want to try, if it ever came back, and if Khora would allow it.

"I think you're reaching," Wilt said, and Khora focused his gaze on her. "We had our suits on. We shouldn't have been affected like that. And that doesn't explain how we brought it back to our ship."

Zed crawled under the console, tracking down the source of the misfire in the lines. The right signals weren't going through. He half listened to Wilt and Khora's discussion, letting the rich tenor of Khora's voice roll through him, striking a warm chord. Ah, there it was. Fricking components were half-melted. Tuputala must've been losing her damned mind trying to keep this rattling deathtrap together. How the hell Khora managed to operate the thing he didn't know. It had been a time bomb waiting to happen.

He poked his head out. "Please tell me how the fuck this thing flew?"

"Wishes and prayers." Khora shot a quick smile at him that hit with a spark of heat before turning back to Wilt. "The suits should block out most dangers I'm aware of, but there are always more we haven't discovered. They must've blocked some, the hallucinations were stronger later…. Though it could be just a matter of time. It's hard to say. As much as I loathe Barboza and his medical opinion, I'd be curious to know what he thinks. Even an imbecile guesses right on occasion."

"What bugs me is the coincidences that cannot possibly be coincidences." Zed peered out from under the console. "Why us? Why did we recover when everybody else succumbed permanently to insanity or was slaughtered?"

"That's troubling you too?" Khora looked at Zed thoughtfully. "I have my team intact. Vidal's got his favorite cronies. Like a chess game."

That resonated with Zed. The situation seemed manipulated, staged, but for what purpose, he didn't know.

"I think you two are drinking paranoia juice," Wilt grumbled. "Keep this to yourselves, okay? I love Quinet like a little brother, but he was off before this. He doesn't need to be seeing more conspiracies. Besides, there are a hundred places on this ship where someone could hide. It's possible we're not alone and others have recovered."

Zed thought of the giant salvage rooms, filled with all manner of junk, or the narrow, winding maze of corridors and honeycombed cells in the prison. That was only half the ship. Wilt had a point. There could be other pockets of survivors. They'd only been looking for a few hours. Somehow, though, he couldn't quite make himself believe that.

"I'll leave Quinet out of it," Khora promised. "How much time do you think you need on the bridge to do what you have to do, Wilt?"

"Let me think on it, and I'll give you a plan," Wilt replied after a moment, and Zed groaned under his breath. He wasn't going to like the plan, he just knew it. "I'll need to disable the weapons and make it look like they're still online. I also want to track the captain's transport. If we can figure out where it is, maybe we can get to it or call it back to the bay."

"I'll talk with Tuputala when she wakes up," Khora said. "It might be time to contact the captain again and arrange a tête-à-tête."

Zed pressed his lips together and jerked on a warped casing. It came away with a clang. Khora wanted to meet with that sadistic son of irradiated space trash. Bad idea. It would take them out of their safety zone. Even if it did get the captain off the bridge.

"I don't think it'll work. Pass me that spanner," Wilt said. Zed heard Khora rummage around, and then she continued. "Why would the captain agree to meet with us? He's not going to trust us, with good reason. I'd slit his gullet myself and smile while I did it."

"That's why he'll meet with us. He'll want to set a trap," Khora replied.

Fuck, it got worse and worse. "What's to stop the captain from regaining control of his suite?" Zed crawled out to glare at Khora. Their gazes met and clashed. Damn, Khora was serious.

"That's where Quinet and you come in. You know the tech to seal the hatchways. He's good at computer coding. Between you two I think we can lock this suite down tight." Khora eyed Zed's angry, worried expression. "I'm not saying we go now. I want to give Vidal time to think about how bad this could get if he doesn't negotiate in good faith. The galley is off-limits unless he wants to try to take out that cook, and there's no way to know how much food has been contaminated. I want him to be hungry and tired. In the meantime, we all can have a rest and continue working on getting the transport running. Fair enough?"

Zed nodded and worked his way back under the console. Rest might make Khora see reason, though he wasn't holding out any hope.

CHAPTER NINE

RIFF WOKE up from a restless dream, pressed against Jakobsen's hard, half-naked body. His heart thudded. Dread clenched his throat. He glanced around to make sure no one had intruded on them. The low light Riff had insisted remain on revealed the large bed and crumpled sheets in Vidal's otherwise neat and clinical bedroom. Riff should've followed Wilt's example and slept on the couch they'd retrieved and stashed in the transport bay. The clutter and noise would've been better than the stark memories here.

Then again, he wouldn't have had the pleasure of his arm around Jakobsen's waist with Jakobsen holding on like he didn't want to let go. Riff relaxed against him, burrowing closer and luxuriating in the rare and welcome comfort and peace after the recent horrors. He breathed in Jakobsen's masculine scent, savored the warmth of his body and the rise and fall of his deep, even breathing.

Riff should get up and return to work. They had a thousand things left to do, and the others needed their rest—if Riff could pry them away from their work on the guidance system. Unless by some miracle that was fixed.

Jakobsen stirred, tensed, and then went still before slowly relaxing. It had to be disconcerting to wake up in a strange bed and be bombarded by other people's memories. Would he just see the two of them since they were the last occupiers, or would it extend further back to Tuputala and Quinet? Riff didn't even want to contemplate Jakobsen picking up on moments between him and Vidal.

Jakobsen rubbed his palm over Riff's arm. "Stop trying to use your psychics," Riff said.

"How'd you know?" Jakobsen turned his head toward Riff.

Because it was human nature to scratch an itch or irritate a healing wound. "You're awake and quiet. Because it's what I and just about every other patient I've known would do." Riff's arm tightened around his waist. "How's it feel? Any pain?"

"No, no pain." Jakobsen paused, and Riff suspected he was reaching again. "It feels odd, but not dead anymore, like there's something blocking me, a patchy barrier."

The description reminded Riff once again of a nerve reawakening after overstimulation, only this was regenerating faster. "The barrier's called self-preservation," Riff replied dryly. "Your instincts know better than your reason does. I'm suggesting you wear your gloves today so that part of your brain can rest."

Jakobsen turned to face him and slid his arms around Riff. "What happens if my ability returns? Are you still going to let me touch you? Knowing I can't stop from seeing what I see?"

Riff stared at him, surprised by the question. Jakobsen drew him in like no one else had since Didier. He appreciated how Jakobsen held his own against Tuputala's obvious animosity and didn't let it affect the job. He believed Jakobsen when he claimed his innocence, which was a laugh. Riff heard many lifers insist they weren't guilty in the face of clear evidence. Tuputala certainly believed Jakobsen hurt a child, but when Riff looked into his eyes, he just couldn't see it.

He'd like to think Jakobsen wouldn't judge him in return for the things he'd done, but that he didn't believe. He traced his fingers over Jakobsen's face, outlined the shape of his mouth.

"I don't know. Would you still want to touch me knowing you won't be able to stop from seeing what I'm really like?"

"Yeah," Jakobsen replied without hesitation. "I'd want to touch you. Despite everything that's happened since the night in the steam room, I keep thinking about how much I want to touch you."

The conviction in Jakobsen's voice stirred emotions Riff had thought were long dead. Before he could respond, Jakobsen kissed him, a long, slow kiss, igniting a craving that had only partially to do with desire. He kissed Riff like he wanted more than a hot, quick release. He kissed Riff like he wanted to learn all the secret places inside of him. He kissed Riff like he was a man, not an object to be used. It unsettled him even as he hungered for more.

Riff kissed Jakobsen back with a rising urgency as thoughts of returning to work fled. Stealing a few minutes for themselves wouldn't hurt.

Riff pulled his mouth away with a shuddering sigh and dragged his nails lightly through Jakobsen's hair. "Rougher." His cock ached and stiffened at the answering throb of Jakobsen's cock against his thigh. "Kiss me like you own me."

"Is that what you want, Riff?" Jakobsen nipped his lower lip, a hard sting that made Riff groan. He slid his hand down Riff's side to grip his hip and tug him closer. "To be possessed?"

"Yes." Riff moaned with pleasure as Jakobsen rolled on top of him, settling between Riff's spread thighs. He had the body of a man who hauled around machinery parts all day. Though he'd cleaned up some before they'd passed out, he still smelled faintly of engine grease and sweat. After Vidal's prissy cleanliness, Riff found it to be an incredible turn-on.

Jakobsen kissed him again with the same hungry intensity he'd shown Riff in the steam room, all devouring lips and possessive thrusts of his tongue. He made Riff hot with need. Jakobsen's hands slid over him, exploring, tracing gentle fingers over Riff's scars. Riff's chest tightened to have Jakobsen tenderly touch the marks that Vidal had laid on him, and he had the urge to shrink away. Then Jakobsen broke off the kiss, and his mouth followed where his hands had touched.

"Don't," Riff said on a strangled gasp. He tugged on Jakobsen's biceps, silently urging him to abandon his body and kiss him again, but Jakobsen remained unmoving. He looked at Riff with his strange, intense gaze. "Hurt me." Riff needed the pain in his body to mask the pain inside. Once he'd enjoyed the pain only because it brought pleasure with it, but that distinction had gotten lost.

Jakobsen shifted his weight onto one arm and slid his other hand up Riff's body to cup his jaw. He studied Riff, rubbing his thumb over Riff's lower lip. He looked at him like he could see all of his wants and fears.

"Are you trying to read me?" Riff demanded.

"No, but right now I wish I could." Jakobsen's gaze darkened as he leaned down to kiss Riff again, a gentle nudging of his lips, a tenderness that made Riff hurt worse than any whip ever could. His protest was muffled as Jakobsen slanted his mouth, kissing Riff deeper and silently demanding a response.

A tremor rippled through Riff, breaking the frozen lock on his body. His arms stole around Jakobsen as his kiss stripped him bare and opened up all the raw and vulnerable places. Jakobsen's hips nudged against Riff's, hard cocks rubbing against each other through their pants.

Pleasure shot through him. He was balanced between the desire for Jakobsen to continue and the fear that he would.

"How do you want me to hurt you?" Jakobsen asked against his lips, groaning as Riff's cock jumped. "Do you have a favorite way?"

Riff was surprised Jakobsen was considering it, and the thought of Jakobsen laying hard hands on him made it difficult to think. "I thought you claimed you weren't into that."

Jakobsen shifted his hips, grinding against him, and Riff groaned. "I'm warming up to the idea, especially when it's clear it turns you on so much. But I have to know if you're going to keep trying to push me away or shut me down when I want to show you more than pain." His lips trailed down Riff's neck, and he kissed the hard beat of his pulse.

"Why would you want to do that?" Riff asked, forcing himself to not pull away.

Jakobsen lifted his head and smiled. Riff's brows drew together. He didn't see that expression often. There sure as hell hadn't been many reasons to do so since they'd met. He liked the way it looked on Jakobsen, and he suspected that before he'd been sentenced he'd been a man who smiled often.

"Because that's the kind of man I am, and I'm going to insist it be a part of whatever this is that's brewing between us."

Riff considered Jakobsen's question, weighing his desire for more roughness and pain against his discomfort with Jakobsen's affectionate side. It was saddening to realize that he was more comfortable with abuse. He remembered a time when it hadn't been like that.

Jakobsen claimed he wasn't dominant, but then there were moments like this when he vowed to have it his way, urging Riff to move out of his comfort zone. Riff hadn't been challenged like this in too long. He remembered how Jakobsen had put a stop to their encounter in the steam rooms with utter finality. When Riff had known pushing him wouldn't work. He'd done it without cruel words or blows. Just like now, Jakobsen was adamant. Riff had a choice. He could do it Jakobsen's way or stop now and walk away. Jakobsen didn't act with authority often, but when he did it was absolute. It was so fucking arousing even as it terrified him.

It was insane to even consider getting involved with Jakobsen and to allow him to push those boundaries. But for all Riff knew, they were going to die soon, and he didn't want to go out with Vidal being his last memory.

"I'm not making any promises, but I'll try," Riff said.

There came that smile again, sexy, unshadowed, as if nothing else existed but the two of them. It punched Riff right in the chest. "That's all I'm asking for." Jakobsen laid a hard kiss on Riff's lips, then knelt up to slowly remove both of their pants.

Riff watched the reveal with avid eyes. Jakobsen's body was blocky, with his shoulders only slightly wider than his hips. Though he was short, he still seemed bigger than Riff.

He reached for him as Jakobsen lay back down, covering them both with the sheet. He slid his hand along Riff's chest, eyes following the path. "You never told me how you liked to be hurt."

Riff's cock jumped hard as a flood of possibilities entered his mind. "I'm a whore for it all. Sometimes I like a quick and brutal whipping, other times I like a slow build, things that take patience like hot wax, then there are the times when I like to feel owned as much as pain, with clamps and collars." He met Jakobsen's gaze, saw the heat there, and it stirred his desire more. He wasn't faking.

Jakobsen's palm slid higher until he was covering Riff's nipple. Riff's breath caught as he felt it harden against Jakobsen's hand. "So if I do this, you'll like it?" He gave Riff's nipple a hard twist that had him crying out softly and arching against Jakobsen at the hot zing of pain.

"Yes."

"What about this?" Jakobsen's lips hovered over Riff's nipple for a moment. Riff's breath caught in anticipation as he rubbed his cock against Jakobsen's hard thigh. Jakobsen's hot tongue circled, his gaze intent on Riff, as he soothed the throb with a lick and light suck.

Riff groaned, catching Jakobsen's head and sinking his fingers in Jakobsen's hair. "Not enough. Make it hurt more."

Jakobsen nipped it hard, and Riff bucked against him with a needy cry. "Yes." Before Riff could demand more, Jakobsen kissed him, one drugging kiss after another until Riff's head swam and he ached with the want for Jakobsen to take it to another level.

The hatchway hissed open, and Jakobsen broke the kiss with a light growl as they both looked over his shoulder. "Sorry to interrupt," Tuputala said, though from her tone she wasn't, and the look she shot

Riff was resigned and angry. "Captain wants to talk to you immediately. I don't think he's going to accept me telling him you're occupied."

The hatchway shut again, and Riff cursed under his breath, pushing Jakobsen's chest. "Vidal always did have screwed-up timing." He had been expecting the man to hold out for at least another day.

"Fuck the captain," Jakobsen rasped, pinning and kissing Riff in a way that made it impossible to think unless it was to beg for more. A hard shudder went through him as all resistance melted away. "We're finishing this."

Jakobsen shifted and pulled Riff on top of him, his hard cock grinding against Riff's ass, rubbing between his cheeks. Riff groaned, pushing back against him as Jakobsen rocked, so close to what Riff wanted that it made the sharp edge of his desire more acute. Then Jakobsen cupped Riff's cock in his hand, squeezing and stroking, and Riff was lost. His breath came in harsh gasps, his heart pounded as he cried out his release.

For a moment they lay quiet together with Jakobsen's hard-on still pressing against him as Riff trembled. Jakobsen's hand skated along Riff's body in a long caress, and his lips brushed Riff's shoulder. Then his hands gripped Riff's hips. "I guess I'm a more possessive guy than I ever thought, because when you go out to talk to him, I want you to still be feeling me."

He thrust hard against Riff, hips driving up again and again. Riff clenched around him, groaning as Jakobsen pressed against and slipped by his entrance, making him crave deeper penetration, though he'd already come.

"Zed…."

Riff writhed on top of him, trying to angle himself so Jakobsen could push inside of him. Jakobsen's teeth scraped his shoulder as he stiffened. Riff clenched, feeling Jakobsen's cock throb, the hot rush of wetness, the scent of sweat and sex. The normalcy of it in the midst of all this chaos and constant dread was a balm to his soul.

Jakobsen laid his chin on Riff's shoulder with a groan. "We're not even close to being done with each other. Go talk with the captain, get us off this ship, because I want you with no worries that he's going to retaliate against you."

Riff squeezed Jakobsen's hands, then rose, not looking at him, his insides such a jumble of conflicting emotions and thoughts he didn't even know where to begin to unravel them. It was easier to concentrate on the problem at hand, and that was distracting Vidal so they could finish repairs. If they managed to survive and escape… well, Riff would deal with Jakobsen then.

ZED WATCHED Khora leave, getting the impression he'd pushed the man's boundaries enough. That certainly hadn't been his intent when he'd woken up to the first moment of peace he'd felt in over a year. He had been safe, rested, unencumbered by visions he didn't want, and Khora was there, curled against him trustingly.

There were a thousand reasons why Zed should've left the attraction between them alone for now. They had enough going on to keep their attention. He was pretty sure Khora had his own reasons as well. But he'd learned a few things in the time he'd had with Khora since the derelict. Life was short. Life was fragile. And he had to grab hold of what he could when he could, or else it all became too overwhelming and a man didn't have anything left to live for.

Zed had no fucking clue what would happen when he walked out of this room, but Khora was his present, and he wasn't ready to leave him. Maybe it had been selfish of them to want to steal a few minutes before going out to face the nightmare, or maybe it was as Khora said, self-preservation.

He sat up and dragged a hand through his hair. He should give Khora a few minutes to settle down Vidal's ire before he appeared. He ran his hands over the bed they'd occupied, touched the pillow Khora had slept on. Nothing. He was still as mind numb as any other nonpsychic. However, when he'd touched Khora, he'd felt the vital buzz of his mind. There were no emotions or impressions, but there was still the sense of his presence, strong and comforting. As much as Zed's ability had made him miserable, it had been an integral part of him, and Zed hadn't realized how much until it was gone. If he recovered it, maybe he could help Khora track down what happened to everyone.

He'd abide by Khora's orders and wear the gloves. He'd never heal if he forced it. Zed cleaned up in the captain's private steam room, forcing himself not to linger, though the surroundings were luxurious compared to the penal steam rooms. There was too much left to do, and those problems occupied his thoughts as much as curiosity over what the captain wanted.

Zed wiped steam off the mirror and stared at his hazy reflection. So much had changed since he'd last seen himself. He should look different, more than several days' worth of stubble on his cheeks. An image flickered behind him, and Zed froze, his hands tightening on the sink as his heart began to drum. He looked down at the sink, drew in a deep breath, and looked back up again, fully expecting the brief apparition to be gone.

Dray Heller stared back at him, his face bruised and bloody, his eyes wild with fear and rage.

Zed jumped back with a yell and spun around to face an empty room. *It's just a hallucination.* That thought brought no comfort. He groped for his new talisman. He had to tell Khora that he could still be sick, but as he left the bathroom, common sense returned. He couldn't run out there naked, babbling about seeing things. That would only make a tense situation worse. He needed to calm down, get himself together, and pull Khora aside the first chance he got.

He got dressed and stripped the bed before remaking it. The captain had extra linens stowed away, all neatly pressed in rigid stacks. The chore helped to calm him. Thinking of Khora distracted him even more.

Zed remembered the feel of Khora's mind, the intensity of his emotions, all that activity locked behind his cool exterior. Khora was like a complicated engine, one that endlessly fascinated Zed as he tried to figure out how it worked. And Khora would take some figuring out. He had touched Zed with no hesitation or coyness, but the submission had been there too, in the pliancy of his body and mouth. The combination excited and intrigued him.

The encounter made Zed rethink what Khora was asking for when he wanted to be dominated. He wanted pain, but maybe not all the time. He also said he wanted to let go, to not be in charge. Zed could understand how that could be freeing for a man who made life and death decisions. Every time he led a salvage mission, everybody looked to him to keep them safe. Right now as they were trying to escape, they all counted on Khora for answers, even Zed. It was a heavy burden.

It would take work to get Khora to accept more than pain from Zed. The scars on Khora's body were minor compared to the scars on his soul. But Zed was more determined than ever to show another side to Khora.

Zed walked out into the main area to face Tuputala's glare and the joy of Vidal's face still on the screen. The captain paused midsentence and narrowed his eyes as his mouth thinned. Wilt and Quinet were missing, probably working on the transport. Best to keep quiet about them—not that he planned on engaging in any conversation. He nodded at Vidal and took a seat next to Tuputala.

He didn't know the captain well, but still to Zed's eyes, he looked strained since the last time they saw him before they took their rest. His eyes were tight and hollowed. Thirty-six hours without a safe food supply, water, or a place to rest comfortably would make an impression.

"Is this all your men, or are more going to pop out of my bedroom?" Vidal asked.

"I believe we were addressing your complaints," Khora replied, ignoring the question. "If you take a look at the surveillance I sent you, you'll see that though the galley is occupied by a maniac, it's just one man. I'm sure your guards will have no issues nullifying the threat. Then you'll have all the food you desire and won't need access to this suite."

"You cannot barricade yourselves in my quarters," Vidal said in a low, intense voice. "That will not be tolerated."

Khora looked around the room, leaned back in his chair, and spread his hands. "Yet that's exactly what I did."

"I'll shut off life support in that area."

"How? It seems that I have all the engineers on my team, and you built a redundancy for that system in your quarters. You're no threat to me in that respect." Khora leaned forward and crossed his arms on the table. "I'll give you the cold truth. We need each other. If we don't work together, this ship is going to be our tomb."

Vidal's expression pinched with anger, though there was a grudging respect in his eyes when he looked at Khora. "I know you have more men than the three with you, and I'm sure by now you know exactly who's on my team. How about an exchange and a meeting? We can discuss our mutual demands then."

"What would you like to exchange?" Khora asked. "I have everything I need here."

"Food enough for six for a week, and in return I'll make sure the water to your quarters stays on. The reservoir I installed is quite small, an oversight on my end, one that I'll rectify as soon as we dock, but in the meantime, it works for my purposes." A thin smile crossed Vidal's face. "My men have enough expertise to do that. You may survive holed up without food, but you'll need water more."

Khora glanced at Tuputala and Zed. "Does he have that capability?" He asked in a low voice.

"Maybe. Let him think we buy it for now." Zed glanced at Tuputala as she nodded her agreement.

"I'll look for the reservoir. See how much we have to work with," Tuputala said and rose from the table.

Khora turned back to Vidal. "I'll see how much food we can spare and get back to you. Then we can discuss a neutral place to meet."

A shaft of alarm went through Zed at the thought of leaving the safety of the quarters for the insanity outside. He'd seen the surveillance, he knew there weren't many remaining outside the walls, but the evidence of what had happened was everywhere. He hadn't realized how walking through it had affected him until he was faced with having to go back. He knew why they had to, but it didn't mean he liked it. One thing was for certain, he wasn't stepping one foot out the hatchway without gloves. Even if his abilities hadn't regenerated fully.

"I thought we could meet in my quarters. There's plenty of room for all our men," Vidal suggested.

"Not happening," Khora replied. "This is my territory now. I'm sure you don't want us invading your bridge. How about the infirmary? It's right in the middle and is defensible."

Once again Vidal's mouth thinned, and his eyes glittered with suppressed anger as he stared at Khora. Then his attention shifted to Zed, and a chill rippled through him. Heller had been antagonistic, but he'd never looked at Zed with such cold resolve. He'd heard rumors of the captain's sadism, seen the evidence on Khora's body, but now he was convinced Vidal would do whatever it took to keep what was his. He wouldn't offer any mercy if given the chance.

"If you show aggression, we'll respond in kind," Khora said with grim promise. "But I'm not looking for violence. I'm sure we can work out a deal that'll be mutually satisfying for both sides."

"You and your deals. One of these days, your scheming is going to blow up in your face." The silky menace in Vidal's voice made Zed cold.

"I'm still alive, aren't I?" Khora retorted. "So are we on or not?"

Zed didn't like this scenario one bit, every one of his instincts shouted this was a bad idea. There had to be another way to shut down the weapons system and to discover where the captain had sent the transport.

The captain turned away, conferring with someone offscreen. Zed caught a glimpse of pale skin and a flash of platinum-blond silvery hair. Then Vidal focused on Khora again. "I agree to your terms. Contact me after you've looked at your food situation and let me know if you still want to trade. In the meanwhile, the water is shut off."

Khora's jaw tightened. "Understood. We can discuss when to meet then." He reached over, tapped the console, and the screen went dark. He opened the comm to the transport. "I need an update. When the hell can we get off this ship?"

"Guidance system still needs a few parts. I made a list. I think we have stability locked down. We have at least another twelve hours of work to do on the engines," Wilt responded, and Khora closed his eyes with a soft swear. "Sorry, but everything on this junk is decades out of date and crumbling. Fixing one system overloads another."

Tuputala returned and shrugged her shoulders. "Captain does have an untouched reservoir tank. I could set it up so we're tapping from it. It's not big, though. What would last him days will go fast with five of us."

Khora turned to Zed. "What did you mean earlier? Is he bluffing?"

"Based on my experience, a ship like this would have an extensive air and water recycling filtration system. Giant reservoirs would take up too much space. There are probably multiple areas set up at strategic points with tanks for the gen-altered algae. Now Captain could destroy the algae or contaminate it, but that would backfire on him."

"A system like that would be too complicated for the captain to cut off manually," Tuputala said. "He'd have to know the innards of the ship pretty damn well to know which pipes are moving water to specific locations."

"I'll pretend I know what the fuck you two are talking about." Khora scrubbed a hand through his hair and stood up. "We'll let the captain think we're buying it. I wouldn't put it past him to try something drastic if he thinks he needs to. In the meantime, Jakobsen, relieve Wilt and Quinet. Let them sleep some. Tuputala, I want to take a look at your shoulder before you help. Then I'll take stock of what food we think we can spare Vidal and his cohorts."

Zed shot Khora a lingering look, but the stubborn man still wouldn't quite meet his eyes. Getting him alone to discuss hallucinations wasn't going to be easy. He'd give him some space while he tended to Tuputala, then speak with him. Khora couldn't avoid talking to him for long. There was too much at stake.

"Understood."

Chapter Ten

"I DON'T like this," Jakobsen said as soon as the access panel to the storage room closed.

Riff examined the quiet, tightly packed space. Spare parts for the machines in the infirmary lined the shelves. The room had somehow escaped the ransacking and chaos. It was a relief to be in a place with no signs of blood or destruction. If they had to wait for Vidal to show, he'd rather it be here, crowded together, than the last room they checked with its dismembered occupant. If they had time to fix…. Riff sighed. They didn't, and the transport took priority.

"You've made your opinion known." Riff met Jakobsen's gaze, silently acknowledging his reservations. He had to admit he shared his suspicions. But this had been the opportunity they needed, and he wasn't going to let it slip by.

"Well, I have to agree with him," Tuputala cut in. "I don't want you in the same section of the ship as the captain. You think that man is going to let you go? As much as you may feel like you were manipulating him, in his eyes he owned you."

"We're not going to let Captain take Khora," Jakobsen replied.

"It's dangerous for you too," Tuputala retorted, her expression hard and angry. "If the captain suspects you're sniffing around, he'll shoot you without even thinking about it."

"I promise not to let my baser instincts get in the way of the job," Jakobsen said wryly with a quick glance at Riff. He believed Jakobsen. That man had a stubborn will. Riff still didn't know what to make of Jakobsen's promise that it wasn't over between them or his reaction to the way Jakobsen treated him. It had him turned inside out. "I don't like the thought of Quinet going with Wilt either."

Privately, Riff was inclined to agree with him on that point as well. Riff was worried about Quinet. Sometimes the man cocked his head as if he was still hearing things no one else could. Riff had also experienced moments where he'd seen things that couldn't possibly be there. Judging from the jumpiness of the others, he wasn't the only one. The situation they were in wasn't just a matter of escaping. If they didn't figure out what happened, Riff would have no way of knowing if it could arise again or if there was a cure. They could escape, only to lose their minds and kill each other. Riff didn't want to go down by his friends' hands. Even more, he didn't want to be the cause of hurting any of them.

He didn't like any of them being separated. Wilt had insisted it would be easier to sneak onto the bridge if she were alone, but Riff didn't know if Vidal would leave behind guards. There was also the matter of the murderous, crazed people still moving about. Tuputala was injured, whether she wanted to admit it or not. He'd considered Jakobsen, but he wasn't sure if Jakobsen had ever been in a kill-or-be-killed moment—except when they were out of their minds. He didn't want to run the risk of Jakobsen freezing if they ran into trouble. Besides, Quinet's nerves would be a liability during negotiations with Vidal.

"Quinet may not be stable, but he'd never deliberately put Wilt in danger," Riff replied. "I worry more he'd cause problems trying to get to her if we took him with us."

"Digging through the computer will give him a problem to focus on." Tuputala poked through some of the spare parts and pocketed one. "We could strike first. If we take out the captain now, the others might fall into line."

"Ambush him and shoot him in cold blood?" Jakobsen's eyes blazed in outrage. "Even if he is a bastard, I'm not going to be a part of that."

Tuputala shot him a surprised look, then glanced at Riff, who responded, "I'd rather not start any more bloodshed. A war will hamper our efforts to get out. If we have to defend ourselves, that's another matter." He met Jakobsen's gaze. "Understood?"

Jakobsen nodded, though he didn't look happy about it. Whatever Tuputala thought about Jakobsen's past and whatever she intimated, Riff didn't think Jakobsen had the stomach for killing. Besides, if Jakobsen heard the drums, however faintly, when he last got into it with Tuputala, Riff didn't want to discover what more violence might spark.

He studied the handheld monitor that showed the now-empty bridge and the equally empty infirmary. He didn't trust Vidal for one moment. Wilt and Quinet appeared on the screen, postures tense as they looked around. Wilt made straight for the console, and Quinet signaled all was clear and moved to help.

"Wilt and Quinet are in place," Riff said.

Movement flickered out of the corner of his eye, a body hanging from the ceiling, swaying in a ponderous arc, but when Riff turned, nothing was there. He clenched his jaw on a new wave of uneasiness. They weren't going anywhere if he didn't discover the cause of this madness. Medical… chemical… there had to be a way of tracking it down.

"Good," Tuputala replied. "I hope they get what they need fast."

"Here he comes," Riff muttered, watching as the captain entered the infirmary with Flaubert, Noyes, and Barboza. They looked as battered as Riff and his crew. The helmsman D and the second guard were missing. "Tuputala, warn Wilt that the bridge is likely to be guarded."

"If it gets violent up there, captain's going to realize something is up. He'll be suspicious when his men don't return," Tuputala replied after relaying the message.

"Good thing we won't be anywhere near the captain if that happens." Riff straightened and met their gazes. "Ready?"

Jakobsen nodded, his eyes grim. "Let's go." Tuputala hefted the gun in her arms and led the way. The murmur of conversation ceased when the infirmary hatchway opened and a tense silence flowed out. Riff eyed the occupants of the room as he stepped through with Jakobsen and Tuputala flanking him.

Vidal turned and surveyed the group before settling his cold gaze on Riff. He was free of the captain. Riff had thought he was so clever when he'd hooked up with Vidal. Instead he'd trapped himself. No matter what happened now, he'd never have to answer to Vidal again and the realization almost made him smile.

Barboza straightened from a crouch with a broken diagnostic machine dangling from his hands. He glared at Riff before staring at Jakobsen with a narrowed, intent gaze. Almost as if Barboza was making a silent promise. Jakobsen shifted back and raised his gun, pointing it toward the doctor.

Riff noted the interaction, vowing to keep an eye on the two of them before surveying the others. He dismissed Flaubert. Tuputala would watch her and turned his attention to Noyes. The refugee stood apart from the others, watching both groups as if they were curiosities on display. The angularity of Noyes's features showed no expression, though the eyes had an avid gleam to them. Noyes somehow managed to be both beautiful and repellent.

"There's no need for violence," Vidal said, breaking the tense tableaux. He gave Jakobsen's raised weapon a pointed glance.

"I agree." Riff holstered his gun, leaving it unclipped and easily accessible. "I have food for you. It's stored in the next room. In return, I expect you to fix that water situation."

"Done," Vidal replied and nodded to Flaubert. "Check that he's telling the truth."

Flaubert shot him a hard glance as she passed them by. She was itching to take them out, but Riff wasn't going to give her that chance. "What else did you want to discuss?" Riff asked as he turned back to Vidal, trusting Tuputala to keep an eye on Flaubert.

"Your terms of surrender," Vidal said, his eyes dark holes of pitiless uncompromise.

"You know that's not going to happen," Riff replied. "Is there anything else?"

Vidal shifted his gaze from Riff to Jakobsen. "What're you doing with them? Tuputala, I get. She's followed Riff around with doggish loyalty for years. You don't belong on their side."

"The only difference between us is we're serving time for our crimes, yet you, Captain Vidal, walk around a free man." Riff didn't want Vidal messing with Jakobsen's head. He was good at finding all the cracks that made up a man's soul and worming diseased, manipulative tendrils into them. He'd known how Riff had needed him, and he'd used that, used Riff's secret pain to hurt him in ways he wasn't sure he'd ever recover from.

Vidal laughed, the sound chilling as he doubled over. Riff eyed him askance. If the madness had returned and it was infectious, they were screwed. Then Vidal lifted his head, and Riff saw the cruel light in his gaze. That, at least, appeared normal.

"Oh yes, you are as guilty as they come. Confessed your crime right in court with no remorse whatsoever."

"Some people just need to die," Riff replied in a cold, flat voice. He caught the quick glance Jakobsen shot him, and Riff felt the sharp sting of his silent judgment. He hadn't cared before what anyone thought of his attitude toward his victims. What a fucking laugh. Those men had been anything but victims. But Jakobsen's opinion troubled him. "This isn't about guilt. Now if you don't have any demands other than our surrender, we can get to mine."

A flash of irritation crossed Vidal's face, and then it was quickly suppressed. "You want demands, here it is. Dr. Barboza raised a good point with me. All the bodies on board this ship pose a health risk. We want you to find and move them to the prison cells."

Riff frowned, his thoughts jumping from one connection to another. It would give him an excuse to examine the bodies and probe Barboza's thoughts on the cause of the mass rage. It would also provide a distraction for them to continue their repairs. Decomposition was a danger, though he didn't intend on staying aboard long enough for it to risk their health.

This could explain part of the mystery of *Pandora*, the lack of bodies. Somebody who recovered from the madness could have jettisoned them. Riff looked at Noyes to find the other man staring at him like he could read his mind. There was something unnerving about the way he watched them as if he were fascinated by the undercurrents between the two parties.

"You want manual labor, as usual," Riff replied.

"That's your only purpose on this ship," Flaubert retorted as she returned and Tuputala shifted to train the gun on her. "They were telling the truth, Captain."

"An honest criminal, how novel," Vidal said.

Riff touched the back of his hand to Tuputala's arm and she relaxed a fraction. "I agree that decomp is a danger and agree to providing help, but only if it's a joint effort. Me and someone of my choosing will work at the task alongside Dr. Barboza and someone of his choosing. We'll bring the bodies to the prison. It'll be up to your team to make sure they get in the cells."

He sensed the sudden tension on either side of him and knew Tuputala and Jakobsen didn't approve. They didn't say anything, but Barboza didn't feel the same restraint. "You're not in any position to give orders. I'm not going to risk my neck by working with you or by slinging bodies around."

"You're right, I can't order you, but I don't have to obey either. If I'm risking myself, I expect the captain to risk one of his top guys." Though Riff was sure Vidal considered Barboza as expendable as anyone else. "Besides, you call yourself a doctor, aren't you the least bit curious to know what we're dealing with? We're going to have to examine those bodies. Unless Noyes has already provided you with an explanation for what happened." Riff shifted his gaze to the quiet man who watched the whole scene with none of the tension that everyone else displayed.

"I'm as lost in the dark as the rest of you." Noyes spread his hands in a helpless gesture that seemed incongruent with his steady gaze. He never blinked. "I have no claim to expertise in human anatomy. There was madness. There was death. And I was alone." The eyes lit up with a strange kind of pleasure that hit Riff with an atavistic chill. "Until I wasn't alone any longer. I have you to thank for that, Mr. Khora. Please allow me to reward you."

Riff took an instinctive step backward. "No need. I'm sure you've thanked the captain."

"Not as much as he deserves, but I'm seeing to that." A quick smile flitted across Noyes's lips, and Riff almost reached for his gun. He wasn't sure what it was about the man, but he set him on edge. Anybody who went through the ordeal he did would end up funny in the head, but Noyes took it to a new level.

"What about your demands?" Vidal cut in. "You already occupy my quarters, and you've obtained weapons. Don't bother asking for my transport back because I have no intention of allowing you to leave. So what is it? A conjugal visit?" His derisive gaze flicked over Riff. "Need a whipping?"

"No," Jakobsen said before Riff could tell Vidal to shove his suggestion down his throat and choke on it. Riff felt a little thrill at the absolute authority in Jakobsen's voice. "You don't have that right any longer."

"I have to agree with him." Tuputala shifted the gun in her arms toward Vidal.

Riff allowed a brief smile of amusement. At least they seemed to agree on something. "Well, if we're done discussing my sex life, we can get down to business." He had what he really wanted, a chance to hunt down what the hell had gone wrong on the ship while providing a distraction so his team could work on repairs, but Vidal wouldn't believe that was it. He needed another demand. "Give me a moment of your time, Captain, one-on-one. I have a proposition for you."

"I hope this is as entertaining as your last one." Vidal gestured toward the curtained-off exam area. "Shall we?"

As Riff turned to close the curtain, he found Jakobsen watching him, his brow furrowed in concern. His eyes and mouth were still red and puffy from the ordeal he'd gone through, which was a reminder they needed to get off this ship.

"Why does he hold such fascination for you?" Vidal asked behind him.

"We need him," Riff retorted, facing Vidal. He looked for signs he'd been hurt during the riot. There were no visible injuries, though he carried himself with a stiffness that implied pain. Riff squelched any empathy he might've once felt. He'd never cared for Vidal, but there had been intimacy and mutual exchange of need. "Him and Tuputala are our best chance of getting this ship running again. Unless you've got a better plan."

"You desire him." Vidal searched Riff's face. "I don't understand why."

Riff barked out a short, humorless laugh. "Don't tell me you're jealous. Are you upset our association has come to an end? Don't kid yourself. He's useful, and I plan on making sure he remains safe, sane, and useful until I don't need him anymore."

"You're not that mercenary. I've been fucking your ass for years. I know what makes you tick. You care about him." Vidal cocked his head with a twisted smile. "Perhaps I should warn him about what happens to your lovers."

Riff ignored the pain of the stab. "I doubt he'll listen. He seems to have formed a powerful dislike of you. Must be my bad influence. He's a violent criminal, same as you and me. I don't give a damn about him any more than he does me. And you're wrong about my mercenary tendencies. Believe me, the relationship I formed with you had nothing to do with tender feelings. I got what I wanted out of it and so did you."

"There is another way in which we differ from Jakobsen," Vidal said with mirth in his eyes and no evidence that Riff's dig irritated him.

"Yeah? Enlighten me," Riff replied, his patience waning. He didn't like the captain's fixation on Jakobsen. He knew what happened when Vidal fixated on a man.

"He's innocent. We're not."

Riff's hands clenched as he stared at Vidal. At first he wanted to laugh the idea off as ludicrous. But Vidal's words mixed with Riff's observations of Jakobsen made the absurdity sound horrifyingly true.

"What the hell are you talking about?"

"Let me clarify. He's not guilty of raping and killing his niece. Dray Heller was furious that Jakobsen had not only interfered with his stepdaughter, but that he'd dared to attack him too, so he had the charges trumped up."

That explained Tuputala's animosity. Jakobsen was lucky she hadn't tried to take him out. Vidal was more of a bastard than Riff had believed. Knowing Vidal's emotional sadism, Riff shouldn't have been surprised, but still it ached to know people judged Jakobsen based on a horror he hadn't committed.

"Why are you telling me?" Riff asked bluntly. Riff was glad to know this information. It would ease tensions between Tuputala and Jakobsen, but he didn't trust Vidal's motivations one second. "What kind of a game are you playing?"

"A man like him is never going to be interested in a man like you," Vidal replied. "Broken, flawed, your star is burning out, Riff."

"And you're reading far too much into it." Riff cocked his head, studying Vidal. "I think you're realizing that you didn't have the hold over me you thought you did, and that's what's burning you."

Vidal's lips thinned. "Get one thing straight. You're not leaving this ship, so if your offer involves that in any way, don't bother wasting your words."

"Why would I want to leave?" Riff asked, spreading his hands as surprise flickered in Vidal's eyes. "I certainly don't want to go back to the military and an endless war. I don't know the first thing about living as a civilian. I sure as hell don't want to be on the run for the rest of my life, waiting for the authorities to catch up with me. I have a job here, a job I do very well."

"Then what do you want?" Vidal asked, his eyebrows drawn together in puzzlement.

"You need help to secure this ship and to get the engines back on again. I have the men who can accomplish both. Me and my crew take over operations for you, get the ship cleaned up, figure out what went wrong. In return, when you get your reward and new prisoners, I head your security with my team. We police the prisoners and coordinate the salvage missions."

Vidal stared at him a long moment. "You do have a rare audacity that I admire, I'll give you that. How does that offer change anything? You still won't be able to leave the ship. You'll still be doing the same job, maybe with a little more freedom. But I don't believe that's all you're angling for."

"It won't be the same," Riff insisted. "I'm not returning to the prison, ever. We'll have our own quarters among your crew. We'll no longer be lifers, and they'll be earning a wage the same as your crew."

"They?" Vidal's gaze raked over Riff. "And what will you be earning?"

Riff moved in closer to Vidal, a smirk crossing his face. "Captain, we're going to be partners, splitting the profits, right down the middle. You need me. You're dead in the water. The engines are down, communication is off-line, and the men you have don't know shit about fixing it. All you can do is send out a distress signal and pray that somebody hears it before you run out of supplies. Pray they'll be friendly and not someone you've pissed off. You could try capturing us, but that could be dangerous. People could get hurt. Killed. There aren't enough of us to be screwing around."

"I've underestimated your ambition." Vidal studied Riff. "Does this mean we're going to be bed partners again too? Or does Jakobsen rule your body now?"

"No one rules my body anymore. And I'm not giving it to you." Riff crossed his arms. "So do we have a deal or not?"

"Straight down the middle? I think we'd have to negotiate that. I may consider ten percent, fifteen if I'm feeling generous." Vidal rubbed his chin. "Let me think on it. You keep up your end, clean up the ship, and I'll give you an answer before we start repairs. Deal?" He held out his hand, evoking memories of another deal years ago that had changed Riff's life.

"Yes. It'll take Tuputala and Jakobsen a few days to run diagnostics anyway." Riff shook Vidal's hand. "As always, it's a pleasure doing business with you, Captain. You won't regret this deal any more than you did the last one. And you might want to think hard about that percentage offer again. I'm not going to be lowballed."

Vidal tightened his grip, pulling Riff toward him. "You might want to use those three days and think of a way to sweeten that deal, my boy. Fifty-fifty is worth a hell of a lot to me. Maybe you can talk Jakobsen into sacrificing himself to me. A man like that would be a challenge."

Denial rose up hot and fast, but Riff choked it down. "I'll give it some consideration."

CHAPTER ELEVEN

ZED CAST several looks in Khora's direction as they made their way back to the captain's suite, trying to figure out what had been said between him and Vidal. Khora's brow was lined in thought. Watching a man think shouldn't be sexy, but with Khora it was, as much as his ability to take charge of a situation, which Zed attributed to his innate passion. He had made a family with this team, whether he realized it or not, and he was hell-bent on protecting them.

Zed wasn't sure where he stood in this family, where he wanted to stand. Tuputala barely tolerated him. He had no doubt she would try to take him out if she thought Khora would be better off. Zed had held himself apart and alone for so long now he'd forgotten how it felt to be part of a tight-knit group, even if only on the fringe.

Tuputala watched Khora as if she wanted to ask questions too, but Khora gave no indication he planned on talking about his meeting with Vidal. "Have you heard from Wilt or Quinet?" Khora asked Tuputala as they entered the more elegant level of the ship that held the captain's suite.

"Not since they left the bridge. We're trying to keep comm silence, just in case." Tuputala shot Khora a grim look, and then her expression turned uncertain when she looked at Zed. "What did the captain mean about him not belonging with us?"

Khora's gaze softened as he looked at Zed. "He may have tried killing the director of the Deneb shipyards, but he didn't touch a child. Vidal admitted your innocence, Jakobsen. I'd misinterpreted the captain's brand of sadism. He gets off on emotional pain more than any other. Everybody sentenced here may be guilty, but for each one of us, there are extenuating circumstances. Regret. Guilt. He enjoys knowing we're trapped with those memories and emotions, sentenced for life to serve on his ship. And when he gets bored watching our little sufferings, he takes one of us aside and lets his cronies have them and sends back what's left."

"Like Bryce?" Tuputala asked softly, her voice sad.

"I suspect so," Khora replied, and Zed's heart twisted at the unspoken pain in his voice.

"What makes you believe Vidal's telling the truth about him?" Tuputala thrust her chin out in Zed's direction.

Zed bit back the need to retort as he considered Khora's words. Extenuating circumstances. Some of his charges had been trumped up, and now that he thought back on it, he saw how that could've been applied to some of the other inmates he'd touched. Definitely not all, but the lingering pain in Khora and Tuputala's eyes said that he wasn't alone. Zed refrained from examining the memories he received from Khora. There were some things that were too private. He'd wait for Khora to tell him.

"Vidal is a twisted sociopath but not a liar, especially when the truth is capable of causing more pain. He told me to hurt me. I recognized the gleam in his eyes when he shared that. Besides, you know your own story," Khora replied softly. "When you look at him, do you see your husband or yourself?"

Sick, sad compassion washed over Zed as he met Tuputala's eyes. He hoped what Khora was hinting at wasn't true, but it would explain Tuputala's rage.

Tuputala looked at Zed again, some of the animosity gone from her gaze, though it remained wary. "So you didn't kill your niece."

"I'm only going to say this once. She's safer if everyone thinks she's dead." Zed stared both Tuputala and Khora down. "So *dead* is how she'll stay. Understand? I'm not giving Heller any chance to touch her again."

Zed recognized the empathy in Khora's eyes as he nodded. There seemed to be a familiar understanding in Tuputala's gaze too. "Loud and clear," she said.

The tension knotting Zed's guts unraveled just as the comm crackled. "Khora, we have a situation," Wilt said. "There are guests at the front door. Quinet and I are pinned down. It's D and a guard I don't recognize. They're trying to break through the security lock. Not having any luck and are pissed off."

"Roger that," Khora replied, motioning Tuputala to take point. "Hold your position. On our way."

Gunfire erupted from farther down the corridor, and they broke into a run. Tuputala peered around the corner. "D's trying to break through the hatchway," she reported as she lifted her gun. "Guard's keeping Quinet and Wilt back around the other corner. I can take them out now, or we can pinch them between us and capture."

"Fire a warning shot. Let them know they're surrounded," Khora ordered. "I'd rather drive them off. We still need to work with Vidal, and that won't happen if we slaughter his crew."

"He's not going to give you the same consideration," Tuputala muttered before firing a single shot. Cries of shock and fear followed. Zed sprinted to the opposite wall and trained his gun on the captain's men. Wilt and Quinet stepped out on the other side of the corridor.

"D, I suggest you get wise and surrender," Wilt called. "Because if Quinet and I don't get you, Jakobsen or Tuputala will."

A squat, grizzled man rose from his crouch in front of the hatchway with an expression of profound anger and disgust. The guard next to him lowered his weapon, looking between them in unease.

"Where's that dickless bitch you call a boss?" D taunted.

Zed advanced as Khora stepped into the hallway with his own gun drawn and replied, "You've got two choices, D. Stay as our guest or get the fuck out of my territory. I'll give you sixty seconds to make your decision, or I'll make it for you."

"Your guest, what a joke." D eased back from the hatchway as the five of them converged on him and the guard from both sides. D began to walk backward down the direct opposite hallway, his gun trained on Khora the entire time, a cruel glint in his eyes. "Soon, very soon, Captain's going to nab each one of you motherfuckers. When that time comes, what happened to Bryce will seem like a day in paradise in comparison."

"You gutless twat." Wilt darted toward D with an inarticulate cry of rage.

"Wilt, no," Khora shouted as D whipped around, firing off a shot that went wild. Wilt backhanded him with the butt of her gun, her expression such a mask of wild fury that the fine hairs on Zed's neck stirred.

Oh fuck. This is very bad. Zed tightened his hand on his gun, as shocked by the sudden violence as he was by the return of the drums beating softly in his brain. D fell back with a shout of pain, and Wilt followed, smashing him again. The guard dropped his gun, clutching his arm where Tuputala had winged it.

The sound of drums increased, and Zed clutched his head. "Stop it. We have to stop this!"

A horrible scream rent the air as another man in a cook's apron charged down the hall and leapt on the trio, slashing at Wilt, D, and the guard with a long knife. The drums beat at almost a frenzied pace, and Zed shoved away the sensation with all of his strength. He had to stop this before they all killed each other.

The guard went down with a gurgling scream of pain. D broke free and stumbled away, bleeding from a wound on his side as the crazy man turned on Wilt.

Zed raised the gun, looking for a clear shot, but she was in the way. "Wilt, down."

"No!" Quinet shrieked in grief and rage as Wilt got off a shot as the cook stabbed her, burying the knife into her body again and again. Zed, Tuputala, and Khora moved at the same time, but Quinet reached him first, jerked another knife from the man's belt, and slit his throat.

Zed caught him as Quinet tried to cut the cook again, pulling him away from the confrontation. "He's dead. You got him," he shouted to the twisting, writhing man. He shook Quinet, searching for signs that the madness had returned.

"He killed her. Why?" Quinet began to sob, dropping the knife onto the floor.

"Let Khora take a look at her." Zed tried to soothe Quinet as his stomach sank. The attack had been brutal.

"That fucker is still alive," Tuputala rasped, and Zed's head jerked around. Tuputala ran past them, chasing after the fleeing helmsman. D looked over his shoulder as Tuputala caught him and slammed him against the bulkhead. The expression in the helmsman's eyes went from furious to terrified as he reached for his gun. Tuputala was faster. "That's for Bryce," she spat as she fired. D slumped to the floor, leaving a smear of blood on the bulkhead.

Shaken, Zed looked down at Khora, who was trying to staunch Wilt's bleeding. He murmured continuously to Wilt, who nodded, her face so bloodless from shock that each freckle stood out. Zed unlocked the hatchway to the suite and shoved Quinet inside. "Grab some blankets and one of the antigrav flatbed trolleys from the bay," he ordered. "It's not safe for Khora to be taking care of her in the hallway. We need to get her inside."

Still sobbing, Quinet bolted for the transport bay. Zed grabbed Khora's med kit, trying not to think about what just happened. The cook must've been lured by the sound of the gunfire. When he returned, Tuputala was checking the bodies of the guard and cook.

"Where's Quinet?" she demanded.

"Grabbing one of the trolleys so we can carry her inside," Zed replied as he knelt down next to Khora, who reached for the med kit with desperate hands. Wilt's face was tight with pain, and black blood stained her lips.

"I'll help him," Tuputala said. "That happened so fast. I don't like how exposed we are."

"How bad is it?" Zed asked, sick worry clutching his throat as Khora shot him a grim look and prepared a syringe. There was so much blood. Wilt's shirt was soaked through. He tried telling himself that some of it had to belong to the guard and cook, but his heart wasn't buying it.

"Her blood pressure's dropping. I think the wounds in her chest missed the heart, but she's got two gut wounds. If the med tank was working in the infirmary, I'd be confident, but it was shattered during the riots," Khora said in a low, tense voice. He gave Wilt the shot and checked her pulse as her eyes fluttered shut. "Come on, Wilt, stay with me. Let's get her inside, then I'll have a better idea of what I can do. Grab me a blanket to put around her."

Zed rose again and glanced around the vicinity. The hallways were empty, other than the three bodies. He checked on the cook to be absolutely certain the crazy fucker was dead, then went to do as Khora requested. He was numb. Fuck, Wilt couldn't die. He was just coming to know her and liked her. She was crusty and mouthy, with a raw sense of humor that made all of them smile.

Tuputala was coming through, pushing the trolley with Quinet by her side as Zed came out of the bedroom, shaking out the blanket. Quinet's sobs had ceased, though there was a wild, frantic look in his eyes that made Zed uneasy. This could get ugly fast, Zed thought as he fell in behind them.

Out in the corridor, Khora had a breather over Wilt's mouth, and her eyes were open again. Quinet darted toward them with a moan of distress and knelt beside Wilt.

"I've got her stabilized," Khora told him, "but we need to get her inside where I can take a closer look at her."

Quinet's nostrils flared, and his eyes glittered like the sharp edge of broken glass. In one fast, fluid movement he pulled his gun and pointed it at Khora's face. "This is your fault. Get away from her."

Khora's eyes widened, his head pulled back, and his shoulders sagged. Zed's heart panged for him as the words hit home. "Quinet, I—" Khora started in a heavy voice, but Quinet interrupted.

"What were you saying to the captain? I saw you on the monitor. You set this up."

Tuputala raised her gun in response and pressed it against Quinet's temple. "Put it down, Quinet. Don't make me drop your brains out of your head."

Zed flanked Khora, also pointing his gun at Quinet, though he felt sick inside. They couldn't start tearing each other apart now. Quinet's gaze was focused on Khora, his hand steadier than Quinet had shown since they found him. Zed wasn't sure if that was a good sign or not.

"I'll tell you everything, word for word, just let me get Wilt inside while she's still stabilized," Khora said, gesturing toward her. "Please."

Quinet glanced down at Wilt, who watched him with bleary eyes, and the gun lowered. When Quinet continued to glare at Khora as he gently lifted Wilt onto the blankets cushioning the flatbed, Zed drew the distraught man away.

"Hey, Khora's going to do his best to help her. You know that," he said softly, stepping in front of Quinet so his line of sight to Khora was broken.

Dark gray eyes, suspicious and hurting, turned on Zed. Quinet stared at him, then nodded and looked away. The tension eased. "I'm fine." He shrugged Zed's hands off him. "Let go of me." Quinet grabbed the handles of the trolley and disappeared inside the suite with Khora.

Zed gripped the bolt around his neck, striving for calm. All it would take was for one of them to break, and he had the craziest feeling something was waiting and watching for that break to happen.

Tuputala carted D over to lie with the other bodies, and Zed joined her. There was so much blood. Zed thought he'd inured himself to it. But the captain's quarters had been clean. To see the hell outside, and to have death and violence right here where he'd considered them somewhat safe, deeply disturbed him. Like their space had been profaned.

Zed rubbed his palms on his pants as sightless eyes stared up at him. He crouched and closed their eyes, grateful he had gloves on. He didn't want to pick up even the slightest trace from them.

"Captain's going to miss his men."

"Probably not for a bit. This is a big ship, any number of things could've gone wrong. We still don't even know if there are lunatics left now that the cook is gone." To Zed's relief, Tuputala covered them with sheeting. "We'll leave them with the other bodies to get ejected."

"Did you have to kill D?" Zed asked quietly.

Tuputala's jaw tightened. "You didn't see Bryce. You didn't see how they fucked him over. They'd killed his spirit before he hung himself." Tuputala's eyes narrowed as if daring Zed to disagree with her.

"I didn't say he didn't deserve it," Zed replied. "I'm just worried about whatever influence we might still be under. I heard the drums when all hell broke loose. Quinet's one step away from losing his shit. I think we need to be careful with our emotions until we can figure out what the fuck happened to us. I worry it won't take much to push us over that edge again."

The hostility faded from Tuputala's expression as she glanced toward the suite. "Some of us more than others. Come on, I don't like Khora alone with Quinet."

Khora was talking quietly with Quinet when they entered. They'd made a thick pallet on the table for Wilt, and Quinet was holding up an IV bag as Khora pawed through his supplies. The worry line between his brows had deepened, etching its way into his skin.

"She going to make it?" Tuputala asked gruffly.

"Her liver has been nicked. I think I can stop the bleeding. She might need a blood transfusion, so I need to test all of us to see who might have the right type. I'm more worried about the perforation to her intestines. I have her on the antibiotics I found. I hope it's enough," Khora said, his gaze haunted.

Quinet made a low, keening sound in his throat. Tuputala laid her hand on his shoulder. "Come on. We have repairs to do."

"No, let him stay with me," Khora cut in quickly. "Wilt might wake up. They'd both be comforted being near each other. He can run diagnostics from here to keep up the illusion that we're going to get the main engines online. Let me test you both first."

"That's what you promised the captain during your conference, that we would fix the ship's engines?" Zed asked with a glance in Quinet's direction, willing him to hear the sense in it. Khora pricked his hand and pushed the blood sample into his handheld diagnostic. "What did you demand in return?"

A tight smile flashed across Khora's face. "That I become the new head of security with you all as my minions. We don't leave the ship, but we're not prisoners either."

The tense paranoia in Quinet's eyes eased, and he glanced down at Wilt, taking her hand. "Uh-huh," Tuputala said, sounding skeptical. "What else?"

"Fifty percent of his profits," Khora said with a shrug as he tested Tuputala. "It'll give the captain something to chew over instead of wondering what we're up to."

"You're too much." Tuputala frowned as Khora checked his machine and sighed. "Neither one of us can donate?"

"No," Khora replied shortly and rubbed a hand over his face. "Just fix what you can on the transport as fast as possible. We need to start going out in shifts to help clean up, but I'll wait 'til the captain contacts us. If I didn't think it was needed, I'd tell him to fuck off."

"You need sleep," Zed said. It had been many intense hours since they last found some rest. Between checking out their water supply, stalling Vidal while they concocted a plan, then finally meeting with him, there had barely been time to breathe, let alone sleep. "Don't forget that after you've helped Wilt. Quinet too."

"You and Tuputala haven't slept yet either."

"Yeah, well we can tinker half-awake," Zed replied. "You're the one we need to think fast on your feet."

Khora looked up at him, his gaze wide open and not hiding behind his usual indifferent mask. It sparked a flood of warmth that made Zed long to protect and shield him. His heart ached with a fierce affection. Khora made it so damn easy to care.

He grabbed Zed's hand and tugged, whispering in his ear as he bent lower. "Thank you."

"Anytime." Zed brushed his lips over Khora's cheek and got the sense of a tired and stressed mind. He wished he could do more to help him. He clapped Quinet on the shoulder, touched Wilt's hand, and then numbly followed Tuputala out to the transport bay.

His scrambled thoughts darted between Wilt and Quinet, but mostly dwelled on Khora. If Wilt didn't make it, Khora would take her death as hard as Quinet. He'd blame himself, and Khora already blamed himself enough. Zed understood. He had felt just as helpless in the wake of Hannah's pain. Maybe he should've gone to safety with her…. He'd replayed that decision over and over and come to the same conclusion. Staying behind had been the best thing he could've done. Together would've increased their chances of getting caught. She was a fighter. She'd thrive in her new home.

As for himself, he didn't know how to deal with everything facing them. He couldn't fix a damned thing for Khora or Hannah, so he'd focus on what he knew how to fix, and that was machines. Then one worry would be gone.

Tuputala switched on the ship's computer and frowned. "Damned guidance system is still fucking up. Why don't you crawl underneath and see if you can track down what the problem is, while I help up here. It's not easy for me to maneuver down there."

Zed popped off the plate covering the access way below the transport. As he wiggled inside, he smelled the acrid sting of burnt wiring. Fresh, must've been from when it was powered up before they left to meet the captain. Whoever had screwed around with the insides of the transport had done more damage than they'd initially thought.

He could hear Tuputala moving around on the decking above him. Then a section of the decking was pulled up, and light and air filtered through. "I think she's fried," Zed called up. "I haven't found the problem yet, but I can smell it."

"At this point, we're going to need to raid the salvage rooms and main bay for parts." Tuputala's voice grew distant as she made her way under the console. "Looks like Wilt finished up what you started. Nice job."

Zed wasn't sure what to make of Tuputala's new attitude. He didn't entirely trust it would last, but he'd take it for now. He aimed his light around as he searched. Tuputala seemed more inclined to conversation now than she ever had before, and Zed figured it might be his only opportunity to get a better feel for the team.

"Wilt and Quinet, they a couple?"

"More like siblings. They were imprisoned together at Xi Tauri," came the muffled reply.

"I don't like the plan for Khora to work with Dr. Barboza outside of the safety of this suite." The thought of Khora going out to collect bodies with only Quinet to watch his back made Zed uneasy. He'd have to make sure it was either him or Tuputala, repairs or no repairs.

"I trust Khora's reasoning." The transport shuddered as power fluctuated and Tuputala cursed.

"I trust his decision-making ability when it comes to the team and our wellbeing. I don't trust it one lick when it comes to his own personal safety."

"I've got to give it to you. You've pegged the man right." Tuputala quieted, and for a while there was only the comforting sound of bangs and clangs of machinery as they worked.

The ozone scent of burned plastic and metal grew stronger, and Zed contorted himself around a bend to face a slag of wires and chips melted and fused together. He cursed under his breath. The entire thing would have to be replaced and a new one cobbled together. They were lucky they didn't blow themselves up when they turned the transport on.

"Make sure the power's off in this grid," Zed called up to Tuputala. "If I get electrocuted down here, you'll never get my corpse out."

"Can't have that. You'd stink up the place for months." Zed wasn't sure how to judge Tuputala's tone. Sarcasm wasn't his strength. The low hum of power ceased, and Zed breathed in a sigh of relief. "Okay, you're good."

"So what gives?" Zed asked as he began the difficult job of dismantling the mess. "One word from Khora about my innocence and I'm not on your list of people you'd rather punt out an airlock than work with?"

"I have a whole damn host of reasons to dislike you," Tuputala retorted. "Only problem is, they seem to be disappearing one by one. So you didn't kill your niece, but you say she's better off dead. Care to clarify?"

Zed closed his eyes. He supposed if there were ever a chance to get in with the team, this was it. Khora might be the head, but Tuputala was the heart; Quinet and Wilt would follow her lead.

"I never laid a hand on Hannah. Her stepdad abused her, and I discovered it. Her mom refused to believe us." The pain of that vicious argument still hurt. "I had to do something and cover our tracks at the same time. She is safe where she's at, but if my sister thought she was alive, she'd look for her and bring her right back to him. She's blind where he's concerned, and I'd rather have her hate me than Hannah be in that situation again."

"So you went after him and caught the raw end of the deal," Tuputala responded, her voice far away as if lost in memory. He started to ask about her story and then refrained. He knew just how personal such questions were. "Bryce was a friend. I don't like someone coming in and taking his place. No matter how much we needed it."

"I get it. I'm the odd man out, a body in a hole that can't be filled." Zed didn't want to know what D had done to drive Bryce to suicide, but being aboard this ship was enough to test the spirit of anyone without further torture.

"Yeah, that about sums it up." More decking was removed, and Tuputala's broad face peered down at him. "How bad is it?"

"It's waking up from a riot and realizing ninety percent of the ship's complement is dead bad." Zed swore as he tried to get the leverage he needed to pry off the damaged interface. "But not waking up after a riot and thinking you're alone and helpless bad."

Tuputala handed Zed tools and pulled out the damaged pieces as Zed managed to work them loose. "There was another reason why I didn't want you on the team," she finally commented.

"You seemed to have a whole stack of them." Zed took his eyes off the mess long enough to look up to see the concern in Tuputala's gaze. He was pretty sure he knew why. "Khora?"

"He's as fucked-up on the inside as that interface. Being attracted to you was bad enough, because the last time he was interested, the captain sold the man off to slavers. Just on the suspicion Khora might be sniffing elsewhere. Then Captain beat him so bad I thought he'd die. But it's more than that. I think Khora gives a damn about you and you, him. And that worries me. You know what he's into. I don't know how much experience you've had with a man like that, but I don't think he knows how to stop anymore. How to say when his limits have been reached. And that's dangerous."

Tuputala's words mirrored Zed's concerns. How the hell was he supposed to know when enough was enough when Khora's only answer seemed to be more? The thought of being alone with him, mixing domination with sex, intrigued and excited him. The thought of hurting Khora, not as much, though Khora's excitement turned him on. If he could still sense Khora's emotions, he'd feel less uncertain about it.

"Was he like this before the captain? Into pain, I mean?"

"Yeah, but he had a healthy relationship with Didier. Captain's warped it and uses it as much to whip his spirit as anything else. The two of them have developed this twisted symbiotic bond. I worry that Khora might let us escape and somehow contrive to stay behind to continue alongside Vidal."

A surge of absolute denial rose up, and Zed glared at Tuputala. "I'm *not* going to let that happen."

Tuputala grinned. "I was hoping you'd think that."

"You're right, I have zero experience with a man like him. I don't even know where to begin. Sounds like you've known him a long time." Zed turned back to his work.

"Long before we ended up in this hellhole," Tuputala responded, but she didn't offer any details.

"I don't suppose you'd care to give me a few pointers," Zed asked with a quick glance up.

"I thought you'd never ask."

Zed closed his eyes as some of his tension drained away. With Khora he'd felt like he was fumbling in the dark, and as much as he wanted to explore the heat between them, he didn't want to damage Khora even more. He knew he had to take control of the situation but wasn't quite sure where to start. Instincts could only get him so far. He'd take any help he could get.

"Why not start with how it worked with him and Didier when Khora was in a healthy relationship?"

Chapter Twelve

"Khora?" Riff jerked out of his meditative prayers at the sound of Wilt's voice. She'd passed out before they'd shifted her to the captain's bed hours ago, and he hadn't expected her to wake up again. He left his prayer beads lined up on the table to keep his count and turned to examine her. Wilt's waxy pallor, the clamminess of her skin, emphasized the desperation in her eyes and Riff's worst fears. The antibiotics weren't enough to fight off the infection, and Riff hadn't been able to entirely stop her slow internal bleed. Wilt was losing this battle. Riff's heart twisted with pain as he felt her irregular, weak pulse.

"Tell me the truth, how bad?" Wilt asked.

Riff stalled, checking her wounds, the stink of perforated intestines hitting his nostrils and awakening memories he never wanted to deal with again. "It's bad. The damage to your liver was worse than I thought, your guts are a mess." Riff scrubbed a helpless hand over his face, his brain scrambling for a solution. "Even if the infirmary wasn't in shambles and Barboza was willing to work with me in surgery…."

"I get it. I'm fucked and not in the way I like it."

Riff's heart panged again as he nodded. There had to be something else he could do, but he'd tried everything, even sneaking out to ransack the infirmary for stronger medicines.

"Hurts like a motherfucker," Wilt said with a raspy laugh and a vague wave toward her midsection. She bit her lip hard, her eyes tightening in pain. "The bastard got me good. I didn't even see him coming."

"I can give you something for that." Riff tried not to hear the echoes of his past in those words but it haunted him anyway.

"Save it. Not gonna need it soon." Riff met Wilt's gaze, her eyes glassy as she bit off another groan.

"It's going to feel like an eternity." Riff's hands shook as he fumbled with a vial of morphine. Wilt was a fighter. She wouldn't go down without a struggle to the last second. He hesitated as he reached for a needle. Wilt wasn't Didier. She wouldn't want to overdose.

Wilt grasped his arm, some strength still evident in her grip. "I know what you're thinking and no. Don't waste that shit on me. You don't need any more ghosts haunting you."

"It's going to be bad." Riff laid his hand over Wilt's. "At least let me give you enough to take the edge off. Running out of morphine is the least of our problems right now."

"It's already bad. Death is one cold bitch. I always liked her." Wilt closed her eyes with a grimace.

Riff chuckled with no mirth, shaking his head as he measured out a dose. "You always did have a way with words."

"I don't want—"

"Fuck you, you're getting it," Riff snapped as he administered the medication. "Quinet can't hear you screaming, and he's right outside the room." Riff couldn't take hearing her scream either.

"Your bedside manner sucks balls." Wilt sighed as the drug washed through her system. "Didn't anyone ever tell you you're not supposed to cuss at your patients?"

"Yeah well, most of my patients are as stubborn as you. It takes cussing to get them to listen." Riff brushed the back of his fingers over her cheek. "Do you want me to get Quinet? He'd want to talk to you. Be with you."

"He's another damn reason why I can't OD. He knows your history. He won't believe you didn't act on your own, and I need him to trust you." Riff winced as he tucked the morphine away, and Wilt patted his hand. "I didn't mean that to wound."

Riff allowed himself a brief strained smile. "I know, you're right. I just wish I could fix this…." His helplessness cut him deeper than any words. What good was all his training if he couldn't save the ones he loved the most? "I'm so sorry."

"What? That you didn't predict a knife-wielding psychopath would jump in?" Wilt lay back, her features drawn. "He interrupted the nice impending brawl we had going with D and his guard. I hope somebody got that bastard for Bryce."

"Tuputala killed him," Riff assured her.

"That's my girl." Wilt clutched his arm again. "You get Quinet off this ship. Promise me." The desperation in her eyes slashed at Riff's already-aching heart.

"I promise." Riff laid his hand over hers. "Did you get it done? Are the weapons shut off?"

"Bet your damn masochistic ass I did." For a moment light gleamed in Wilt's eyes before fading. "The weapons system seems to be online, but it'll misfire if they try. Took me a while, I had to mask what I was doing, lay in false trails. I made it seem like I accessed life support. I got the location of the captain's transport too. It's not far. I sent the coordinates to our ship, just gotta get the bitch moving."

Riff squeezed Wilt's hand. He was being selfish, taking her time and energy when the others would want a few minutes with her. "You did more than enough. You let me worry about getting the transport going."

"See that you do." Wilt's fingers tightened around Riff's before going limp. "See you around, Riff."

"Good-bye, Cybil." Riff rose and leaned over to kiss her forehead. "*Om Nama Sivaya,*" he whispered. When Riff entered the main room, Quinet had his back to him, muttering to himself as he worked at the computer. "She's awake," Riff said. Quinet jumped with a yelp and spun around in his chair. "Why don't you sit with her while I get the others?"

"Is she going to be okay?" Quinet asked anxiously, leaping up. Riff shook his head, pressing his lips together as he clasped Quinet's shoulder. Quinet's eyes widened, stricken with grief and fear.

"She's dying. I'm sorry," Riff replied quietly, helplessness, grief, and anger coiling in him, serpentine and quiet.

"The captain, he did this," Quinet accused as they entered the bedroom. "He sent the guards and that crazy cook." Quinet seized Riff's shirt. "You have to kill him. You have to hurt him back."

Riff covered Quinet's hands with his own. The last thing they needed was some blood crusade, deserved or not. "The surest way to hurt him is through money. We abandon him here with nothing, and he suffers longer, knowing we bested him."

"Don't you dare talk around me like I'm not fucking here," Wilt growled, diverting Quinet's attention. "You listen here, Marty Quinet. I have a few words for you."

Riff slipped away and headed toward the transport bay. The sounds of banging, cursing, and sparking electricity greeted him. Tuputala was welding along the underbelly of the transport, and Jakobsen was nowhere to be seen, though his curses were heard. Tuputala shut off the welder and yanked off her mask, giving Riff a searching look. Riff shook his head, and Tuputala's expression darkened.

She pounded on the side of the transport. "Jakobsen, get your pint-sized ass out here."

"Joey, if you want a chance to say good-bye, I'd do it now," Riff said.

Tuputala nodded and took off at a run. A few moments later, Jakobsen emerged from the transport with an irritated expression that disappeared when he saw Riff. He glanced around for Tuputala, and his gaze saddened.

"Do you want to go see her?" Riff asked. "She's fading fast."

"No, I'm not going to take time away from the others. That's not fair." Jakobsen walked toward Riff, searching his face. He wiped his hands on a rag that was only marginally less grease-stained than himself. "How are you holding up?"

Riff shrugged. It was what it was. "I couldn't save her." That's not what he'd meant to say, and he looked away before he could see the contempt on Jakobsen's face.

Jakobsen laid his hand on Riff's shoulder, and he felt bolstered by his quiet, solid presence. "I'm sorry."

"Thanks." Riff wanted to turn and sink into Jakobsen's embrace for one long moment, and the unwelcome urge made him stiffen.

Jakobsen pulled Riff into his arms, and Riff resisted, trying to step away. He didn't need any more emotional entanglements. He had to concentrate on what else they had to do. "We need to go out there. Get extra clothes for us all… extra weapons while we take care of the bodies. We had a deal. Vidal's going to insist we keep our side. We've been quiet too long, and he's not patient." Riff was babbling, but he couldn't seem to make himself stop.

Jakobsen's arms tightened around him. "Stop thinking so much. Give yourself a few moments to grieve. She deserves that," he added as if he knew the arguments Riff was about to offer.

Riff relaxed against him, allowing himself the comfort. Jakobsen smelled of oil and sweat, which was probably better than how Riff smelled. They were going to have to go on without Wilt with her smartass mouth and her knack for getting computers to do whatever the hell she wanted. They were going to have to convince Quinet to leave without her. Riff didn't have the slightest idea of how to accomplish that, but he'd made a promise.

Jakobsen's hand rubbed over his back, and Riff stilled his thoughts. Despite his grief it felt too good to be held like he mattered. He couldn't fight all the feelings Jakobsen awoke in him. Not right now. Finally, he pulled back, and Jakobsen let him go. Jakobsen cupped his cheek, brushing his thumb over Riff's cheekbone.

Jakobsen kissed him, a heated, tender kiss that melted Riff's remaining resistance. He could become addicted to the way Jakobsen kissed him. The hatchway opened, and Riff pulled back to look at Tuputala as she entered. Her shoulders were bowed down in grief, though her gaze was determined. Quinet trailed after her, a lost child in her shadow.

"Is she…?" Riff asked, and Tuputala nodded with a grim twist to her lips.

"Captain contacted us," Tuputala said with an angry grimace. "Barboza and Flaubert are waiting for you at the prison. They want you to stack the bodies at the entrance, and they'll take it from there."

"I need you," Riff said quietly to Jakobsen, who nodded.

"See if you can find those parts we talked about," Tuputala said to Jakobsen. "Quinet, I could use your help talking to the transport's computer to track down problem areas."

"Yeah, I'll take a look," Quinet replied in a daze. "When Wilt wakes up, she'll help."

Tuputala shot Riff an alarmed look as he watched Quinet shuffle aboard the transport. He'd have Tuputala keep a watch for signs of hallucinations. It could just be the shock and grief Quinet wasn't ready to accept, or it could be another symptom that he wasn't quite well. This might be enough to tip him back over that ledge for good.

"Get some rest," Riff advised. "Him too. I have a tranquilizer in case he needs it. We'll clean the room and take her with us. We've all been up for a while. Let's not make mistakes at this point because we're tired."

"I'll make sure he goes down. There's not much else we can do here without those parts." Tuputala shot a pointed glance at Jakobsen, but the edge she had toward him had disappeared.

They grabbed one of the antigrav flatbed trolleys and pushed it into the main room. "Wrap up the other three in sheets. I'll take care of Wilt.

If we shroud the bodies as we gather them, it might keep Barboza and Flaubert from looking too closely."

"Eventually they're going to ask us what happened," Jakobsen replied as he followed Riff into the captain's room.

"I know. I'm surprised Vidal hasn't yet." Riff stopped when he saw Wilt. Her pain-ravaged features relaxed now in death. Riff sighed, the ache in his heart renewed. Jakobsen squeezed his shoulder and grabbed sheets as Riff retrieved a blanket and gently swaddled Wilt's body. She should be cremated, but the ship didn't have the capabilities, and Riff couldn't see any way around leaving her with the others.

He forced himself to move along, and by the time he'd picked up the room and remade the bed, Jakobsen had the other three on the flatbed. "We're going to need more linens if we're going to wrap everyone we find."

"We pass a laundry on our way. We should be able to find plenty there."

"Laundry?" Jakobsen asked with a strange note in his voice, but he didn't offer any details when Riff pressed.

After he gave Tuputala a tranquilizer and grabbed the blood samples he'd taken from all of them, Riff and Jakobsen left for their shift. Jakobsen offered to take turns carrying Wilt, but Riff insisted on doing it himself. He didn't want her touching D or the man who'd killed her. The horror around them had ceased to make an impression. Riff was numb to the evidence of blood and violence. Wilt's vigil had left him battered, and his thoughts kept drifting back to Didier and the screams that echoed in his memory.

The laundry room was large and dim; the scent of the chemicals used in the cleaning masked some of the death and decay. The violence had continued inside here as well. A man hung from a line, and Riff shuddered as he looked away. It was too much like finding Bryce. Like finding Didier bleeding out. Watching Wilt getting stabbed. Too many friends gone.

Out of the corner of his eye, Riff caught the flicker of a shadow. He froze, then turned slowly, his heart hammering. He scanned the deep shadows around the broken shelving. The deeper pools between the machines. White strips of linen had been shredded, splashed with blood. Nothing would ever scrub away the blood on the ship.

Jakobsen abandoned the flatbed and went inside as Riff hovered in the hatchway, reluctant to move past that swaying body. Coming here had been a mistake. What they needed would be as ruined as it was everywhere else.

He caught another quick flicker of Wilt disappearing around a rack of hanging towels that were oddly untouched. Riff started to call to her on instinct when the punch of loss hit him again and he realized he still carried her body. He wanted to shrug off the hallucination, call it an effect of the ordeal they'd been through, the tiredness that was now making him clumsy, but in his heart he couldn't quite do that. He kept thinking, what if they were carrying a disease that could kill off most of a space station or plague a world? That question haunted him most of all.

"Jakobsen?" Riff called out as he set Wilt down and followed him inside. "Come on, we're not going to salvage much here."

"I need to find him," Jakobsen replied, his voice muffled.

Curiosity overrode Riff's jangling nerves, and he followed the sound of Jakobsen's voice. There had only been a few workers here, and not one of them stirred. Jakobsen was checking the bodies, his expression grim, until he paused by one stripped bare, with napkins shoved down his throat and shears stabbed into his chest. Jakobsen's gaze turned sad as he pulled the napkins out of his mouth.

"You know him?" Riff asked in a hushed voice as he knelt down next to Jakobsen.

Jakobsen shook his head. "I know of him. He took care of the prison's laundry. The sense of him was on every damn sheet, every towel." Jakobsen closed his eyes with a sigh, and Riff removed the shears. At least he'd died fast. Most hadn't. "He was kind of simple, just wanted to work. It's crazy, but if it hadn't been for his calming presence, I think I would've lost my fucking mind the first few weeks I was here."

Riff still found that strange. The idea that Jakobsen could understand so much from a person merely from touching something they'd touched. It should bother him, but after everything they'd been through, he couldn't summon up any outrage over the invasion. Hell, Jakobsen still wanted to be near him despite dipping into Riff's mind. That said enough.

It was clear from Jakobsen's genuine grief he'd known the man despite what he said. He touched Jakobsen's shoulder, and those hazel eyes focused on him. "I'm sorry."

Jakobsen's eyes darkened. He slipped off a glove and skimmed his bare fingers over Riff's jaw before drawing him close. Riff tensed, then forced himself to relax. "What do you sense when you touch me?" he asked, despite his fear of the answer.

"Not as clear as I used to. Compassion… so much sorrow, like you carry around everyone's hurts, not just your own."

Riff pulled back, and Jakobsen let his hand fall away. "Come on, we'll take him with us."

"I'll wrap him, you find us some linens," Jakobsen said as he tugged his glove back on.

It didn't take long, and there weren't many workers in the rooms, so they went ahead and gathered them all. The thought of leaving that body hanging silently gave Riff the willies. Like it could somehow turn into Bryce, step down, and haunt him even more than he was. Riff shivered as they left and turned toward the salvage rooms.

"Are you really going to be able to get the transport to work with cobbled-together parts?" Riff asked.

"We're almost done with repairs. Believe me, she'll make it to Vidal's transport," Jakobsen replied.

Jakobsen opened the hatchway to the salvage room, and the stench of rotting flesh rolled out stronger than before. "Ugh," Jakobsen said, his face twisting into a grimace. The skittering of rats lent urgency to their job.

"It's going to be miserable working in here," Riff said. "Tie a cloth around your nose and mouth. That'll help some."

Jakobsen grimaced and fished a couple of rags out of his pocket. They were marginally cleaner than the one he was using earlier, and the scent of grease helped to filter out the stench.

"Let's stay within sight of each other," Jakobsen suggested. "We don't know if the cook was the last nutjob."

Riff nodded and laid Wilt down in the prep room. She'd be safe there for now. He watched Jakobsen as he began scavenging for parts. They had to get off this fucking ship before Riff lost another one of his own. He turned away and took on the ghastly task of loading bodies onto a flatbed and gathering tissue samples.

"Do you think you can fix one of the diagnostic machines in the infirmary?" Riff asked.

"Maybe, if it's not too damaged. We can swing by there when we drop off this load." Jakobsen approached, eyeballing the full cart with a grim gaze. Silently, Jakobsen helped him push it to the hatchway outside the prison cells where they piled the bodies. They heard the echo of voices arguing from the twisting corridors, though they didn't see Barboza or Flaubert.

Afterward, they swung by the infirmary. While Jakobsen tweaked one of the machines, Riff tried to find anything else they could use that hadn't already been destroyed or taken. When Jakobsen was done, Riff started the tests and computer analysis. By the time Jakobsen finished his scavenging, they might have some answers.

As they headed back to the salvage rooms, the flatbed humming along with them, Jakobsen flexed his fingers in the gloves, his lips tightening. "I cannot wait to get off this ship. I keep trying to anticipate the next bad thing to fuck us over."

"Yeah, me too," Riff replied as they turned down the final corridor. The lights flickered as the great engines of the ship throbbed to life. Jakobsen and Riff froze, then exchanged glances. "That wasn't us."

"The failsafe could've finally kicked in," Jakobsen replied as he began to push the flatbed again. "Or we're not as alone as we thought. We did suspect someone was in Engineering."

Great. It wasn't that Riff minded the thought of someone else being alive, it was that he didn't know what the fuck to expect from them. He trusted his team—though Quinet's instability concerned him—and not one person outside their group.

Riff couldn't escape the feeling of running out of time. If Jakobsen didn't find everything he needed this shift, they'd have to go out again. In the meantime that would mean fewer people to work on the transport, more time for Vidal to come up with a trap. Riff's offer would only distract him for a short while before he decided he wouldn't share any of his profits. His pride wouldn't let him allow a prisoner to go free. Especially one whose bond he'd purchased and who he'd have to pay a decent wage.

Riff had filled the flatbed a few more times and delivered his burdens before Jakobsen came to him with a look of satisfaction. "I have what we need," Jakobsen said, his voice cutting through Riff's exhaustion and fears. "Let's get Wilt and lay her to rest. Then we can call it a day. We're going to be no good if we fall over or get sick again."

"I want to stop by the infirmary and see if those tests I started yielded any results. I don't trust Barboza not to hide the information from me or worse, destroy the results because he thinks I'm an idiot."

"Do you think you'll find anything?" Jakobsen asked, falling into step beside him.

"I don't know. If we do I hope it leads to a cure or immunization. We can't be carriers." Riff stopped and looked back when he realized Jakobsen was no longer behind him.

He stared at Riff in shock, his normally ruddy face pale. "And if we are?" Jakobsen asked. When Riff hesitated, grim resignation settled into Jakobsen's gaze as he answered his own question. "If we are, none of us are going anywhere."

Riff hated to think like that, hated to think of what he'd have to do to ensure that, but there it was. "Do you think I'm crazy?" he asked. Maybe this was another delusion. And he was putting them all at risk by trying to prove he wasn't ineffectual.

"No more than any of us. We know that something put this entire ship into a killing rage. We all heard the drums, so wild they drove out every thought, left only emotion…." Jakobsen's voice trailed off, and Riff looked at him sharply. His gaze was clear, though, haunted, not unfocused as if he was hearing them again.

"What are you thinking?" Riff asked.

"That you're right. We need to figure out what happened before we leave. We can't take the risk of spreading this. So do what you need to do. And I'll figure out what else I can do. Wasn't Wilt or Quinet going after the captain's log on *Pandora*? Maybe that would give us some clues. Were they able to retrieve it?"

Riff tried to remember, but the details were hazy, as if he was trying to remember a dream. If they had, the information should be on the central computer. "When I check the test results, you check the computer."

Once again, Riff carried Wilt as Jakobsen pushed the flatbed. It seemed wrong to treat her like the others, but the best Riff could do was say a quick prayer she would be the only teammate he'd bury in these coming days. When they reached the prison, they heard no sound of Barboza and Flaubert from within the network of cells and winding corridors. Given the time, it was possible they had ceased work for the day.

"Think it's a trap?" Jakobsen asked as Riff cradled Wilt's body.

"I don't know, but I'm not leaving her out here for those jackals to touch. Make sure nobody locks me in. I've got this."

Riff sensed Jakobsen's eyes on him until the turning of the corridor obscured him from his line of vision. The penal wing gave him the heebie-jeebies. The unnatural silence. The obvious evidence of violence and death. All those men and women, trapped and crazy. It terrified Riff to his core. He laid Wilt down on her bunk, touched her head a brief moment, and walked away.

A look of relief crossed Jakobsen's face when he reappeared. "Still want to go by the infirmary?"

"Yeah, checking the results won't take long."

The infirmary was quiet with no evidence that Barboza had stopped by. Riff had scorned his skills and motivation before, but this took his callous disregard to a whole other level. Maybe Riff's taunts had hit too close to home and that's why he was so damned defensive. If he'd lied about his credentials, Vidal would skin the man.

Riff studied the computer analysis of the tests he'd run and frowned. There wasn't anything in the blood or tissue samples to indicate an illness. The results should've been a relief, but they only led to more questions. The only oddity was the elevated levels of epinephrine. Their blood had been clean of any toxins as well. But... how many days had it been since they'd woken up? Time enough for it to clear maybe. Riff rubbed his hands over his eyes. His sense of days was screwed.

"So get this," Jakobsen said, cutting through the tired circle of his thoughts. "There's no Noyes on the ship's manifest. Looks like it was out on a pleasure cruise with some corporate heads, their mistresses and friends, and the crew. He isn't listed among any of them."

Riff frowned. "Was the captain's log recovered?"

"Yeah, I think so." Riff stared at the test results as he listened to Jakobsen work, his fingers tapping in a soothing rhythm that echoed in his tired brain. Jakobsen whistled, long and low, breaking the spell. "Get this. Last entry has them responding to a distress call. Where they discovered a single survivor in a hiber unit."

He met Jakobsen's shocked gaze, and then both of them turned toward the hiber unit sitting innocuous in the corner. "This establishes a pattern," Riff said. "The ship *Pandora* ran into, then *Pandora*, now us. That's three at least. Signs of violence, an empty ship except one survivor, Noyes." He shuddered. Now that man was awake with them as their numbers were dwindling.

"But how? Why?"

Riff crossed to the hiber unit with Jakobsen by his side. "If we can figure out the how, then maybe we can keep it from happening again. The why… I'm not sure I want to know. You check for any hidden sections where a weapon, a poison, or a bioagent could be hidden."

"I thought you said it didn't look as if we'd been poisoned."

"Just do it," Riff said, pounding his fist on the counter. "There has to be an answer. I don't know everything, dammit. It might be something that I have no way of detecting. That I don't have the damned skill set to track down."

"Okay." Jakobsen set his hands on Riff's shoulders and shook him lightly. "Get it together. I'll help. We're both wiped and short-tempered."

Riff drew in a deep breath and closed his eyes. He wanted to lean into Jakobsen, feel his arms around him, but he tensed and pulled away. "You're right. Thank you."

"Have you considered psionics?" Jakobsen asked, tapping his temple with a troubled frown.

Riff considered the possibility. That might explain some of the mysteries, but he'd never heard of abilities strong enough to affect an entire ship. "What do you think? You'd be more familiar with the capabilities than I."

Jakobsen frowned, his gaze going inward. "I'm not sure," he said finally. "I know abilities can grow by quite a bit. Mine did. Stress and trauma seem to make them expand as well. It'll be interesting to see if mine come back stronger. I really kind of hope not. I think anybody who'd be able to warp the minds of so many would have to be batshit insane themselves. Which might explain a lot. Noyes seemed off, not crazy, but what do I know?"

Riff turned toward the hiber unit and pulled up a record of Noyes's information while he'd been sleeping. As far as he could tell, he'd been the only one to use the hiber unit, on and off over several years. Jakobsen skated his fingertips down Riff's back and got to work searching for a hidden compartment.

The more Riff looked at the unit's readings, the more he got a sense of wrongness. All of the vital statistics were a little off, not quite working in harmony. Riff couldn't explain the impression he got, that Noyes was more a copy of a human than really human. All the parts were there, just not put together perfectly.

There had been human mutations in space before, but they'd never encountered aliens. He wasn't against the idea they would exist; he just didn't think they'd look humanoid. With all the millions of ways life evolved, it wouldn't make sense for alien life to seem so familiar.

He straightened, his back cracking, joints and sinews aching. He needed to sleep before he began making up the boogeyman too. "Did you find anything?" he asked as Jakobsen rose from his crouch with a disgusted expression.

"No, it's tight as a drum. You?"

Riff shook his head wearily.

Jakobsen took his arm and steered him away from the hiber unit. "Come on, let's go back. I don't care anymore about the answers. I just want to get the fuck off this ship."

Riff couldn't agree with him more.

CHAPTER THIRTEEN

ZED LINGERED in the steam room, letting the heat soak out the aches of body, mind, and soul. As tired as he was, his thoughts wouldn't stop spinning, skipping from the final repairs needed to wondering about Noyes. Tuputala was still recovering from her wound. Quinet was one step from taking a nosedive straight back into insanity. And now Wilt was gone.

He closed his eyes, conscious of Khora in the other room, trying to get some sleep. Khora hadn't said one word since they left the infirmary, and frankly Zed was worried about him. It was easier to focus on Khora than worry about them all. Khora he could do something about. He should've lured him into the shower with him, given them both a chance to unwind, but he'd already showered and crawled into bed by the time Zed finished talking with Tuputala.

Zed shifted, resting his forearms against the wall. Flashes of emotion, flickers of scenes rolled over him, too nebulous to identify, for which Zed was grateful. He didn't want to know the captain's moods. His abilities were starting to come back, though now it was stronger with living beings. Strange, how that was the opposite from the way it developed the first time. He'd take it, though. He'd rather touch Khora and know what he was feeling than someone else. One person was easier to filter, easier to block with clothing, than trying to keep himself from touching anything, ever.

He stepped out of the shower and dried off before donning fresh clothes. Anxious to lie down next to Khora and pull him into his arms, Zed went to join him. The bedroom was dark and empty, the bed stripped of half the blankets and pillows.

He stared at the bed a long minute, then grabbed a pillow and blanket for himself and went in search of Khora. He wasn't in the main room or the galley. Tuputala wouldn't let Khora show his face in the transport bay, so that left only one place. Zed hesitated before the hatchway that Khora had blocked off from everyone. He was pretty sure that was the room where Vidal had put all those whip marks on Khora's body; he just wasn't sure what to expect inside.

Khora sat against a back corner, the farthest spot away from the hatchway. His arm wrapped around his knees as he stirred a small pile of beads with a faraway, haunted look on his face. Zed stepped inside and shut the hatchway. He expected Khora to snap at him to go away, but instead those ink-dark eyes focused on him with what almost seemed to be relief.

"I couldn't sleep in that room," he said.

"I can't sleep either," Zed admitted. "Pretty wound up."

Zed glanced around the pristine room, the walls painted a disturbingly bright white. Every light blazed. There were leather straps with buckles hanging from the ceiling, several other devices with restraints that he supposed were meant to hold Khora in a certain position. Benches, tables, and other pieces of furniture that Zed had never seen before were scattered about. It was interesting to see firsthand what Khora craved, though Zed knew he was desperately missing one huge element. That was the side Zed was determined to show him.

One of the walls had the smooth, glossy texture that said the captain communicated with his crew right where everybody could see what he was doing to Khora. It infuriated him. He suspected Vidal used it as another layer of control and humiliation, but he also suspected that Khora didn't give a rat's ass who saw him bound and naked either.

Zed wouldn't want to share that image with anyone. He'd want to keep it to himself, like he wanted to keep Khora. He didn't want to just fuck him and go on his way. He wanted to stay by his side, comfort him when Khora needed it, support him, and, yes, even dominate him. The thought of watching Khora surrender all that control he kept locked up made Zed hungry to see it. He got a taste of it in the steam rooms; now he wanted to experience it for real.

They shouldn't be in here. They had this time to sleep. They'd need it. But they were both too wound up to rest, and sex was a stress relief. Zed crouched down in front of Khora. "Do you want me to leave?"

Khora's gaze slid from Zed to someplace over his shoulder before focusing on him again. "No. Stay, please."

His hands slid up Zed's arms, his touch firm and warm. Zed sensed the chaos inside him, the mind that would not rest. Zed ached to run his hands over him, to kiss him, but he held himself back. He mimicked

Khora's touch, sliding his hands down to grip Khora's forearms. Zed dove into the sense of him, realizing he'd never be able to think of Riff as just Khora again.

"What do you want?" Zed asked, his voice low. Riff glanced away again, a quiver of uncertainty running through him, and Zed tightened his grip. "Look at me. Tell me."

Riff met his eyes again. "I want you to hurt me, and I want to fuck." The way he said it, the heat in his eyes had Zed's blood stirring. There was no uncertainty now. Riff wanted this bad.

"You want me to hurt you because it feels good to you," Zed said, and Riff nodded. "What are the other reasons?"

"It makes the screaming stop," Riff said in a hoarse voice, his gaze unfocusing again. A chill went through Zed. What haunted Riff so much?

"Who's screaming?"

Riff shook his head, so Zed tried a different tactic.

"Are they screaming now?"

Riff shook his head again. "Not since we recovered our sanity." A faint, humorless smile touched his lips. "I think we've been too busy for me to brood."

Zed suspected there was more Riff wasn't telling, but he didn't push for it now. Zed dropped his gaze to Riff's lips and the urge to kiss him grew stronger. Kissing Riff was a pleasure he didn't want to quit.

"What do you see when you touch me now?" Riff asked, his gaze searching Zed's face. Once again, Zed sensed that electric zing of sexual awareness. Riff definitely knew what he wanted.

"Enough heat to set me on fire. Hunger that matches my own."

Riff smiled then, his eyes lighting up with sensual promise that chased away the shadows. He took Zed's breath away. "Sounds like we both need a little release."

"I'll hurt you, but I won't abuse you." Zed was determined to make that distinction clear.

"I asked for it," Riff said with a shrug. "By both word and deed. I knew what I was doing."

"Maybe you did, but I'm saying that's a line I'm not willing to cross," Zed replied, making sure Riff met his eyes so he'd understand Zed meant every word.

"Fair enough," Riff replied. "Now that we've got the ground rules established, are you going to kiss me or just look at me?"

The way Riff challenged him with that little twist of insolence made Zed's blood heat even more. It was sexy as fuck.

"You'll know when I'm ready to kiss you," Zed promised. He rose, tugging Riff to his feet as he glanced around the room, trying to figure out how he wanted him. Most of the furnishings seemed devised so he'd only have access to half of Riff's body unless he moved him around, and he didn't want that. Which left him with the straps in the middle.

Riff saw the direction of his gaze. "I don't want to be bound. Let me hang on to the straps." Zed sensed the quick wash of fear and saw it echoed in his eyes. He understood. Zed could still feel the straps on his own skin from when he woke up and found himself helpless.

"I don't want to bind you." Zed kissed each freshly bandaged wrist. "In fact, I find the idea of you taking it without being held down really sexy."

Zed stripped his shirt off, his eyes hot on Riff as the other man did the same. The hard scarred body combined with that razor-sharp mind of his turned Zed on with a punch of lust. He wanted to ease back all of Riff's layers, get to know him on every level.

"You're looking at me like you want to pounce me," Riff said, eager expectation reflected in his eyes.

"You're looking like you want to be pounced." Zed raked his gaze over him again, anticipation building. "Take the straps, Riff."

Heat flared in Riff's eyes, scorching him to the bone. He walked to the middle of the room with full confidence and grace as if he knew Zed couldn't look away from him. He grasped the straps above the buckle, wrapping them around his palms twice. Zed stepped close to him, trailed his fingertips down Riff's arm, along the play of muscle under his skin. Riff called to him the way gravity called to a falling object.

"Are you going to kiss me now?" Riff asked in a husky voice.

"Soon enough, though your mouth tempts me very much." Zed continued the slow caress down Riff's ribs. Riff's desire fed Zed's own. "I wanted to lay down a few more ground rules."

"Yeah? Like what?"

"If you want me to whip that hot ass of yours until it's burning red, then fine, I'm all in, but you will be thinking of me when I do. Not him, got it?" Zed wasn't concerned about Vidal. He was sure Riff didn't want to think about the captain any more than Zed did. It was the other man that concerned him. The man Riff punished himself for.

Another quaver of uncertainty struck, and dark brown eyes fringed with those oh-so-black lashes widened. His gaze traveled over Zed's naked chest down to the unmistakable bulge in his pants. Riff wet his lips, his eyes going hot again and his hands tightening around the straps he held on to. Zed ached to really touch him, but he was coming to understand this was like foreplay. If he played this right, when he finally did touch Riff, they were going to combust.

"Yeah, I understand," Riff whispered.

Zed stepped closer and cupped Riff's jaw. He rubbed his thumb along the stubble. As tempted as he was by Riff's mouth, he had to make one other thing clear. "We're doing this because we want to, because we desire it, not as a punishment. Not for Wilt or Bryce or Didier."

Riff looked away as a shaft of denial lanced through him. Zed trapped his head between both of his hands, forcing Riff to look at him. "It doesn't matter why we do it," Riff insisted.

"Trust me, it matters. Because it goes right back to the first rule, and if you're thinking of punishment, then you're not thinking of me."

Pain filled Riff's gaze, and he tried to pull back again. He carried enough guilt and sorrow to bring a man to his knees. One day he had to get that story out of Riff, but Zed didn't think he was ready now.

"It doesn't matter because you don't really want to do this," Riff said, tamping those emotions down. "You're humoring me so you can fuck me."

Zed touched his mouth to Riff's, tracing his lips with his tongue until he ceased trying to pull away. "You're so wrong. When you looked at me with that raw and naked expression and asked me to hurt you, I realized I wanted it very much. I'd walk through fire to get you to look at me like that again. I like the idea of walking that line between pleasure and pain, that you trust me to do it."

Zed pulled back, staring at Riff's lips for a long moment before pinning Riff with a hard stare. "So do we have a deal, or does it end now?"

Riff stood tense for a long minute, resisting. Then he relaxed, leaning his cheek into Zed's palm. "We have a deal."

Zed's heart jumped.

"Now kiss me like you mean it."

"You're awfully bossy." Zed grinned and kissed the corner of Riff's mouth, moving back as Riff tried to capture his lips. "Is that the way this is supposed to work?" He continued to kiss around Riff's mouth, savoring the anticipation, the catch of Riff's breath, the way he trembled when he finally stopped trying to anticipate Zed's lips.

"Please, Zed, kiss me," Riff said, his voice heavy with want.

The sound of his given name made Zed ache with the need for that deeper intimacy. "Riff…." He touched his forehead to Riff's and stared into his dark eyes. Heat and tenderness slid through Zed in a slow, deep wave. He kissed his way to Riff's mouth and memorized the feel of it before parting his lips and deepening the contact. He didn't understand what hold Riff had over him, but he didn't want it to end. Riff moaned, his lips softening as he let Zed dictate the slow slide of their tongues. Unencumbered by the usual images Zed received when he touched, he was able to fully experience what Riff felt, and his full-on surrender to desire made Zed hungry for so much more.

Zed pulled back and stared at the haziness in Riff's eyes a long moment before dropping another soft kiss on his lips. As much as Riff's response had him wanting to take more, to demand until Riff gave him everything he had, Zed wanted to savor him first.

He stepped back and looked at Riff. He clung to the straps like he didn't know how to let go. Golden-brown skin gleamed with a light sheen of sweat, and he watched every move Zed made as if he were a lifeline. Zed knelt in front of him and pressed his lips to Riff's stomach before tracing his tongue around his navel. Riff trembled, making a soft sound.

Zed rested his hands on Riff's hips, his fingers dipping beneath his waistband to touch the hot skin there. He let his head fall back as he looked up at Riff. Riff swallowed, the knot in his throat bobbing.

"If you keep looking at me like that," he said, his voice hoarse, "you can do whatever the hell you want to me."

"I plan on it anyway." Zed rubbed his cheek against Riff's stomach, then dragged his pants and underwear down a couple inches. He could smell how aroused Riff was, hot and musky, making Zed want more. He didn't know when they'd have a chance like this again, and losing a couple hours of sleep was worth taking his time.

He scraped his teeth against Riff's hip, breathing his scent as Zed slid Riff's pants down, leaving them tangled around his thighs. He turned his head, pressing an openmouthed kiss against Riff's shaft, the heat making his lips tingle.

Riff made a low guttural sound in his throat. "Are you trying to make me beg?"

Zed rubbed his lips along Riff's shaft, lifting his eyes to watch Riff's face. "I hadn't thought of it. Would you beg for me? Somehow I can't picture it, but I'd be definitely willing to experiment to see what it would take."

He kissed the already slick head of Riff's cock and dragged his tongue around the glans, still keeping his gaze on Riff's face. Fuck. The expression there scalded him inside and out. It made Zed want to beg to be allowed to worship him. He tasted him again with a hot flick of his tongue, and Riff moaned, his lips parting.

"For you I just might," Riff said on a low breath.

Zed dragged Riff's pants the rest of the way down and helped him out of them, trying to regain his equilibrium. He needed to be in control right now and not overcome with lust.

He slid his hands over Riff's body and rose. There had to be something he could use in the captain's stash to get Riff ready for him. Because when he was done giving Riff what he wanted, he'd be more than ready to take what he wanted in return. Strapping Riff's ass was one thing. He didn't want to hurt him when he fucked him too.

Zed found lubricant and a beautifully shaped, elegant dildo. He was going to enjoy this very much. Riff's gaze dropped to the toy, and he shifted, leaning forward, his biceps bulging as his arms took some of the weight of his body. He bent slightly at the hips, offering Zed all the access he wanted. As willing and eager as Riff was, Zed wondered what it would take to get him as wanton and hot as he had been the night in the steam rooms. He might not have been acting like himself, but Zed was sure it was a reflection of a side locked deep inside him. One rarely shown.

He rubbed his hand over Riff's taut, muscular ass, imagining it reddened and hot. He tried an experimental smack with his hand. The sound of skin on skin was as erotic as the low hum of pleasure that came from Riff's throat.

He glanced over his shoulder at Zed, his eyes alive and laughing. "Trying to get into the spirit of the moment?"

"Something like that," Zed replied, encouraged by the pleasure in Riff's expression. He smacked Riff's ass a few more times, watching the way his handprint stood out before blood rushed to the surface. He caressed Riff's skin, trying to understand what he felt, and the rush of pleasure mixed with the anticipation for more washed away Zed's lingering reservations.

"I'm new to this whole domination thing," Zed whispered against his ear. "But I like it. Your excitement has got me burning so fucking hot." A shiver rippled through Riff. "I want you to be stretched and ready for me when I am ready to fuck you." He rubbed the lube-slicked toy against Riff's entrance.

Riff groaned and tilted his head back to rest on Zed's shoulder as he widened his stance. "Do it."

"You are one hot piece…. damn Riff, the sexiest fuck I've ever had the pleasure to touch," Zed rasped, nipping Riff's throat as he pushed the toy into him. He'd never been this turned on, but the dichotomy between the man who took charge so effortlessly when he led his team and this man so willing and eager to submit to whatever Zed did to him had set his brain on fire.

A small, helpless sound escaped Riff's throat. "More."

Zed nipped his throat again, twisting the toy deeper as Riff sagged against him. He slid his arm around Riff's chest, seeking out his hard, tight nipples. "Is this what you want?" he asked, tugging on one roughly.

"Close," Riff breathed, arching his body so that his chest pushed against Zed's hand as his hips tilted back, rocking against the toy. "Make it hurt."

"Like this?" Zed rubbed his lips against Riff's jaw and twisted his nipple.

Riff cried out, his body going taut as he circled his hips. "Yes… just like that."

Zed dragged his tongue over Riff's throat, feeling like he could get lost in him and his every reaction. He was a fever in his blood, addicting and dangerous. Zed wished he had a mirror so he could see every flicker of emotion on Riff's face. He caught Riff's mouth, kissing him again, hungry this time, demanding, and Riff kissed him back, their tongues tangling and stroking together.

Fuck, Zed wanted him. He wanted him now. His whole body ached with it, but he'd promised. He twisted hard on Riff's other nipple, swallowing his cry as Riff's mouth softened, his lips becoming pliant as his body swayed against Zed's. Zed circled Riff's throat with his hand and broke the kiss, turning Riff's head to the side.

"Do you have a preference for how you want to be spanked?" he asked, kissing Riff's throat. The captain had a whole array of whips, paddles, and implements Zed couldn't even put a name to.

Riff shook his head fractionally. "Nothing there is personal, so it doesn't really matter."

Zed looked at the tools Vidal had wielded to give Riff what he needed while twisting it into something unhealthy. He couldn't use any of them on Riff, but he suspected Riff didn't want just his hand either. He thought about Riff's words and the clue they provided…. Something personal.

"Would this work?" Zed rested his hand on the leather belt around his waist. It wasn't his own. Lifers weren't given belts, but he had been wearing it around his waist for the last few days.

A hungry expression entered Riff's gaze, and he wet his lips. "Yeah, I'd like that." The look he shot Zed was full of pleading. "Please."

Zed undid the buckle, so turned on by the need in Riff's eyes. It reminded him he had to set limits now. "Twenty strokes."

"Forty," Riff countered.

"It's not a barter, Riff. Twenty or none." Zed removed his hand from the buckle.

Riff's eyes narrowed, testing him, weighing to see if he was bluffing. Zed hoped he didn't press because he'd hate to disappoint him, but Riff had to realize Zed was serious. He'd witnessed more than once that Riff was the kind of man who liked to push every boundary there was.

RIFF STARED at Zed, at war with himself. He had no doubt Zed meant every word. He remembered the steam room, how Zed had shut down their interlude with absolute finality. He'd do the same thing here, leaving him needy and wanting.

He looked away, weighing his options. This wasn't like being with the captain. Zed was more controlled, and he demanded far more than anyone had in a long time. Was the pain and sex worth that vulnerability? Riff was acutely aware of his absolute nakedness, body and soul. Zed understood him more than he should, considering their short time together. That psychometrist ability of his, even stunted as it was now, revealed too much of Riff while Zed remained a mystery.

In the end it was Zed's silence that decided him. He'd laid out his terms and was giving Riff the time and space to make his own decision. Besides, Zed was right to limit the strikes. Riff couldn't be a bloodied, bruised mess and still expect to be on point, mentally or physically, and considering the nightmare they were in, he needed to be at his best.

"Make them count," Riff said with far more pleading than demand in his voice. He knew his expression was raw and naked. He couldn't seem to project his usual façade. He was too tired in body and spirit. And this precious time with Zed, this release and honest desire, was giving him just what he needed.

Zed's expression softened. "I will," he promised, "just keep your mind on me."

It was impossible not to. Zed commanded his attention with the way he looked at him with his intense hazel eyes, with the little things he kept saying, the way he mixed in gentle tenderness with the rough, and how he kept touching Riff like he could read his soul. All of which held Riff right there in the moment with him.

Riff watched Zed remove the heavy leather belt, moving with the lazy grace of a natural hunter. If he was uncertain, it didn't show. He was all sexy dominant male and as turned on as Riff. Zed folded the belt in half, approaching Riff as he watched mesmerized.

Zed paused in front of him, sliding his hand along the curved arch of Riff's neck. Riff turned his head and kissed Zed's palm. In the short time they'd been together, he'd come to crave the way Zed touched him like that. Commanding, affectionate…. And it wasn't just about reading Riff's emotions, because Zed touched him like that even with his gloves on.

Zed kissed him, somehow hard and possessive while remaining tender. Riff didn't know how he did that, but it made his knees weak. He sighed against Zed's mouth as he broke the kiss, leaving Riff's lips tingling. Zed walked around him, trailing the leather over Riff's bare skin. He shivered in anticipation, turning his head to watch Zed's progress.

Any worries he had that Zed would be tentative were lost in the first volley of hard smacks. Riff gasped, his hands tightening, white-knuckled around the straps, as stripes of heat blossomed across his ass. The shock burned into pleasure and Riff groaned. He looked over his shoulder at Zed, who rubbed his hand over the red marks, soothing the sting so only the heat remained.

Their gazes locked, and Riff's breath caught at the intent way Zed looked at him. He wasn't faking for Riff's sake. He really was into it.

Zed straightened, and Riff braced himself, clenching his buttocks, which in turn shifted the toy inside him. Another series of five smacks came one right after another, harder than before, without giving Riff a chance to draw a breath in between. He turned his face into his arm, his whole body tensing, then shuddering in release as the pain and pleasure washed over him again.

Zed slid his arms around him, his hips pressing against Riff's ass so the bulge of his cock was apparent. He kissed Riff's throat as his hand slipped lower to stroke Riff's cock. "What does it feel like for you?"

"You can't tell with that magic touch of yours?" Riff asked, rubbing his cheek against Zed's.

"Just that you like it and that you're as excited as I am," Zed replied as he continued to tease Riff's cock with firm tugs. "But that doesn't tell me as much as I want to know."

"It hurts like a brand on my skin, all the nerve endings awake and tingling. It pushes all thoughts out of my head so I can't think about anything other than the pain and the anticipation of more." Riff savored Zed's closeness. His hips moved so that he thrust into the circle of Zed's fist. It felt so good, the hot fire across his ass mingling with the pure pleasure of Zed's touch.

"Then why ask for it if it hurts like that?" Zed asked, his lips feathering along Riff's jaw.

"It feels so good to not think for a bit. It's peaceful and comforting to not be in control. Cleansing." He turned his head, inviting contact, and Zed took it, claiming his mouth in a kiss that took his breath as surely as the leather belt had. "You're not planning on stopping halfway through, are you?" Riff murmured as the kiss broke.

He felt Zed's lips curve against his own. "No, I'm just trying to understand. I never thought I would be so turned on by using a belt on a man. Then I met you, and you changed everything."

There was a note in Zed's voice that spoke to Riff's own loneliness. It unsettled him. As much as he tried to tell himself he didn't want anything more than pain and sex, his heart said otherwise.

Zed released Riff's cock to cup his ass instead, squeezing and reawakening the burn. Riff wanted him so bad he was finding it hard to think about anything else. He hadn't expected Zed to get so into it, and he hadn't expected to be into the moment with him either. Zed invited an intimacy Riff hadn't felt in a long time.

"Count out the last ten for me," Zed said, touching his lips to Riff's shoulder.

Riff swallowed back a whimper of want before Zed took it as a sign he didn't crave it and braced himself in anticipation of the onslaught. The strikes came fast, one after another, each one building on the pain before it, as Riff counted, the numbers falling from his lips in rough pants.

The last strike was hard enough to make Riff cry out and almost orgasm. The sound of the belt hitting the floor sent a tremble through him. Then Zed was in front of him, his hazel eyes hot with an inner fire. Riff stared at him, trying to pull himself out of the haze of aching desire and lingering pain.

Zed's arm came around him, holding him tight, as his hand cupped the back of Riff's head. "Let go of the straps, Riff. I've got you."

Riff forced his grip to loosen, feeling like he had to peel each finger off. He was conscious of every inch of Zed's body pressed against his own. Hot and hard all over. "Damn, your eyes make me weak."

"Just my eyes?"

Riff shook his head mutely, unable to talk as he tried to process everything from the fire heating his ass, to the desire running rampant, to the other conflicting emotions Zed made him feel, things that caused his heart to pound, dangerous things.

"Would you slap my face?" The impulsive request surprised Riff. Nobody had done that to him since Didier, and he would've knocked out anyone who tried. That was intimate, too personal to share, and Riff almost took the request back.

Zed's eyes narrowed as he studied Riff for a long moment as Riff held his breath, waiting. "Let's save a few things for another time," he said, gently touching Riff's broken nose.

Riff looked away in mingled disappointment and relief. Then Zed lightly smacked Riff's hard cock and Riff gasped. That was just as shockingly intimate as what Riff had proposed, and though done lightly, it ached more with unfulfilled need. Zed did it again and Riff groaned. It was followed immediately by another, a little harder, making Riff's head swim with desire. He opened his eyes and focused on Zed, who was watching him intently. If he didn't fuck him now….

A faint smile of satisfaction touched Zed's lips. "Now that look I recognize."

Riff's heart pounded as he grabbed Zed and kissed him roughly. Zed growled against his lips, and then they were moving, Riff holding on to him as Zed propelled him back until they met the wall. Riff moaned, going boneless as he was pinned between Zed and the hard surface. He raked his fingers down Zed's back, to the waistband of his pants, feeling the other man's hunger in his devouring kiss.

With shaky hands he undid the front of Zed's pants and reached in to caress his cock. "Why the hell aren't you naked yet?" Riff demanded.

"You've been keeping me too busy with your orders. 'Spank me, make it harder, slap me around….' When did I have time to get undressed?" Zed pulled away with a grin. He pushed Riff back against the wall when he tried to follow. "Where do you think you're going? Stay right where you are."

Riff leaned back against the wall at the rough tone. The toy inside him was an irritation at this point, a reminder that he needed more while Zed took his sweet-assed time getting around to fucking him. He kept his eyes on Zed, watching him as he stripped out of the pants, idly stroking himself. Damn, Zed had a beautiful body. Riff hadn't taken the time to fully appreciate it while they were in the steam rooms.

Zed was several inches shorter than him and all muscle, but he carried it in a compact, graceful way. He didn't have the captain's lean neatness or Didier's bulldog look. His shaggy brown hair fell into his eyes, giving him a rough, wild look, and his fair skin was flushed. Riff loved it, along with the reddish scruff that had thickened in the last few days.

Zed grabbed the lubricant again and crooked his finger at Riff, who approached on shaky legs. He'd never been one to crawl, but damned if Zed didn't make him think of doing just that.

Zed cupped the back of his neck, and Riff swayed toward him. "What do you want, Riff?"

Riff gripped Zed's biceps, need drumming in him as he tried to figure out what angle Zed was going for. Wasn't it obvious… or was he looking for Riff to beg?

"It's not a trick question." Zed's eyes drifted down to Riff's mouth, looking as hungry as Riff felt. "I want to fuck you so damn bad. I just want to make sure I'm not leaving out anything you need."

"Oh no… no, fucking's good," Riff said. Whatever else he was going to say was lost as Zed kissed him, completely scattering his thoughts as desire went supernova. Zed's arms came around him, and then he was bearing Riff down to the floor and the pile of blankets they'd left there. Riff rubbed his hips back against the blankets, savoring the burn and ache as much as the thrumming desire and Zed's hard body over him.

Zed's hand slid between Riff's thighs, twisting the toy as Riff curled his fingers into Zed's back and moaned into his mouth. Then the toy was gone, leaving him with an aching emptiness. Riff whimpered, sliding his legs up to frame Zed's hips in invitation, but instead of his cock he felt Zed's slick fingers penetrate him, thrusting deep and hard.

Riff tore his mouth away, shifting and panting. "Not enough."

Zed scraped his teeth over Riff's throat. "This is for me. I want to make us both so crazy we forget where we are," he rasped, continuing the hard thrusts. He kissed Riff again, mimicking the motion with his tongue.

"Fuck, already there." Riff shifted his legs higher and slid his hand between their bodies to stroke their cocks together. "I've been there with you from the moment you told me to grab those straps." Riff nipped Zed's chin. "Fuck me, please. I've been dying to feel you fuck me for what feels like weeks now."

He groaned as Zed twisted his fingers inside of him, pressing the bundle of sensation that sent him into overload. He writhed, nipping blindly again as he rode the wave of pure sensation.

"Where do you go when I do that?" Zed asked. "Where does that beautiful mind of yours go?"

"To the stars," Riff gasped as Zed did it again.

"That's where I want to take you all the time," Zed murmured. Then his fingers were gone, and the pressure of his cock filled Riff instead.

"Yes," Riff panted, winding his body around Zed so he couldn't withdraw. Before he could make further demands, Zed drove into him hard and fast just like he craved.

Riff slid his legs down, braced his heels, and rocked up to meet every one of Zed's thrusts. He tried to capture each sensation in case it was his last, the feel of Zed moving over him, the heat and sweat, the scent of them mingling together. He kissed Zed, drinking in the taste of him and the sound of their bodies slapping together.

Zed hooked Riff's legs, pressing them back and down, pinning him, owning him, fucking him deeper. Riff opened his eyes to find Zed staring at him, pinning him with those eyes as much as he was with his body. Riff clung to his biceps, his cries getting higher as pleasure bombarded him to the point of pain. It was too much. The intensity. The ache of his backside from the belt. The feeling of being with someone who actually gave a damn, who made him feel safe and comfortable in his own skin. All of that came together in a rush of wild exhilaration. Desperate need and pounding tension for more built to a rush that sent him over the edge as he came hard and fast and oh-so satisfying.

Zed groaned, his thrusts faltering as Riff squeezed around him. "Don't stop," he groaned. "Don't stop."

"Still making demands," Zed said and captured Riff's mouth. He drove into Riff again, making him cry out at the intensity. It heightened his pleasure, drawing out his orgasm. Then Zed's body tensed, and Riff clenched around him again.

Zed tore his mouth away. "Oh fuck," he groaned, grinding into Riff as he came.

They were both trembling and panting. After a few moments, they untangled themselves. Riff grabbed a towel to clean them off as Zed sat up and arranged the blankets and pillows into a comfortable nest. Riff sank into it gratefully, too spent to think. He closed his eyes, reaching out to touch Zed and reassure himself that he was near.

"Do you want me to shut off the lights?" Zed asked.

Riff's eyes flew open. "No," he said, too sharply.

Zed shot him a considering look as if he were trying to ferret out Riff's secrets.

"Leave them on, please."

"Okay." Zed settled down behind him and curled his arm around Riff's waist. Warm lips brushed the nape of his neck, and much to Riff's surprise, he found himself relaxing enough to sleep. His body was a heavy weight of satiation, and it dragged him down. He focused his thoughts on the sensation of Zed's closeness instead of the thousand and one worries plaguing him, and felt himself drift off.

Chapter Fourteen

"Khora! Wake up. We've got a huge problem."

Zed jerked out of his sound sleep at the alarm in Tuputala's voice. Riff sat up, untangling himself from Zed's arms. "What's wrong?" he demanded as he reached for their piled clothes.

"Where's Quinet?" Zed asked as he noticed Tuputala was alone. The fear in her eyes froze him.

"Gone." Tuputala shook her head, and curls escaped her loose braid. "We finished repairs, and I said something about now being able to leave and he freaked. Wouldn't stop talking about Wilt, insisting that we had to get her. I was just about to tranq him, but he got to it first and zapped me. I passed out before I could even open a comm line."

"You let him tranq you?" Zed asked in disbelief, then held up his hands as Tuputala turned a savage look on him. "Never mind, we'll find him. Any idea how long you were out?" He felt pretty rested, though that could've been the adrenaline surging through him.

"Probably no more than half an hour," Riff replied for her, stuffing his feet into his boots. "Any sign of Quinet on the monitors?"

Tuputala looked sick, and Zed's heart sank. "He took them out before he left. I'm sorry. I should've nailed him with the stuff when he first started getting agitated. I was so close to finishing the repairs, and I let myself get caught up."

"Don't," Zed replied. "We're all doing the best we can do. Don't kick yourself while you're down. Did Quinet get the transport computer running?"

Riff shot him a surprised look as a relieved expression crossed Tuputala's face. "Yeah, computer's good, the interface is repaired. Quinet also programmed the coordinates Wilt gave us. I'm not willing to trust the transport in a chase situation. If we can switch ships and send our transport on a different course, I think we can elude the captain completely. He may have somehow gotten his engines up, but his navigator is dead."

"Sounds like a good plan, but first we have to find Quinet." Riff straightened and turned to Zed as he finished getting dressed. "We're going to have to split up. Tuputala and I will search. You get the transport loaded with what's left of our food, clean water, tools, anything you think we'll need. I don't know what the captain's transport has, and we'll need enough to get us to the nearest planet. If you can, get the damned monitors running too. Then you can keep an eye out for us."

Zed bit back a protest. He did not like the thought of any of them being alone, especially Tuputala and Riff, but there was too much ground to cover to do it together. Fuck. "Understood."

Tuputala tied back the straggling wild curls around her face. "Crazy bastard could've gone anywhere. He thinks we're hiding Wilt from him."

"Check the engine rooms. That might be the first place he'd go, thinking we sent her there to fix something. That or the salvage rooms," Riff suggested, though he didn't look convinced.

"I'll grab our weapons." Tuputala disappeared from the hatchway.

"This isn't your fault any more than it was hers." Zed stepped closer, silently willing Riff to look at him.

"Yeah, keep telling yourself that," Riff said, his eyes haunted.

Zed caught Riff's arm. "What other solution was there? Drug him and lock him up? That wouldn't have been fair either, and maybe it would've made him deteriorate faster. Or maybe you should've stayed up with him until you put yourself in his state."

"Don't try to be reasonable with me," Riff snapped. "I'm not in the mood for it."

"All I'm saying is, Quinet needs you at your full game, not having should'ves and could'ves crowding your head." Zed dropped his hand. "Now go find him and take care of your damned prickly self when you do."

To his surprise, Riff kissed him hard on the lips. "I don't like you," he murmured, though his tone and the wash of confused emotion from him belied that sentiment. Zed kissed him again, as much to soothe his own anxiety and fear as Riff's.

"Keep telling yourself that, Khora. Next chance I get, I'm going to make you eat those words." Zed watched Riff walk away and tried to reassure himself the man knew what he was doing. They were so close to escaping, and the need to get off the ship was a raw itch under Zed's skin. Quinet's ass had better not be far away.

He checked the monitor links and found that Quinet had buried them under so many traps and self-replicating blocks Zed couldn't hope to unravel them quickly. He was good, but Quinet was better.

"We're not going to have visual anytime soon," Zed reported grimly, grateful they still had communications at least.

"Tackle the other tasks, then," Riff replied over the comm. "We'll keep you updated. In case Vidal grabbed him, change the codes on all the locks. We don't want any more surprises."

The thought of Quinet in the captain's hands made Zed wince. He was fragile. It wouldn't take much to break him. Zed cursed, and his hand tightened into a fist. Riff would find him. He had to.

"Will do." Zed cut the link and spared a few minutes for recoding the locks. He loaded the antigrav flatbed with whatever he thought they would need, stripping the galley bare of water and food. He gathered all of Riff's medicines, retrieved the extra weapons, clothes, and linen they'd gathered, and headed into the bay.

The transport looked pretty good, considering the state she had been in. The fried wiring had been replaced and the deck plates were back where they belonged. Zed checked the navigation system and had to smile when he found the stolen gyroscope part jury-rigged into place. He ran another diagnostic and fired the engines, pleased to hear how the they hummed to life. He couldn't believe how well Tuputala had integrated the gyroscope. The designs were very different. He turned on navigation, checked the coordinates Wilt gave them and the course Quinet set. When it was time to leave, he didn't want any delay.

Zed ordered himself not to check on their progress. They'd let him know if they found anything. But fuck, it was hard. Tuputala and Riff were outnumbered by the captain's men, and Quinet might not want to return. He busied himself with loading the supplies onto the transport and making sure they had full tool kits.

Then he remembered the beads Riff had left in the room they'd slept in. He went back and looked down at the pile and neat little line he'd started. He'd seen Riff wearing the beads on a bracelet, and for him to carry them around like this told Zed they meant something. He understood the need for a tangible talisman. He carefully gathered the beads so they wouldn't be forgotten. He'd restring them as he figured out the mess Quinet left behind with the computers.

As he worked, his thoughts flitted back to Riff and the others, worry weighing heavy on his mind. The occasional chatter told him they were still searching. He didn't like it, but there was jack shit he could do about it. Other than maybe spank Riff when he returned, but he'd like that too damn much.

He was surprised at how into it he'd gotten, but he'd have to be dead beyond any hope of reviving not to respond when Riff looked at him like he did or when he sensed the hot rush of his desire. And it wasn't just how turned on Riff was that convinced him; it was how relaxed he'd been afterward. How he'd curled up in Zed's arms and allowed himself to fall asleep. The pain did satisfy a need within him, and that eased some of Zed's uncertainty. He was navigating unfamiliar territory, going on instinct.

Zed banished the problem of Riff as he finished restringing the beads and renewed his attention to the monitors Quinet had fucked up.

Zed rested his palms on his knees, glaring at the computer. "You think you're a stubborn bitch," he muttered. "You've got nothing on me. Might as well give in now."

He went back to work, tackling it from another angle. If he recoded and shunted…. Zed buried himself in the fascinating puzzle. It wasn't the same as struggling with parts and tools or the joy of coaxing an aging machine into working again, but it did draw him in. There was something therapeutic about finding another way.

A young girl's laughter caught his ear, and Zed swiveled around with a frown. That couldn't be right. There were no kids on the ship. Tuputala had been certain. Agitated thoughts clouded his mind. What if she was wrong? She was wrong and kids were being hurt.

Zed drummed his fingers on his thigh. Damn her. She'd lied to him.

A slim figure in a space-station jumpsuit skipped up the gangplank into the transport. She had a short mop of glossy brown hair and a sad smile. "Hannah?" Zed called sharply, jumping up from his chair. The image faded, and Zed shook his head against the sudden aching in his temples. They needed to get off this damn ship. He was losing it as bad as Quinet if he thought he saw his niece.

"Khora, you there?" Zed said into the comm, clutching his talisman. "I think it might be starting again or maybe some echo effects. I don't know. But I'm seeing shit that cannot possibly be here. Come back. We'll figure out another way to search."

He tried to think back to how he'd felt before the riots. He thought he'd seen someone on the derelict, but that quick glimpse had looked more like Noyes than anyone he'd known. The only other hallucination he'd had was Hannah's stepfather. But if it was a hallucination, would he be aware? He sure as hell hadn't been last time.

"Khora?" Zed called again, when there was no response his growing sense of alarm buried everything else. "Answer me, dammit. Tuputala?"

"I'm afraid I had to disrupt your communications since you shut down my ability to call for help," Vidal cut in. "Tit for tat, or so the saying goes. I never really understood that one."

Zed closed his eyes on a silent curse. Where the hell was Riff? He'd know how to communicate with the bastard. All Zed wanted to do was punch him in his sneering face. "I was never very good with words myself," Zed replied. He accessed the computer again, his fingers flying as he tried to lock out Vidal. "I guess it was only a matter of time before you started hacking into systems."

"Well, it was a mistake to purchase the bonds of lifers who showed remarkable technical aptitude instead of having more of them among my own crew," Vidal said as Zed headed toward the suite. He might have a better chance through the main interface. Zed paused long enough to change the locks on the transport bay doors as well. Just in case. Of what he wasn't sure, but if Riff wanted him to double the layers of security since Quinet went missing, Zed would triple it. "I won't make that mistake again."

"If you take Khora up on his offer, you won't have to worry about it," Zed countered. "We can help, and we will as soon as Khora gives the go-ahead."

"I don't make deals with lifers," Vidal said, his voice as cold as the vacuum of space. "You and your friends had your romp. I'm taking back what's mine. I have Marty Quinet. Josephenia Tuputala has been injured. All that's left is you and Riff, and you're both alone."

"Vidal, you fucking bastard, I swear—"

The icy finger that raced down Zed's spine as the line went dead froze his fury. He had to warn Riff. They had to rescue Quinet and Tuputala and get off this ship before the captain found other ways to block them. He accessed the interface and heard the main hatchway to the suite open. Zed spun around, Riff's name on his lips. Noyes stepped into the room, Flaubert right behind him.

Zed and Flaubert went for their guns at the same time. "Drop it, Jakobsen," Flaubert ordered.

Zed tightened his grip on the gun. "You first."

They stared at each other in a tense standoff. Noyes chuckled. "Well, hasn't this gotten to be interesting. Really, there's no need for violence, is there?"

There was something in the nuance of his words that made Zed's gaze flick to him. If he took out the guard now, he could overpower Noyes and get to his team. All he had to do was kill the guard. Zed's finger tightened before he came to the horrific realization that he had been about to shoot Flaubert in cold blood. For what? This was a standoff, not a shootout.

All those thoughts raced through his head. A gun went off, and searing pain struck his shoulder. Zed fell back with a pained cry, his gun falling from nerveless fingers. He touched his hand to his shoulder, staring in disbelief at the blood on his fingers. The motherfucking bitch shot him.

"Captain, Jakobsen is down," Flaubert said. She lowered her weapon with a self-satisfied smirk.

"Good. Restrain him and wait for me." Vidal's voice cut through the scene. "I'll be there as soon as we've secured Khora."

"The captain's got plans for your so-called leader," Flaubert said, her eyes gleaming in anticipatory pleasure. "Maybe he'll let you watch while he tears him apart."

Rage flashed through Zed. He yanked the spanner from his tool belt and chucked it as hard as he could. The spanner hit Flaubert between the eyes and she dropped to the deck in a boneless heap.

Zed stared at her in horror as blood began to seep out from under her. He'd been aiming for her gun arm… hadn't he? Zed reached for the threaded bolt, clenching it to will away the hallucination. But this wasn't his imagination. More blood pooled under her.

"Well, that was interesting," Noyes said. Zed snatched his gun back up and pointed it at him. Noyes stared back at him with no fear whatsoever. It was disturbing. "Thank you again for the rescue. I was trying to get to your side, but it was difficult to escape the eyes of the captain."

"How'd you get in here?" Zed demanded.

"Any lock can be broken given enough time." Noyes glanced at Flaubert with avid curiosity lighting his eyes. "The captain is not as helpless as he'd have you believe."

Zed knelt beside Flaubert, careful to keep Noyes at a distance. His shoulder was one agonized throbbing pain. Better not to think how bad it might be. He fumbled, trying to check Flaubert's pulse and breath with his bad hand while keeping the gun steady on Noyes. She wasn't breathing, and there was a depression in the middle of her head.

He'd killed her.

Zed rose to his feet unsteadily, his thoughts reeling. He had to figure out what to do next. He didn't want Noyes with him. He didn't know what it was about the man, but he gave Zed the heebie-jeebies. He didn't trust him for one second. Maybe Noyes had picked up on the fact that Vidal was a sociopath, but he still couldn't see Noyes wanting to defect to them.

And call him cruel, but Zed didn't want him even if he was innocent.

"It was either you or her," Noyes said in a low voice that meant to soothe but seemed to buzz in his head instead. "Why should you feel guilt over her death?"

"Get out," Zed demanded. For a moment, the pressure in his head increased. His hand shook as terror gripped him. He didn't know how Noyes was doing it, but he was dead certain that somehow the man was the cause of all this madness. Zed clutched the talisman hard enough to cut into his palm, struggling to fight off that pressure. "What the fuck are you?"

The pressure ceased, and Noyes grinned. "What do you think I am? Who am I, Zed Jakobsen?" He took a step closer and Zed retreated. The man was lean, urbane, yet somehow utterly terrible in his alienness. "While we're at it, who are you? Mechanic? Killer? Lover?"

With each label he moved closer, and Zed scrambled back, his heart hammering. He had the feeling that if Noyes touched him he'd lose his shit.

He swallowed around a tight and dry throat. "Stay the fuck back."

"Did you know your sister despises you?" Noyes said in his compelling, sensual baritone. "She wants you dead."

It terrified him that Noyes knew so much, as if he could read minds as easily as Zed once read objects. Was this how people felt about him, like he was an invasive monster? If he touched Noyes, what would he see? Zed shuddered and retreated around the table.

"I don't think too much of her either," Zed replied. "She didn't believe her daughter. She'd rather stay with a monster than upset her comfortable world. So I don't give a fuck about how she feels."

The maneuvering led him closer to the main hatchway. Just a few more feet and he might have a chance. "I've been on many ships, but nothing like this one," Noyes mused, his gaze intent on Zed. "So much contained violence. So much hate and anger. It almost got out of control."

Zed's pulse raced, and the need to escape clawed at his thoughts. "Oh, it got out of control. I know you had something to do with it. I don't know how, but you did."

The unnatural grin widened. "You think I'm a puppet master? Nothing like that, I'm afraid, more like… a scientist, an explorer. I want to know what makes you, you. How do your little minds work? Always scurrying, always going. Little mice in a labyrinth, trying to gnaw their way to their own demise. What makes you tick, Zed Jakobsen? If I peel back your skull, what will I see?"

"You aren't gonna see shit, asshole." Zed bolted for the hatchway. He didn't know how to force the man out. Hell, he wasn't certain Noyes couldn't dance right back in no matter how much security they had. The only thing he could do was locate Tuputala, Riff, and Quinet and find a way back to the transport. Noyes and Vidal could live happily ever after in their little psycho world.

As the hatchway opened, someone moved up behind him. Zed spun around to face Dr. Barboza. Shit. He'd forgotten about him. Before Zed could lift his weapon, sharp stings struck his thigh and arm. He glanced down to see tranquilizer darts piercing his flesh. Urgency fought against the rapid wash of the drugs.

He lurched toward the doctor. "Run. Get out of here before he sees you."

Barboza steadied him as he stumbled to his knees on a wave of dizziness. "Delusional, it seems, maybe from the wound. I'll have to get the bullet out before the captain questions him."

Zed clutched at the doctor, trying to get his tongue to work, but it felt too thick for his mouth. Noyes emerged from the suite, watching Zed with keen eyes.

Terror gave Zed the strength to tighten his grip and shake the doctor. "Kill him. You've got to…."

Barboza shook his head and pried Zed's hands from him. "I'll get him secured, and then help Captain with that garbage Khora. Personally, I think he should just kill him and be done with it. The man's more trouble than he's worth."

Zed's head swam as he struggled to stay awake. Hands grasped his legs and began dragging him back into the suite, past Noyes. Those eyes stared at him, bored into him, exposing every secret in his mind as Barboza continued to drone on.

"It's too bad about Tuputala. I should've waited until she had cleared that catwalk. Nasty way to go. I had to be sure, you know. I couldn't risk her seeing me. She's dangerous."

Zed's eyes closed on a wave of grief. Riff was going to lose his shit.

Barboza dropped Zed's legs, and then Noyes was kneeling next to him. Zed's mouth opened on a silent scream. *Don't touch me. Please God, no, DON'T!*

Zed fought the drugs rolling over him. Had to warn Riff. Noyes cocked his head, studying him. *No, no, no.* Cold fingers brushed his check. Zed screamed as the darkness swallowed him.

Chapter Fifteen

If I were Quinet, where would I go?

Riff paused outside the infirmary, trying to collect his scattered, worried thoughts. Quinet hadn't been in any of the salvage rooms, and Tuputala had searched every niche and compartment he could hide in. They'd had no choice but to split up then. Riff didn't like being away from the suite this long, and he sure as hell didn't like the entire group left isolated and alone. He was going to kick Quinet's ass when he found him, after making sure he was okay.

He'd hoped Quinet had gone to the infirmary, still thinking that all Wilt needed was more medicine. But that theory hadn't panned out either. Riff frowned, tapping his foot. Quinet knew they were supposed to clean up the bodies and bring them to the penal wing. If he'd finally accepted the fact that Wilt was dead, he might've gone to look for her in their cell.

Zed had been quiet too, except for occasional technical comments to Tuputala. Based on their quick conversations, it sounded like Tuputala hadn't exaggerated. They were ready to go. If they could fucking track Quinet down.

"Jakobsen, any luck with the monitors?"

"Not yet, but I'll get back on it once I'm done with the other stuff. I'll let you know if I break through."

If Zed managed to dismantle Quinet's code, Riff was going to kiss that man senseless. Stress had his temples pounding and made his blood seethe. They'd been so close. When he got a hold of Quinet…. Riff frowned, shaking off the sudden violent thought.

"Heading to the prison," Riff said to Tuputala. It was time to stop tiptoeing around and finish this. "How's it going on your end?"

"Still in the engine room. Nothing so far, but no sane man would be hanging around here. It's the aftermath of a war zone. Noyes better be worth a helluva lot of money, because Captain's going to need it to get this bag of bones moving again." Riff heard the sound of clangs and a vicious curse from Tuputala. "If Quinet's here and still as out of it as he was, I wouldn't lay odds on his survival. Whoever was in here setting fires also laid traps."

Riff considered their options. His gut instinct told him Quinet was in the penal wing. As much as he wanted to dismiss the idea, it was based purely on his fear of being trapped there. Quinet was seeking comfort, seeking Wilt. And comfort meant familiarity.

"Meet me at the entrance to the prison cells. Barboza and Flaubert might be working in there. I need you to cover my back so I don't get locked in."

"I'm pretty sure there's someone down here with me. Maybe more than one," Tuputala replied in a tense voice. "Don't think it's our boy, though."

"Get the fuck out of there, then," Riff said as concern spiked again. "Do you want me to meet you?"

"Don't worry about it. I'll beat you there." Riff frowned as the comm cut off.

What if Quinet wasn't there… what next? Everything in Riff screamed to get off this ship as soon as he could, but he couldn't leave one of his team behind. He'd made a promise to Wilt. She would haunt his ass until his dying day if he did.

Riff fingered his wrist where his beads should be but felt the bandages instead. One damn problem at a time. First, finding Quinet and dragging him off the ship whether he wanted to come or not.

The ship was quiet, too quiet, which only added to his nerves. The engines had shut down again. Even the rats had disappeared. Riff hadn't heard from Vidal since they woke up. Vidal wasn't the kind of man to sit back and let anybody run his world. He was plotting, waiting for one of them to slip up, and Quinet had given him the perfect opening to screw them all over.

Half the lights had gone out, and as Riff moved through the silent, bloodied corridors, shadows flickered and whispered in a seductive dance. It made him think of Zed. Zed scared him. Scared him more than any nightmare this ship could produce, because Zed was making him care again. Bastard.

The hatchway to the entrance was open, the guard station empty. The bodies Riff and Zed left at the end of their shift were gone. So at some point Barboza had returned.

Riff paused just inside the hatchway, straining to hear. "Quinet? You down here?" he called softly. He remembered the silence that had greeted him the last time he woke up here. The utter stillness. The hair rose on the back of his arms in a prickling wave.

"Tuputala? You coming or not?" Riff said into the comm and static crackled. A shadow stirred, and Riff took another couple steps inside. "Quinet? Is that you?"

Bryce stepped out, his face bloodless so that the bruises stood stark against his throat. Guilt twisted Riff's heart, even as his instincts shrieked. Bryce ducked around the corner, and heart thudding, Riff followed. When he got to the corridor, he found it empty. Riff dragged a hand through his hair, trying to think through his confusion. He was looking for someone else. Quinet.

He glanced through the porthole into the first cell and closed his eyes with a sigh, lightly banging his forehead against the glass. Anything that was not bolted down had been swept out into space— personal belongings, bedding, bodies. Vidal hadn't waited one minute before ejecting them, not even asked for a moment of silence to remember them.

The need to know for sure had him running, moving deeper into the penal wing. Every cell he glanced in showed the same emptiness. It infuriated and terrified him to know Vidal had this power the whole time. With a press of a button, he could start over again with a whole new batch of prisoners if they became troublesome. So easy to kill with a button instead of looking his victims in their eyes. He'd watch them through his cameras, tapping his fingers the way he'd tap that crop against his leg. *Tap. Tap. Tap.*

Breathing hard, Riff stopped in front of Wilt and Quinet's cell. He didn't want to look. He didn't want to see it cold and empty like the rest. If he didn't look, he'd never know. Riff steeled himself and peered through the porthole. Wilt lay on her bunk, the shroud pulled away. She'd been tucked in as if she were sleeping.

"Quinet?" Riff called, reaching for the handle of the hatchway. A bloody fist thumped against the porthole. "Fuck!" Riff jumped back with a shout.

Quinet appeared, his face pressed against the glass as he glared at Riff. "Go away."

Riff felt in his pocket for the tranquilizers. "Come on, man, we've got to go. It's time. Wilt wants you to go with us."

"No!" Quinet thumped the hatchway again, angry determination glinting in his eyes. "You lied. You want to take her away. You want to toss her like trash. Like the others. All wrapped up as a present for the hungry god to eat. So hungry and cold…."

Riff looked over his shoulder at Wilt's body. Blood stained her hand and the blanket covering her. "Are you hurt too? Let me take a look at you."

A look of confusion crossed Quinet's face. He bowed his head and lifted his hands, blood flowing from the long, deep wounds on his arms. "I think I had an accident."

Ice squeezed Riff's chest, driving out other concerns. He reached for the hatchway handle again, only to find it digitally locked. "Tuputala, can you override the controls on the cell locks from the guard station?" Silence greeted him. "Jakobsen, can you hear me? I need help."

"Can we take her with us?" Quinet asked in a childlike, quiet voice. "Promise? I'll go if you promise."

"Yeah," Riff replied, his voice tightening. "Just as soon as we can get the hatchway open we can all leave." Quinet let his hands fall to his sides as he turned to walk back to Wilt. There was so much blood. "Quinet, do me a favor." Riff waited until Quinet looked at him. "Put pressure on your wounds. I'll help as soon as I get in there, but I need you to slow down the bleeding."

Quinet shook his head and knelt down beside Wilt. "Tired. Hurts."

"Tuputala, answer me, dammit." Riff yanked on the hatchway. He didn't know one fucking thing that would help him hotwire the console. He wasn't going to watch another teammate die in front of him. "What did you do, Quinet? What did you use to cut yourself?"

"The man told me to do it," Quinet whispered, laying his head down on Wilt's arm.

"What man? Who?" Riff demanded, trying to make sense of his words. "The captain? Did Vidal put you up to this?"

"The man… the man with the foreign eyes." Quinet draped his arm over Wilt's body and closed his eyes. Riff watched the slow rise and fall of his chest, dread a sick weight in his stomach. He wasn't making any sense. He'd finally snapped.

"Tuputala? Jakobsen? Please. I've found him. He needs help. I can help if I can get to him." Riff pounded on the hatchway. "Somebody fucking answer me."

They're all dead, a voice whispered. *They're all dead, and you're alone. All alone until somebody finds you.*

Riff shuddered, dragging a hand through his hair. He drummed on the hatchway. "Let me in!"

"I'm afraid I can't allow you to do that." Riff's heart began knocking at the sound of Vidal's voice. "Your teammate is ill, and I'm not going to run the risk of contaminating the rest of us. As a medic, I'm sure you understand."

"I can help him," Riff snarled, yanking on the hatchway. "You don't know what the fuck you're talking about. I ran the tests. None of us are contagious. Open. The. Fucking. Hatchway."

"You don't dictate demands to me," Vidal snapped. "You've forgotten who's in charge. It's not you. It was never you."

Riff closed his eyes, resting his forehead against the porthole as he waited for Vidal's stab. It would hurt. Whatever he had planned, it would cut deep. "Please," Riff replied, his hand trembling as he tried the hatchway handle again. "Let me go to him."

"He's beyond your help. In every way."

A klaxon went off, pounding through Riff's skull. The decking shuddered. Riff's head jerked up and he stared sightlessly into the cell with an inner scream of denial. Warning lights flashed along the corridor and in the cell.

Riff focused on Quinet as his hands tightened on Wilt's blanket. The decking shuddered again, and the bunk shifted.

"You can't!" Riff screamed. "He's still alive."

"He's insane," Vidal replied in a flat voice. "You knew it and still let him join your team instead of locking him up. This is on you."

The back wall of the cell began to part, opening up to the vacuum of space. "No! I'll turn myself in. Just shut the damn doors." Riff beat on the hatchway until his hands throbbed with pain. Until his blood pounded with the fire of his fury.

"I don't believe you, Riff. I don't believe you for one second."

Riff knew it didn't matter if Vidal believed him or not. If Quinet was sane and healthy or not. Vidal would still open the doors. He'd do it because he enjoyed watching the pain Riff was in.

"Please don't," Riff begged, clinging to the porthole, tears stinging his eyes. He was so close. If he could get through the hatchway, he might have a chance.

Riff fought the hatchway as the rear wall opened farther. The plain thin mattress on the top bunk shifted and was swept out into space. Quinet wrapped his arms tight around Wilt and buried his face against her shoulder as they were dragged forward.

"No!" Riff screamed, straining his throat with the force of it.

Quinet didn't even try to save himself, didn't grab for the bolted-down bunks. And then they were gone. Sucked right into Quinet's hungry god.

Riff stared at them as they spun away from the ship until they were only specks and disappeared. Helplessness and sorrow transmuted to rage as he whirled around. "I'm going to kill you," he swore, staring at the closest camera.

"You seem to be in the habit of killing your lovers." There was a smile in Vidal's voice. "I'd better watch my back."

"Don't worry. I'll make sure you see it coming." Riff bolted for the prison entrance. He had to find Tuputala and Zed and find out why they didn't answer. Vidal could've been blocking the comm signal, or it could be something else. Then they'd leave. Leave Vidal to starve and pick off the corpses he had left to him.

Ahead a hatchway slammed shut. The sound echoed hollowly down the corridor. Riff put on a burst of useless speed. His heart hammered so hard he felt lightheaded as he rammed into the hatchway with his shoulder. He was trapped. Trapped with no one near, no one coming to his rescue.

"Zed? Joey? Where are you?"

"We have Zed. I'm afraid he was wounded when we captured him. He might not be right in the head anymore." Riff closed his eyes, picturing Zed how he'd last seen him, staring him down with promise in his eyes. He'd better be okay, or he'd take it out on Vidal's spleen. "But he's sufficiently coherent for my purposes. He'll live long enough to tell us how to release the locks you put on all the vital systems."

Vidal was noticeably silent about Tuputala, which meant she had to be alive and free. Otherwise Vidal would gloat over it to hurt him more. Please, let her be alive.

There had to be another way out of the prison. Riff's thoughts raced as he tried to think of something. Trickery might work. If he disabled the cameras, he could wait for whoever fetched him.

"Now just sit tight and Dr. Barboza will be there soon." Riff stifled a hot, vicious bolt of pleasure. Dr. Barboza… he wouldn't mind getting his hands on him. "Can I trust you to be a good boy?"

"Yeah," Riff said with a veiled smile. "I'll be good."

"Typical and exactly what I thought," Vidal replied. A hissing sound filled the corridor. Riff looked around wildly as gas slipped through the ventilation system. "You'll be more docile when you're struggling to draw a breath."

Rage flashed through Riff again. He wanted to rail at the captain. He wanted to claw his way through the hatchway. None of that would get him out of this situation, and it would only quicken the loss of oxygen. He had to remain calm. He had to wait for his chance. Riff clutched his head in his hands, trying to escape the feeling of being trapped as he struggled to control his breathing, one long, slow breath at a time. There had to be a way out of this. There had to be a way to make Vidal pay and pay dearly.

Chapter Sixteen

Thump. Thump. Thump.

Zed woke up to utter darkness weighing down on him, pain stabbing his shoulder, and the sense that the drums had returned. It was quiet, though, except for the rapid pounding of his heart. He was naked and bound, propped up against a wall. It was cold. His skin prickled from it, and his extremities ached. He straightened, trying to get his bearings. Something was different with his head; it hurt, but not like the pain he experienced when he'd woken up after the riots.

He sat on a smooth, slick surface, but he didn't get any kind of a reading from it. His ability had started to come back, now nothing. But it didn't feel dead, more like when he held his talisman and let all the input flow over him instead of pounding against his brain. Or when he encountered people with strong mental shields.

There wasn't one pinprick of light for illumination. When Zed moved he felt the tug of a wide bandage on his skin. At least he wasn't bleeding anymore, though the thought of Barboza's hands on him made him want to retch. Zed lifted his bound hands and felt his mouth and eyes. Relief flowed through him. They hadn't been stitched shut again.

He heard hoarse, rapid breathing and froze, his thoughts flashing to Noyes, of being alone with him in the dark. Zed shivered. Noyes had touched him. He'd touched him, and Zed had seen… a nightmare made flesh. Noyes wasn't human. He was the shell for something…. Zed struggled to remember, but the more he tried, the more afraid he became. No, he couldn't open that memory.

"Who's there?" he called softly after a long, agonizing moment. He'd rather know than sit in the dark and wonder.

"Zed? It's me," Riff replied in an odd, subdued voice. "Are you hurt? Vidal said you were."

"Flaubert shot me." And he'd killed her in return. Zed couldn't quite bring himself to say that. Killing Heller would be one thing. Killing Flaubert had served no purpose, because here he was, bound and captured. "It hit my shoulder, burns like hellfire, but I don't think anything's broken. Noyes was there." He heard the fear edge back into his voice at the name. "He did something… I can't remember. He's not what we think he is. He's not human."

"What makes you say that?" Riff asked, his voice still far away, as if he couldn't quite focus on the conversation.

"He touched me." Zed bit back a spurt of fear at that. He had to concentrate on something else. He tried to judge how close Riff was by the sound of his voice. Not too far, maybe he could get to him. "How about you?"

"No. They knocked me out too fucking easily." Again Zed heard a *thump, thump, thump*. The heavy sound of a melon hitting a solid, muffled object. Zed's heart jumped, and then the sound ceased. "They killed Quinet. Cycled him out with Wilt," Riff said in a lost voice. "He was still alive."

Zed swallowed hard around the lump of grief, shock, and sorrow. God, Quinet. And Tuputala too. He had a vague memory of Barboza saying he'd shot her. He tried to remember the details, but they were a drug-induced blur. He decided to keep his mouth shut. Riff had lost enough and didn't need another blow. Quinet and Wilt. Riff and Tuputala. They were tight. Unravel one and you unravel the rest. He bet Vidal had known that.

"I'm sorry, Riff," Zed said quietly. He inched his way toward Riff's voice, trying to scoot as best as he could with bound hands and feet. By the time he reached Riff, his shoulder felt as if it were being repeatedly gored with a screwdriver.

The thumping sound came again, and Zed realized Riff was pounding his head against the padded wall. "Where are we?" he asked in an attempt to distract him. He needed Riff to keep it together. They had to get away before Noyes returned.

"Captain's fun room. He'll leave us in here, waiting for the darkness and loneliness to wear us down." Riff's voice sounded so hopeless that Zed's heart twisted. He'd focused so much on how Vidal had threatened to beat Riff to death that he'd never considered all the other ways Riff could've been hurt. "Then he'll come for us."

"Good thing we're not alone." Zed reached out and clasped Riff's hands. They were freezing cold, and there was no impression of him at all behind that mental shield. Zed fumbled over Riff's wrists, trying to make sense of the knots.

"What happened to your niece?"

Zed stiffened, then went back to trying to loosen the ties around Riff's wrists. "That's a conversation for another day. After we're off this ship."

"We're never getting off this ship." Riff laughed, the sound unnatural in the dark, and another chill went through Zed. "What? Don't trust me? You can tell me."

Zed leaned his head against the wall and closed his eyes against the darkness pressing down on him. If Riff had lost his mind…. He tested his mental shield and felt it thinning. He reached out, grasping Riff's hands again.

The memory of screams rolled over him. Agonized screams of the dying. Of someone Riff had cared for with a deep abiding love. More screams. Screams that filled Riff with vengeance and vindication.

That was what Riff heard when he was alone in the dark. Zed tightened his newfound shields before the emotions and memories could take him over too. "Hannah's stepfather was abusing her in his office. She tried telling her mom, but her mother accused her of lying."

"But you found out about it."

Zed turned his head toward the sound of Riff's voice. "I was isolating myself. My ability became too much to handle when I started sensing people's emotions and memories. I was in a relationship that had gone very bad because of it. So I volunteered to do some external work. It's quiet in the evac suits when you're out in space. I needed that quiet. When I returned I found Hannah hiding in my cubicle. She didn't want to tell me at first. She was afraid I wouldn't believe her too. But I saw…. God, Riff, I saw what he did to her. I felt what that bastard did."

Zed's heart ached at the thought of his niece. He was never going to see her again. Never see the woman she'd become. "Heller wielded too much power on that station. I'd never get him arrested, especially when my sister refused to listen. So I snuck Hannah off the station. Sent her to where I knew she'd be safe. Then I went after Heller, confronted him in his office. He was so damned condescending, so damned righteous in his power. I snapped and tried to take him out, but his security was too tight. When I wouldn't give up her location, no matter what Heller did, he found another way to make me pay. But she's safe. That's all that matters."

"And Vidal knew all that. It amused him, the sadistic fuck." Riff's voice hardened, chasing away the hopelessness that had consumed him before. His fingers stroked Zed's cheek. "I'm sorry about your niece."

Zed inched closer to Riff, determined to get his story as well before it ate him alive. "What happened to you, Riff? Why're you here?"

Riff tried pulling his hand free, but Zed tightened his grip. "Now it's your turn. It's like you said, do you trust me? I heard the screams. I heard how the sound hurts you. Talk to me."

Riff didn't try to pull away again, but he didn't speak either. A moment later Zed heard the *thump, thump, thump* of his head against the wall. "Hey, stop it," Zed said, his voice sharp. "This might be our last chance to get clean with each other. You need to talk this out, not punish yourself more."

The thumping stopped, but it was a long, cold moment before Riff spoke. "We were on leave in some back-hole planet with a sad excuse for a garrison. We didn't really care where we landed. We just wanted to be planetside." Riff's voice sounded far away, like he had been transported to the past along with his words. Zed lowered his shields again and let himself be swept along with Riff's words and memories.

"Didier liked to gamble. It was his biggest vice and the one he couldn't control. I was horny as fuck and pissed that he wouldn't leave the tables, so I left him to have a few drinks. He won big, and it pissed off the local yokels. They followed him to our room, beat the hell out of him, then gutted him and left him to die."

Zed rubbed his hands over Riff's, trying to get some warmth into them. "And you found him," he said, seeing all too well the horror of that moment.

"Screaming. He wouldn't stop screaming. Nobody came to help. If we'd been on our ship, I could've saved him. But they were days away, and the shithole of a planet had only the bare necessities. Not what I needed. He was hurting so much. I couldn't see him like that. He begged me to make it stop."

Zed squeezed Riff's hands. "What did you do, Riff?"

Riff went quiet again, a tremor moving through him. A sound caught in his throat, a strangling note of distress. "I overdosed him on morphine. He just slipped away. Just went to sleep and then was gone."

Zed brought Riff's hands to his lips. His fingers were so cold, like they'd never be warm again. Zed got the sense he'd lived that nightmare over and over again since the madness had come over the ship. He'd tried so hard to save them all, and his failures weighed him down.

"They came back." Riff's voice hardened. "Drunk and looking to hurt him more, or maybe looking for me. I don't know. Three of them and one of me, but they were drunk, I wasn't. They were injured because Didier had fought back, I wasn't."

Riff killed them. Zed didn't have to be told that to know. He saw Riff striking back, knowing right where to hit. But those weren't the deaths that preyed on Riff's soul. They weren't the reason he'd sought out Vidal and had him whip scars onto his body. He'd taken what had been a pleasure for himself and turned it into an endless punishment.

"I—"

"Don't." Zed squeezed his hands. "I don't care about those other motherfuckers. As far as I'm concerned, they got what they deserved. You think that too. That's not what's eating at you. Didier is."

"I killed him."

"He was already dead," Zed replied matter-of-factly, hoping it would cut through Riff's self-torture more than gentleness would. "You said it yourself. He was already dead. His body just hadn't caught up to the truth yet. He was in pain. You eased that pain. He didn't die alone and hurting. Next time you think you should be punished, think about that."

"I should've made him come with me instead of sitting down at that table."

"Was he your lover or your child?" Zed replied in the same implacable voice. "It wasn't your job to make him do anything. He's a grown man who made his own decisions and mistakes, just like you and me. What-ifs don't mean a single goddamned thing."

Some of the tension left Riff's body, and he scooted closer until he was pressed up against Zed. "Tuputala thinks I shouldn't blame myself either. How did I end up with you two on my side?"

"She has her moments of wisdom," Zed replied roughly, trying not to think of what might have happened to her. "You blame yourself for too much. For Bryce, Wilt, Quinet. You've got to give yourself a chance to grieve and move on. You block it off and imprison yourself in the moment."

"You're reading me, aren't you?" Riff asked, though there was no rancor in his voice.

"Do you want me to stop? It's come back. I seem to have more control, though I'm not sure why." Zed's thoughts touched on Noyes again and he shuddered.

"It's a little too late. You probably already know every damned secret I have. There's a helluva lot more to be concerned about than having my personal demons exposed."

Riff's hands drifted over Zed's chest until he found the outline of the bandage. He traced the edges, his touch gentle and sure. "If Dr. Barboza didn't do a good job patching you up, I'm going to take it out of his hide." The words were said lightly enough, but Zed heard the underlying fierce protectiveness. He was a healer who killed, a protector who failed. No wonder he was screwed up in the head.

And now Zed had killed too, and he couldn't bring himself to feel bad about it either. They were just trying to survive. All of them, the captain's crew included, but Zed wasn't going to let their survival be at his expense anymore.

"Remember the last time we were in this room?" It seemed so long ago that Riff had asked him to hurt him, to fuck him, and though it had been rough and hot, it had been tender and sweet too.

"I'm never likely to forget it," Riff said with a rusty laugh.

"Me neither. Hold on to that memory, Riff. Don't think about the other times you were locked in here, in the dark or when he was trying to break you. I'm the one here with you. Everything outside of this room may be fucked-up, insane, and evil, but what's between you and me isn't."

It was sure as hell easier to focus on comforting Riff than worry about what awaited them. Vidal would want to know the code to the transport bay. He was going to play them against each other. He was going to enjoy hurting Riff any way he could. Which meant he'd probably be giving Zed to Barboza. The thought of being with that man again made his insides clench with fear. He'd been tortured before at the hands of Heller and his men, but he suspected Barboza would be far worse.

And somewhere out there, Noyes was waiting and watching, enjoying every fucking moment. Zed shuddered again, biting back the fear that threatened to overwhelm him. What had he seen when Noyes touched him? What made him think that if they didn't escape they were better off dead because the only other option was endless madness?

Riff's hands moved to his face, and the light touch of his fingers gave Zed something to focus on other than his fear and helplessness. This wasn't over between them, and they'd find a way to save themselves. Then Riff's mouth followed the path of his hands, and he was kissing Zed.

Every time Riff had kissed him, it had been full of demand, it had been meant to push his buttons. He'd allowed Zed to kiss him tenderly, but he'd never initiated a kiss like this until now. It had taken going to hell for Zed to find what he'd unknowingly been searching for his whole life. He looped his hands around Riff's neck and kissed him back, trying to show in that contact what he felt and wasn't sure how to express.

"You scare me," Riff murmured as he pulled back. Zed sensed that fear as if Riff was on the edge of tumbling into a void. He also sensed the deeper emotions that Riff struggled to hide, the care that Zed echoed.

"With everything that has happened since we went on board the derelict, I'm the one who scares you?" Zed asked.

"You make me want what I had before. I didn't think I could feel like this again."

Zed stroked his fingers over Riff's hair. He touched their foreheads together, matched his breath to Riff's. "I feel it too."

CHAPTER SEVENTEEN

LIGHT FLOODED the room, and Riff jerked awake. He looked around in confusion as Vidal and Barboza entered. He couldn't believe he'd fallen asleep. He'd never done that before, but then again, he'd never been left in the dark with anyone else either.

Zed tensed next to him and straightened. "Where's Noyes?" he asked in an undertone.

Riff looked beyond Vidal and Barboza, but he didn't see the other man. He shook his head slightly. "He's close, I'm sure."

"Don't you two look cozy?" Vidal scowled at them, his brows knotted. Pissed that Riff hadn't worked himself up into a mess or because they were so close together? "That'll make matters easier. This is the way it's going to work. We're going to ask you questions. Answer truthfully and you won't regret it. You lie or choose to remain silent, the other one gets hurt. Understand?"

"Don't you dare say one word on my behalf," Zed said under his breath as he shot Riff a hard glance. "Don't give him a damn thing."

"Now, torturing Riff won't work. But I do know how to fuck with that clever mind of his." Vidal tapped Riff hard on the top of his head. Riff couldn't look at Zed. The sick taste of fear coated his tongue. *No, not Zed, please not Zed.* "If I hurt you, I hurt Riff. Now I'm not sure where the best points are to hit a man to do the maximum damage, but you know, don't you, Riff?"

Riff's thoughts flashed back to the men he'd killed, how it had felt to lash out in that precise killing rage. And the screams. Vidal loved to make him remember just so he'd beg to forget.

"There's a problem with your scenario." Zed's hard voice cut through Riff's nightmare. "Riff doesn't know the codes to the transport bay. I changed them after he left."

"And Zed doesn't know what Quinet did to lock us out of the other functions. He's not here to help because you killed him," Riff ground out between clenched teeth.

"Quinet no longer had a grasp of reality. Even if you could've made him focus on the task, I didn't want him free to roam around my ship." Captain Vidal stood back and surveyed the room. "Barboza, bring Jakobsen to that bench and strap him down."

Riff saw the quick flash of fear in Zed's eyes before he suppressed it. He no longer bore the marks of his earlier imprisonment in the healing pinpricks around his eyes and mouth, but the nightmare still lingered. This might awake repressed memories Zed didn't need. The situation was fucked-up enough as it was.

Barboza cut the ropes around Zed's ankles and dragged him to his feet. Zed fought and made Barboza work for each step until Vidal came to help him. A shadow moved out of the corner of his eye, and Riff turned his head to see Noyes slip through the ajar hatchway. There was something about the man that made him feel more naked and vulnerable than he was, which was saying quite a bit.

"Get him out of here," Zed shouted, straining against the hands holding him down. "Riff!"

Riff looked at Noyes again, who watched Zed with a slight smile on his lips and a profound fascination in his gaze. Zed screamed, fighting harder and almost breaking loose. Something had happened between the two of them when Riff had gone hunting for Quinet. Something that had terrified Zed to his core. He'd said Noyes had touched him. He couldn't remember what he'd gotten from the man, but whatever it was had left an imprint on him.

Noyes caught him looking and came over to crouch in front of him. "Riff!" Zed shouted, his entire body taut as he struggled. "Riff! Get away from him! Don't let him touch you."

"Shut him up," Vidal snarled.

"What did you do to him?" Riff asked in a shocked whisper. He'd never seen Zed so afraid, not even when he'd rescued him in the infirmary.

"Nothing more than a conversation," Noyes replied with an unblinking gaze. "Mr. Jakobsen seems highly excitable."

Zed's cries broke off with a harsh gurgle. Riff tore his gaze away from Noyes. Vidal had his hand clamped over Zed's mouth as he pinched his nose closed. Barboza laid his weight on Zed's legs and chest. Zed bucked, still struggling. Barboza managed to buckle one arm down and moved to the next while Zed fought for air. Riff's hands tightened into fists. He was going to rip them apart.

"What would you do if you were free right now?" Noyes asked in a low, compelling voice.

"I'd kill them all," Riff swore, unable to stop himself from watching Zed's struggle to breathe.

"By yourself? Naked and unarmed?"

Riff forced himself to meet Noyes's gaze. He flinched from the truth of the words as much as the calculation in those eyes. Noyes touched his wrists, his hands cold and unnatural, like a reptile. Riff didn't want to know what Zed had seen when those hands had touched him.

"I would find a way. Believe me."

Noyes cocked his head. "I think you would try and fail. They are as desperate as you, just fighting to survive."

"If you're trying to evoke my sense of sympathy, it's as dead as Quinet. Vidal can rot in his ship." Riff straightened, helpless fury writhing as he watched Zed's struggles weaken. "If you accidentally kill him, we're all stuck here," he called to Vidal.

Vidal removed his hands, and Zed's chest heaved as he drew in deep, gasping breaths. Despite the situation he was in, he stared at Riff like he was the one in the most danger. His gaze screamed at Riff to run.

"If I free you, will you let me into your head?"

"What?" Riff looked at Noyes, trying to understand. "What do you mean?"

"You're an enigma. Vidal, I understand. I've seen his type before. Barboza too." Noyes smiled with his too-white perfect teeth. All the rest of them looked battered and worn, but not Noyes. "I need more time to study. You're all so fragile. But you and Zed, you're different."

"Get away from him," Zed shouted, renewing his struggles, and another chill went through Riff. Zed sounded scared out of his wits. "Don't listen to him, Riff!"

"What happened between you two?" Riff demanded. "What did you do to him?"

"Do we have a deal, your mind for your freedom?" Noyes asked intently.

Riff had the terrifying feeling Noyes wasn't speaking metaphorically. He shook his head, his throat dry, his heart hammering. "I'll take my chances with the devil I know."

"It will be Vidal and Barboza, then. How disappointing."

Vidal slapped his hand over Zed's mouth again and pinched his nose. "Noyes, Barboza, strap Riff down across from our boy here. I want them to be able to watch each other."

"I prefer to witness rather than dirty my hands. You're doing a fine job on your own." Noyes tugged at the bindings on Riff's feet, releasing them, and Riff's eyes narrowed.

Barboza grabbed him roughly and hauled him up. Riff stumbled toward the other bench, his mind racing. What kind of a game was Noyes playing? Riff couldn't tell what side he was on, but Zed didn't trust him, so Riff wasn't going to either. He fought the urge to take down Barboza with a blow to the throat. Vidal was standing over Zed. Riff knew what Vidal was capable of doing if he resisted. Barboza shoved him down on the bench and jerked his arms over his head, hooking his bound wrists down.

"Get out, both of you," Vidal said in a tight voice as he released Zed. "You're distracting me."

Zed drew in a shuddering breath as Vidal eased up on him. Barboza hesitated, staring at Zed with an avid gaze that made Riff sick. He moved closer, touching Zed's ankle. "Let me have this one, Captain, while you work on Riff. I can get him to talk." The fear that rolled off Zed was palpable. "We have some unfinished business together."

Vidal looked at Riff as he considered it. Riff pressed his lips together to keep the denial locked inside, but Vidal noticed it anyway and smiled. "Why not? We are on a timetable."

"No!" Zed lashed out with the legs Barboza had neglected to strap down. One heel caught the doctor in the temple, the other jabbed his chest. Barboza fell back, staggered, and went down, the back of his head hitting the corner of Riff's bench with a sickening, squishy thud.

"How careless," Noyes murmured into the sudden, shocked silence. "I'll have to reevaluate the odds."

Vidal stared down at Barboza with an expression of aggravated displeasure. Riff lifted his head, trying to see if Barboza was dead or just knocked unconscious. "If you're not going to be useful, Noyes, get out."

Riff kept his gaze on Zed, who watched Noyes until Riff heard the hatchway close. Then he looked at Riff with bleak eyes. "The biggest danger you face is Noyes," Zed said in an urgent, hoarse voice. "You should've shoved him out the airlock."

"I didn't realize you were the paranoid type." Vidal dragged Barboza out of the way, leaving a smear of blood on the floor. He didn't even check to see if the doctor was still alive. It was as if Barboza had ceased to exist the second he stopped being useful.

At that moment Riff knew they were fucked if they didn't find a way out of this. Vidal hadn't recovered his sanity, maybe he'd never had it to begin with, and all he lost was his control. The only thing that mattered to him was making them hurt. They could give him every answer he wanted, and he'd still kill them, even if it meant he'd die along with them. Lingering alone on this broken ship.

Vidal retrieved a thin-bladed knife from a box, and Riff broke out in a cold sweat. Vidal hadn't used the knife often, but it had been brutal when he had. Some scars never faded.

"Fuck you, Vidal. Get away from him, or I swear to God, I'll rip you in half." Zed shouted more curses as Vidal paused next to Riff. The point of the knife dragged along his thigh, leaving a burning line in its wake. Riff swallowed hard and stared up at the ceiling. The tip paused next to his cock, then gently scratched his scrotum. Riff went ice-cold. He couldn't look at Vidal. He didn't want to see the anticipation and satisfaction in his eyes.

"Now, this is simple. Riff has two balls, and Zed, you have two legs. You are the one I need whole. Riff can afford to lose a few nonvital parts. For each leg you allow me to strap down, Riff here gets to keep a part of his body that gives him so much pleasure. Do we have an understanding?"

"Yes." The word was ground out, stony and furious. Riff glanced at Zed, whose hazel eyes blazed with a fury that should've incinerated Vidal. Zed straightened his legs, his body tense as Vidal approached. Zed made a soft sound of distress as the first leg was strapped down. Riff wanted to tell him to fight, to do to Vidal what he'd done to Barboza, but Barboza's death had been more mischance than calculation. Vidal strapped down Zed's other leg, and Zed strained against the restraints, his breath coming faster.

"Good boy." Vidal rubbed the top of Zed's head. "Maybe you'll have the chance to fuck Riff again and have him enjoy it." Zed jerked his head away with a snarl. Vidal looked at Riff. "I can't believe you picked him to replace me. Do you care about him?"

Riff's gaze flicked to Zed, then back to Vidal. "He's a means to an end, same as you are." He didn't have much hope that Vidal would buy it. Once he had an idea in his head, he was incapable of letting it go.

"Nice try." Vidal set the knife aside and balled his hand into a fist. "Now, let's start off with something simple, a demonstration of good faith to show me you're willing to cooperate. Why did you send Wilt to the bridge?"

Zed looked at him and shook his head fractionally. Riff pressed his lips together, anxiety roiling in his stomach. He had to find a way to get Vidal to take it out on him instead. "You want to know why I looked for someone else to satisfy me? Because you weren't doing it for me anymore. You promised you would make the screaming stop."

"You want the screaming to stop?" Vidal strode over to him and wrapped his hands around Riff's throat. Riff's muscles jerked as his breath was cut off. "I can make it stop right now. I don't need you alive."

"Wait, no, stop," Zed shouted as Vidal tightened his grip. "Wilt went on the bridge to install listening devices. We—"

"Don't lie to me." Vidal turned on Zed with a snarl. He dug his fingers into the bandage over Zed's shoulder and Zed screamed.

Riff flinched, jerking against the bonds holding him. His wrists burned from wounds reopened, and fresh blood stained Zed's shoulder. He'd woken up just like this, alone in the penal wing, with his arms bound above him, only then he didn't have Zed's cries of pain in the background. Remembered fear and urgency lent him new strength. As the bandage tore away from his left wrist, he felt the bindings loosen.

The nauseating thud of bare knuckles against flesh woke more sickening memories that made Riff choke on his bile. That's how it sounded when he'd beat those men to death. He tore at the ties around his wrist until blood slicked his skin and his wrists were on fire. His left hand finally slid free, and Riff fought with the knot on his right hand with slippery and sticky fingers. Just a little more.

"Tell me what I want to know." Vidal paused his pummeling of Zed's ribs and stomach. Even if Zed gave him what he wanted, there was no reasoning with Vidal. He'd kill Zed before feeling like he was beholden to him. "What are the codes to communications and the transport bay?"

"Go fuck yourself," Zed replied with a groan.

"Wrong answer." Vidal drove his fist into Zed one more time and then turned to Riff, grabbing the knife. Riff glared at him. Vidal could carve all the lines he wanted into Riff's flesh and he wouldn't give him a damn thing.

Vidal smiled and tapped the point of the blade under Riff's eye, where the skin was tender, past the protection of the bone. "Right or left?"

A fresh wave of cold sweat broke out over Riff's skin. "Wilt was on the bridge to find the coordinates to your transport," Zed said desperately, breaking the tense moment.

"Bullshit." Vidal looked over his shoulder at Zed. "You have a transport."

"It's fucked. It was fucked before this mess happened," Zed continued, his words tripping over themselves in an effort to get out. "We've been trying to put it back together again, but we can't rely on it to get us far. Why do you think we're still here?"

"Zed, don't," Riff said in a soft voice.

"Shut up!" Vidal snarled. The point of the knife dug a little deeper and Riff flinched. "Did Wilt get the coordinates?"

"Yes, but Quinet scrambled them when he locked us out of the damn computer. We're as stuck as you are."

Vidal was silent a long moment as he looked between Zed and Riff. "I believe you." Zed relaxed. Riff didn't. He knew Vidal too well.

"Right or left, Riff? Choose one, or I'll take both." Vidal would. Riff's stomach lurched with sickening fear.

"No!" Zed screamed and fought harder.

Riff had one hand free that Vidal hadn't noticed. It was his off hand. If he could just get the leverage he needed, distract Vidal somehow so he could get his other hand free….

"I'll stay with you," Riff said, digging his fingers into the knots.

Vidal stroked his cheek with the flat of the blade. "You'll stay with me regardless."

"There's a difference between being coerced and submitting. We both know you prefer it when I submit." Riff stared up at him, pleading for a last-minute miracle. Tuputala coming to the rescue. Noyes with another creepy offer. Even as he discarded those possibilities, he calculated the odds. When Vidal took his eye, he'd turn his concentration back on Zed, giving Riff the time to get free.

Vidal kissed Riff, a slow invasive kiss that repelled him. Riff forced his mouth to soften, to allow the intimacy as he loosened another knot. He tugged experimentally on his wrist. Close. Not quite enough.

Vidal straightened with a narrow-eyed look down at Riff. "You're used goods. You can't give me what I want. Right or left? Last time I'm asking."

Riff drew in a deep, shuddering breath, steeling himself. "Left."

Vidal smiled, that cruel, cold smile Riff knew too well. The smile he saved for his most sadistic moments when he was savoring the anticipation before the strike. Then Vidal abruptly turned away and realization struck with breathless force.

"No," Riff screamed, reaching desperately for Vidal's collar, and fell short. "No, don't. Don't. Take mine."

His shouts mixed with Zed's screams as Riff yanked frantically on his wrist, fighting the knots. The last binding fell away, and Riff uncoiled himself from the bench, one thought burning in his mind: This had to end.

He grabbed the back of Vidal's shirt and dragged him away from Zed. Vidal fell back with a cry and jerked free. He spun around to face Riff, blood-stained knife in his hand.

"Don't you dare touch me. You're nothing." Vidal slashed at him with the knife. Riff grabbed for something he could use as a weapon, and his hand closed over the hilt of a whip.

Vidal darted away as Riff lashed out with it. Vidal cried out, his hands coming up to protect himself as he stabbed the blade toward Riff. Riff struck again and again, vicious blows that kept knocking Vidal back farther until the tail wrapped around his wrist. Riff jerked, and the knife fell from Vidal's grasp.

Vidal's eyes widened as Riff struck again before closing the distance between them. He held up his hands, stumbling back. He was disheveled, with his hair mussed, uniform untucked, and a red welt standing out on his pale cheek.

"Wait, no, stop, Riff, you need me."

"No, I thought I needed you." Riff caught Vidal's shoulder, spun him around, and wrapped the whip around Vidal's throat, pulling it tight. "I was wrong." Vidal clawed at his hands, making terrible sounds as his heels drummed on the ground. Riff tightened it more until he went limp, his weight dragging against Riff's body.

Riff released him, shaking as he looked down at Vidal, who stared up at him with empty, lifeless eyes. He shuddered and bolted to Zed. The gaping, bleeding hole in the left side of his face was a mocking ruin. Riff stared down at Zed, at the pain etched in his face. Not again. He couldn't fix this.

"Zed...."

Riff glanced down at Vidal again, hearing him saying over and over in his head, *"You seem to be in the habit of killing your lovers."* Or getting them maimed. The warmth that Zed managed to light inside of him shriveled into a cold, lifeless ball.

"Riff." He looked up at the urgency in Zed's voice. "You have to untie me before Noyes returns."

It was the fear in Zed's voice as he said Noyes's name that got Riff moving again. With shaking hands he loosened the straps holding him down.

Zed sat up, gingerly touching a hand to his face with a sick expression. "How bad is it?"

Riff forced himself to look at Zed as a medic. If he could just distance himself, wall away his feelings, this would be so much better. But it was hard. Too much had happened, too many losses.

"It's a mess. I'm going to have to make sure there's no lingering tissue left inside that could cause an infection."

He met Zed's gaze, helpless to fix it and sick with that knowledge. "There's no way to save it. There are too many nerve connections there, I—"

"I'll find a way to cope. There are bionics, there are options, but we have to get off this ship first." Zed pulled him close. "Stop blaming yourself."

Riff turned his face into Zed's neck, trying to control his shaking. He had to get it together. This was not the time to have a mental breakdown. Zed wrapped his hand around his nape as Riff ran his hands gently down Zed's sides, checking for bruising and broken bones. That had been a vicious beating.

"Are you okay?" Riff asked softly. He pulled back and checked to make sure the bleeding from his shoulder had stopped.

"I'll survive." Zed looked intently at Riff and gave him a hard pat on his cheek. "How about you?"

"Pretty fucked-up, but I'll survive if we get off the ship." Riff glanced around the room, searching for their clothes as his thoughts whirled. Zed looked about as ready to fall apart as Riff felt. "Is the transport ready to go?"

"More than ready. The coordinates are locked in. We just have to get on board. Do you have a plan for getting by Noyes?"

There it was again, the edge of fear in Zed's voice. He'd said Noyes wasn't human, but that couldn't be possible. "No, I planned on winging it. Shoot first and worry about it later. We need to find Tuputala and get the hell out of here."

Zed caught his hand. "Riff—"

"Don't say it." Riff's heart squeezed with sudden denial. "Don't tell me she's dead."

"I heard Barboza say that he'd tried to tranq her and she had a bad accident. It didn't sound good. Barboza didn't even try to check on her, and they wanted us alive."

"Barboza's a negligent fuck, and our lives mean nothing to him. If it happened in the engine room, then retrieving Tuputala would've cost him too much effort. Especially if he considered you and me an easier option."

"I'm not saying we don't go look for her," Zed replied. "I don't want to leave her behind if there's a chance she might've survived. But you need to be prepared."

"No," Riff said forcefully, pounding his fist into his palm. "Nobody else on this team is going to die."

Zed didn't answer as they pulled on their clothes. Riff held on to the whip and retrieved Vidal's knife. They were the only weapons they had for now. Vidal, the arrogant ass that he was, hadn't thought to bring a gun with him. He was too used to having his back guarded.

He gently scooped up Zed's eye from where it had fallen, miraculously unscathed, somehow still beautiful in its rawness, the iris still gleaming a brilliant hazel.

"Leave it," Zed cut in.

"But...." Riff trailed off. There was nothing they could do to save it; already it was dying, losing moisture. But it seemed a crime to leave it behind. To leave any part of Zed behind in this fucked-up nightmare.

"Leave it," Zed insisted. "We have more important things to focus on."

"I could've kept this from happening," Riff replied. "I had one hand free. If I'd moved faster…. I figured the loss of an eye would be worth the sure knowledge of a lethal strike. I didn't know he'd pick you."

"It's not your fault. I told Vidal to fuck off, not you. I let my anger and fear get the best of me, and you almost lost the eye because of it. It was a flip shot. He could've taken it from either one of us, and he didn't know which one until he made the final decision. He had to touch me to cut me. I know what I'm talking about. He was trying to calculate which one of us it would fuck with more."

Zed spoke sense and he probably wouldn't shut the fuck up until Riff agreed with him. Sure enough, Zed continued. "I'd rather that you waited for the sure moment, because if you'd made a move before you were ready, then both of us would be dead now, or worse."

Riff nodded and set Zed's eye down on the bench. "I'm ready. Let's find Tuputala and get the hell out of here."

Chapter Eighteen

ZED'S WHOLE face screamed like a rusty nail had been driven into his temple and was being jiggled about. He never imagined being able to feel emptiness, but that's the only way he could describe it, like there was a gaping maw dug out of his skin. The hole was probably not that big, but it seemed enormous, and his hand itched to touch, as much as the thought made him ill. Add in the aches from the bullet wound and the beating and he was amazed he could stand. Adrenaline and fear coursed through him in one hell of a powerful motivator.

"Don't touch it," Riff said as he opened the hatchway to the main suite.

Zed snatched his hand away and looked warily around the room. It seemed quiet, but he didn't trust for one second that Noyes wasn't around, studying, testing. He'd watched that entire scene play out. Zed didn't know how, but he knew it with a gut instinct that made his psychic senses flare.

He kept turning his head, trying to see out of the corner of his eye. The lack of peripheral vision fucked with him and left one whole side vulnerable and exposed.

"Where are my medical supplies?" Riff asked as he searched the room. He was steadier now, that was a good sign, but he seemed distant and withdrawn. "Do you want something for the pain?"

"Your supplies are packed on the ship and no, not if it's going to muddle with my head." Zed found a gun and clipped it to the holster with relief.

Riff frowned as he grabbed Zed's chin with a gentle, firm hand. "We need to cover it before we go wandering about."

Zed tried to distract himself as Riff worked ripping apart a clean sheet. This ship was a death trap. Sooner or later it was going to claim them all. Tuputala had been recovering from that injury on her back before she'd gone to the engine room. He didn't like the thought of abandoning her without knowing for sure, but leaving the suite was suicide.

"What if I get the cameras back online?" he suggested as Riff laid the bandage against his skin. As gentle as he was, Zed's nerve endings screamed. "I had an idea before Barboza ambushed me. We can scout out the engine room first, search for Noyes."

"It'll take too long," Riff replied without giving it any consideration. "We can get to the engine room and get back before you break through Quinet's lock."

"The engine room is huge. I overheard you talking. Tuputala said it was dangerous, there were traps and fires. We won't be able to search it quickly. Not if we want to do it right."

Riff's jaw tightened as he tied a cloth around Zed's bandage. "And you wouldn't get a clear view through the cameras even if you were able to get them online."

A sense of heavy dread blossomed in Zed's heart as he stared at Riff. "We cannot go off half-cocked, just because you have an inclination to be reckless." Riff was hurting as much emotionally and mentally as Zed was physically. Vidal had really done a number on his head before he'd started torturing them. He wasn't in a position to be thinking clearly.

"And your paranoia has gotten the best of you. Noyes hasn't done a damn thing to us except for being a creepy fuck. Anybody would be a creepy fuck after they went through what he did. You say he's not human, but where's your proof? What did you see when he touched you?"

Zed shook his head. "I can't remember. But it was bad. You have to trust me on this."

"Vidal is dead. Barboza is dead. And Noyes isn't here. Hell, we could take this ship for ourselves instead of running away."

Zed straightened, his abused ribs twinging. "You are out of your mind. You want to stay on this ship now? There is nothing sane here."

Riff glanced away and shook his head. "I want to find Tuputala, and you're too much of a coward to help me."

"I didn't say I wouldn't help. For fuck's sake. I'm saying we have to use our heads." Riff turned away from him as if he didn't exist, completely tuning Zed out. He caught Riff's arm, turning him around to face him. "You will give me the respect I'm due."

A contemptuous note entered Riff's gaze. "Why, because I let you fuck me once?"

"No." Zed reined in his hot anger. That's what Riff wanted to see, wanted to find the buttons he could push into overdrive. "Because I've given you my loyalty and proven it. Because I've worked my ass off, doing my damned best to get us off this ship. Because I've backed you even when I didn't always agree with your decisions, because I thought you were the best man to lead our team. You might want to think about all that."

Zed headed toward the main console, leaving Riff to stew that over. For once sinking himself into a puzzle didn't ease his troubled mind. Riff had been the first person not to judge and label him since he'd been arrested. He'd picked Zed for their team because he knew he could do the job. Maybe attraction had been a factor, but Zed didn't think it had been his primary consideration. All that crap with their sickness had just pushed it to the forefront, brought issues, emotions to the surface that had been long buried. Riff had treated him like a man, not an object of contempt, and how he treated him had not changed when he suspected he was innocent. Why the change now?

He could hear Riff muttering to himself in a low, angry voice but at least he was staying in the suite. The pressure increased, the pain in his temple spreading out to stab the back of his brain. Suddenly shaking, Zed rested his hands on the console, trying to steady himself. The pain became a drumming, and his heart rate sped up to match.

Zed clutched his head with a groan. Noyes was somewhere near. Flashes of memory filtered through the mental barrier he'd erected to hide behind. A long, slender form. A crawling chaos of lashing limbs. Noyes was pitting them against each other, studying to see who would strike first.

"Riff. Get on the transport."

Riff turned toward him, rage flashing in his eyes. "I knew it. I fucking knew it."

"You're so goddamned stubborn." Movement flickered out of the corner of his right eye. Zed turned, tracking the movement, the slight dark figure with laughing eyes. He knew those eyes. That laugh. He'd heard it again and again during the madness. He'd seen the truth when Noyes had touched him, and the truth was pure, primal, ugly emotion. "Noyes is here."

Riff straightened, and the anger in his eyes disappeared. He backed up, touching Zed on his shoulder. Zed drew his gun, training it on Noyes, and he vanished.

Hannah appeared, her eyes wide and guileless. "Uncle Zed?" She held up hands red and wet. "Riff hurt me."

Zed lowered the gun and looked at Riff, who edged back, his eyes widening. "What did you say to him?" Riff snapped, glaring at Hannah.

Zed's hand shook and bile burned his throat. Riff had been the cause of every misfortune, pain, worry, and injury he'd had since he'd met him. Riff found Noyes, being where he shouldn't have been. Riff insisted on bringing the bastard back, releasing the plague on everybody. He'd baited the captain, Barboza. He thought he was so fucking smart when he was just bringing ruin to them all.

"Don't say one word to her. Don't even look at her," Zed snarled.

"Look at who?" Riff's brows drew together. "There's no one there but Noyes. He's fucking with your mind."

The pounding in Zed's head drummed louder, the noise of violence and lust. Riff took a step toward Hannah, and Zed raised the gun. This was wrong. The wrongness screamed at him, and Zed tried to fight it. "Don't move, Riff, I swear to God, don't fucking twitch. You go near her and…."

Riff froze and then turned his head slowly toward Zed. He looked at him with eyes suddenly old and tired. "You want to kill me?" The gun wavered, and the pain in Zed's head increased, stabbing, tearing. Riff stepped closer to him and grabbed Zed's hand, steadying it. He pointed the gun to his temple. "It's okay, Zed," Riff said in a voice both sad and relieved. "It's okay. Just do it."

A deluge of emotions, images, and memories flooded Zed. Riff's compassion for his fellow prisoners, his grief over his fallen teammates, the tenderness he felt toward Zed, which he was so desperately afraid to show and feel. Riff hadn't stolen the medical supplies out of greed. He'd rescued Noyes because it had been the right thing to do. He'd carry the guilt and grief for his loved ones' deaths with him for the rest of his life. And despite his words, he did castigate himself for the murders he'd committed. He was a medic, first and foremost. His innate gentleness had been buried, smothered, starting with his years as a field medic in an endless war.

Zed tried to pull his hand back, stricken by the bleak look in Riff's eyes, but Riff wouldn't release his hand. "Zed, please," he said, his voice raw.

This man was used to all kinds of pain, the kind that he craved and the kind that he'd internalized. He carried emotional and mental scars as long-lasting and vivid as the whip marks on his body. Zed could learn to give Riff the kind of pain he needed, but he refused to add to the rest.

"I'm sorry," Zed whispered.

Riff nodded, closing his eyes as his hand fell away from Zed's. "Lead me from darkness to light, from death to immortality." Riff whispered the prayer under his breath. Zed kissed him hard on the lips, steeling himself for what he had to do next. He sensed Riff's shock, his confusion, and then the hot wash of his emotions regarding Zed, terrifying and tender and heated.

Zed shot Hannah. It was one thing to know intellectually that the little girl was only another hallucination, but his heart and memories weren't buying it. She must've sensed his intent because she dodged. The bullet slammed into her hip, and she fell back with a shriek that tore into Zed's ears. He'd nailed Noyes, but it wasn't a killing shot. She sprang back up in a crouch, watching them with glittering eyes.

The gun flew out of Zed's hand as an unseen mental force ripped it from him. It spun away, coming to rest near the main hatchway. "Is that what you did to Quinet? Made him so tired that all he could think of was to end it?" Zed demanded. "Are you doing the same thing to Riff?"

Hannah shrugged, her eyes unnatural, alien. They didn't match her face. "The feelings are already there. All of those foul corners of your fragile minds that you try so desperately to hide and lock away. I bring them out into the open. What you do with those feelings and urges is entirely up to you. That's the fascinating part."

"What the fuck are you?" Riff said harshly.

"Wouldn't you just die to know?" The gaze shifted between Riff and Zed. "Tell him, Zed. Tell him what you saw when I touched you."

Zed clutched his head. No, he didn't want to remember. He'd never been so afraid. Not when he'd woken up strapped down with his head swathed in bandages. Not when he'd first been alone with Noyes. Not when Vidal had offered him up to Barboza. Not even when Vidal had stood above him, knife in hand with Zed knowing he was going to take his eye. Nothing compared to the terror that seized his heart now, threatening to stop it cold. The fear thrummed in him. A living creature with starving eyes, coming for him.

"He's not human, Riff. What we're seeing isn't what he really looks like. He's a nightmare come alive. An avatar for something impossibly old that we cannot hope to understand and remain sane. Alien isn't even right, it's something more."

"I've never encountered bonds like the ones between you two or with the rest of your team. Even in your madness and hallucination, you didn't go after each other. And you, Zed, you have a rare ability. You access a part of your brain that most don't, and you've gotten stronger since I touched you. I want to study you longer. If you two come away with me, I'll let Josephina Tuputala live."

Hannah vanished, and Noyes took her place with no apparent sign of injury, though he was careful to keep his body angled to protect his wounded side. His greedy gaze snared them both. Zed's instincts screamed at him to reject the offer, but if he did and Tuputala died as a result, he wasn't sure Riff would ever forgive him.

"No deal," Riff said flatly. "No rewards. I don't trust any of your offers. If Tuputala were still alive, she'd be here. We were locked up long enough for Vidal to go looking for her. I don't know why, but you seem to need our acceptance, and I'm not giving you that."

Those cold, inhuman eyes turned on Zed. "I'm with Riff, no deal."

"Then I have no use for you anymore."

Zed gasped as the drums returned, pounding in his head, his whole body, driving out reason and fear. He fell to his knees, vaguely aware of Riff next to him, screaming, his hands pressed over his temples as if he was trying to squeeze out the sound while trapped in a vise. Zed struggled to move toward Noyes, emotions crashing through him like discordant cymbals. Rage and lust. Fantasies bombarded him, cruel and sickening, all the things he could do if he'd just stop fighting.

He glared at Noyes, at all the images flickering around him. People he longed to tear apart, flay alive. Heller. Barboza. Vidal. Tuputala stumbling through the hatchway.

Riff grabbed Zed's leg, yanking him back, fists pummeling into Zed's bruised body. "Riff, no! It's me." The punches faltered.

Riff stared at Zed, his face screwed up in an expression of agony as he lifted his fists again. More images flickered around them, faster now. Flaubert crawling toward him with her head caved in. Barboza with a needle and thread. Tuputala hefting her gun and blowing out Noyes's brains.

Zed gasped again as the drums stopped, the pressure on his head cleared. He stared at Tuputala, waiting for her to vanish too. But she remained, her hair a wild mess, favoring one of her legs as she leaned against the bulkhead. His gaze shifted to Noyes, ichor puddling around him.

"Is that really you?" he asked, looking back at Tuputala.

"Who the fuck else would I be?" Tuputala growled. She leveled the gun at Noyes and emptied the clip into him. "If you're done asking stupid questions, we'd better get to the transport."

Riff rocked back and forth, shaking his head. "It's over? Is it really over?"

Zed crawled over to him on shaky limbs and wrapped his arms around Riff. "Yeah, it's really over." He kissed Riff's forehead, forced his hands down, and made him meet his gaze. "Let's get out of here."

Riff and Zed helped each other to their feet. He felt battered all over and inside out. Tuputala and Riff didn't look much better. Zed unlocked the bay hatchway, and they stumbled to the transport. Zed locked his gaze on the small ship like it was a gateway to salvation.

Riff and Tuputala slid behind the helm as Zed entered the code to open the main doors. They were so close. The need to escape thrummed, cutting off thought, and Zed forced himself to calm down and make sure the shield was up so everything wouldn't get sucked into space with them. One mistake and they could all die right at the moment of escape.

"Engine looks good, coordinates are set," Tuputala said, fingers flying over the console. "Good job, Jakobsen."

"You too. You are one badass lady." Zed clapped her shoulder. "I'm glad you're back."

Tuputala's hands stopped moving. "Quinet?"

"Gone," Riff said in a hoarse voice.

Zed squeezed his shoulder as Riff fired the engines. The transport lifted and skimmed lightly out of the bay doors. "If you've laid the coordinates in right, we should rendezvous with the captain's transport within an hour," Tuputala said as she sat back.

"I laid them in right," Zed replied. "Run a scan. Our sensors should pick it up at this range."

Riff leaned forward and brought up the monitor. Moments later it beeped as it picked up the other transport. "It looks safe and sound. She's sitting pretty, waiting for us to collect her."

Tension in the small cabin ebbed. Zed leaned down and flicked on the rear monitor. The prison ship spun in the vacuum, getting smaller as the distance between them increased. And then it was gone. Riff drew in a deep sigh of relief, sat back, and reached up to clasp Zed's hand. Zed soaked in the warm wash of his emotions, the relief and lingering fear, the comfort he got in Zed's nearness.

He wrapped his arms around Riff and leaned down to whisper in his ear, "All that you're feeling, it's like that for me too."

Riff glanced up at him, his eyes softening, then going sad as he touched Zed's left cheek. "Yeah?"

Zed laid his cheek against Riff's hand. "Yeah."

Epilogue

Beep! Beep! Beep!

The high-pitched alert of the computer jerked Riff out of a nightmare-plagued sleep. He froze, his eyes still shut as he tried to separate dream from reality. Zed was behind him, his arm draped over Riff, his warmth a balm for Riff's racing heart. They were on the transport. That welcome reality sank in. Riff sat up with a yawn as Zed stirred on the makeshift pallet next to him.

"Wha…?" he asked in a sleep-drugged voice.

Tuputala propped herself up on her own pallet in the tiny room they'd converted into sleeping quarters. "That had better be good news, or I'm going back to sleep."

"I'll check it." Riff squeezed Zed's hand as he rose. The last several weeks of uneventful travel had given them all a chance to recover from their wounds, but they were still on edge, and it had been difficult to get any restful sleep. He hoped being planetside and having a change in their routine would help snap them out of the horror that continued to haunt them.

He scrubbed a hand over his face, rubbing the sleep out of his eyes as he made his way over to the cockpit. The monitors continued to flash and beep, announcing the proximity of a likely system. Riff flipped the alarm off, sat down, and pulled up the details, trying not to get his hopes up. The last two systems they'd explored hadn't panned out, but as he scanned the data, his pulse jumped with renewed optimism.

"Hey, you two, I think I have something here," Riff called back, excitement threading his voice.

The rush of footsteps announced their arrival. "What is it?" Tuputala demanded as she slipped into the copilot's seat.

"Did you find a place for us?" Zed demanded from behind him.

Riff brought up the data onto the bigger screen so they both could see it. "Sadir, small planet with its own established government, so no damned Marine garrison." That had been the problem with the last two systems they'd checked. Riff knew his fellow Marines. They were a suspicious lot, for good reason, and they tended to dig into strangers' pasts until they uncovered what they wanted. He'd had no hope of staying under their notice for long.

"Looks like a good mix of urban and agriculture," Tuputala added. "Not so small that we'd stand out and not so big that they'd have a heavy stake in the Planetary Councils and Courts. Their shipping and commerce seems to be robust enough that they have plenty of people coming and going."

"They're a pretty new government. Are they looking for settlers?" Zed asked, leaning over Riff's shoulder.

"The usual. Experts in their fields, families, singles looking to start families," Riff replied.

"Shouldn't be too hard to find work. Even if we moved out to one of the smaller communities, people always need medics and mechanics," Zed said.

"Did you get the work done on our new IDs?" Tuputala asked with a worried glance.

"Yeah, along with all the appropriate licenses if we choose to stay. Thank Zed for the hacks. They helped immensely and so did your templates." Riff tapped on the controls, bringing the transport out of its skim cycle as they neared the system. The stars became normal, some pinpricks, others blazing orbs of light against the utter dark. "The planet's not that far from the Deneb Shipyards, relatively speaking." Riff turned in his chair toward Zed. "Is that going to be a problem?"

Zed shook his head, the makeshift patch over his left eye giving him a rakish, dangerous appearance. "Shouldn't be. Most people from the shipyards went to the spaceport instead of heading to out-of-system planets. Heller and his wife preferred the luxury cruises or visits to the capital. I don't see any of them visiting a younger settlement."

Hellar's wife, Zed's sister…. Her memory still caused Zed pain. Riff could sense that without Zed having to say a word. Zed carried his emotions in his stance and the look in his eye. Over the last few weeks, Riff found he could read Zed almost as well as Zed could read him.

"Besides, we might not stay," Tuputala said. "We're just looking at options and a good, long rest. If there are no Marines, we have a little breathing room."

Riff started to weigh those options against their skills, the money they'd have available to them, and what they each thought they wanted. Being confined together as they'd been had left them with little to do other than dream, and talk, and grow closer. Whatever they did decide, it would include all three of them.

"It'll be my first time planetside," Zed said, cutting into Riff's thoughts as Tuputala laid in a course for the planet. "What should I expect?"

"There's going to be a lot more light, so you might want to consider a hat to shade your eyes until we can all get some glasses. Sadir's primary is bright. Gravity will be a bit higher than you're used to too." Riff shot Zed a quick grin as he thought of all the different sounds and smells of planetside, the way a breeze felt. He loved being on a ship and traveling, but it was a blessed release to get a chance to put his feet on the ground on occasion. "It'll be amazing. There's really not much I can say, you have to see it for yourself."

Riff checked the chronometer, did the calculation, and smiled. Back home the festival of Diwali was just beginning. The thought filled him with many happy memories. After everything they'd been through, he considered that an auspicious sign. He'd have to talk Zed into helping him decorate the transport with lights. He hadn't had a chance to celebrate since he'd been imprisoned, and now he looked forward to it and the start of a new life.

"Well, I know what I'm going to do. I'm going to the bathhouses. Then I'm getting laid. Then I'm going back to the bathhouses. Then I'm sleeping for a solid twenty-four hours, even if I have to drink myself into insensibility to do it. And God help anyone who tries to wake me up." Tuputala turned a ferocious glare on the two men next to her.

Riff and Zed exchanged amused glances. "Actually, that sounds like a pretty fucking perfect plan," Zed replied, rubbing his hand through the scruff of his hair. "I want one night of sleep where I'm not dreaming of being chased. We could all use that."

Riff touched Zed's hand. They'd all had the nightmares, but Zed had them the worst. Whatever he'd seen when he'd touched Noyes had left a mark. None of them were unscathed, and the mental scars lingered. Riff relived all those moments of helplessness when he hadn't been able to save his teammates, to save Zed. He remembered how close he had been to giving up at the end…. Sometimes he could still feel the cold metal of the gun as he begged Zed to shoot him.

But Zed didn't give in, and in the end Riff hadn't given up. They'd survived. Riff shook off the bad memories. He tried living in the past, and it had almost killed him. Dwelling on regrets and guilt didn't work. He'd learned that lesson. By some miracle they were alive, and he refused to take away from the elation of this moment.

He touched the *tulsi mala* that sat once again on his wrist thanks to Zed. "Yes, we deserve a long break. Then we can decide what we're going to do next."

The planet grew bigger as they neared, a vast orb of oceans and landmasses. Riff tore his gaze away from the view and concentrated on the information before him. Sadir had a new government and was heavily involved in the trade routes that intersected throughout all the known systems. Both were good indicators that the black market was healthy. Riff expected a payload from selling the captain's transport. As nice as it was, it wouldn't do for long-term deep-space travel if they chose that option. And thanks to the captain's paranoia, they'd found a sweet stash of credits, enough to tide them all over for a bit while they decided what to do.

With that kind of money, they could easily set themselves up on Sadir if they wanted or buy a ship of their own, one in need of a little work Zed and Tuputala could easily handle. Riff hadn't mentioned the idea to the others yet, but he was thinking more often of setting up his own salvage gig. He knew the work. He knew the contacts, who and where he could sell what they gleaned. They could get rich even with a small operation.

"We're being hailed," Tuputala said, her voice tense. The transport shuddered as they broke the atmospheric barrier and then stabilized.

"Give them our new IDs," Riff ordered, still scanning the rush of data. "Ask for permission to land in… Svyatilishche. It's almost morning there."

A few moments later, Tuputala sank back, a broad smile crossing her face. "We're clear to land. Hot fucking damn!" Tears shone in her eyes as she turned and caught Riff, then Zed in a rib-cracking hug.

Excitement, the release of stress had Riff's hands trembling as he took over piloting. Zed squeezed his shoulder in silent support. The transport flew over a region of lakes and long dark green belts of trees.

The city they were aiming for lay in the western territory and rose on the horizon, a rambling, sprawling chaos of greening terraces and sky-raking buildings. The spaceport lay on the outskirts, and Riff angled the ship in that direction as the coordinates for their bay popped up.

"There it is." Zed leaned over, stabbing his finger toward the array of hangar doors set into a tall hillside. One set had opened, the landing lights around it twinkling in the early-morning light. The bright mood in the cockpit chased back all the shadows. Here was a chance for all of them, a new life, a new beginning. His thoughts kept returning to that idea of restarting and moving on.

Riff slowed the transport, and minutes later they were setting down. Tuputala let out a whoop of delight and was out of her seat before Riff had a chance to power the ship down.

"Don't wait up for me, boys. I'll check in in a few days."

"Don't forget to bring a commlink, and don't spend all your damn credits in one day," Riff called out after her, swiveling his chair around.

"Aye-aye, boss man, you've got it," came a muffled reply. "Try not to bang each other up too much while I'm gone. Keep the bruises to acceptable levels." Riff heard the sound of the transport's ramp lowering, and then she was gone.

"She's going to be back the moment she realizes she forgot her new IDs and her allotment of the credits," Riff said with an exasperated look toward the rear of the transport.

Zed laughed, scraping his hand through Riff's hair before leaning down to kiss the top of his head. Riff leaned into him, wrapping his arms loosely around Zed's waist. They were here. He could hardly believe it.

Zed returned his embrace, and Riff closed his eyes. He'd worried that his feelings for Zed, Zed's feelings for him, would have been a lie. Once the danger was over and boredom set in, the stress of being confined in close quarters, surely that tenderness and heat would've faded, but it hadn't. Zed understood him, maybe a little too well, and Riff knew Zed, the good and the bad. The last weeks together had proved their initial attraction hadn't been a lie.

"You are thinking some pretty deep thoughts for a man who should be running around in a state of jubilant glee. Don't we have our own credits to burn through?" Zed asked.

Riff tipped his head back, studying Zed's face as his heart beat faster, and a sweet warmth filled his heart. "How do you know what I'm thinking?" he teased.

"I have no idea what you're thinking," Zed said, lacing his fingers behind Riff's neck. "But I can sense you thinking from ten feet away."

"Mmm." Riff rose and drew him closer as Zed's hazel eye gleamed. "But you can still tell what I'm feeling."

"Loud and clear." A soft smile crossed Zed's lips. "I love you too."

"You bastard." Riff leaned in to kiss him. "You took my words. I was going to say it… eventually."

"You were taking too long. I'm an impatient man." Zed kissed him again, deeper, sweeter. "You tell me when you're ready. It's enough that I know, and now you know too."

Yeah, now Riff knew too, and it filled him with a sense of security he had not felt in a long time.

Zed broke away and captured Riff's hand, his face bright with renewed excitement. "Come on, you're the expert here. I fully expect you to show me what's so exciting about being planetside."

"I think our first stop should be some new clothes and some real food." Riff was dying for something that didn't come out of a protein pack or a rehydrated meal. "Then maybe we can find a quiet, comfortable place for just the two of us."

The corner of Zed's mouth quirked in a wicked smile that made Riff ache with need and want. The lack of privacy on the transport had gotten old fast. Zed caught his hand. "You ready?"

Riff laughed and followed Zed out. He had a hunch there were some interesting times ahead. "Ready."

MARGUERITE LABBE has often been called both Trouble and Sunshine by those who know her. She's not sure how she manages to make both those nicknames work together, but apparently she does. She's a New Hampshire girl who married an Alabama boy, an Air Force brat who has somehow managed to settle herself firmly in Southern Maryland, with one overgrown son and two crazy cats.

Marguerite loves to spin tales that cross genre lines, where stubborn men build lifelong ties of loyalty, friendship, and family no matter the odds thrown against them, and where love is found in unexpected places. She has won the Rainbow Award for Historical Romance with Fae Sutherland, as well as the Rainbow Award for Paranormal and the Rainbow Romance Award for Excellence, also in Paranormal.

When she's not working hard on writing new stories, she spends her time reading novels of all genres, enjoying role-playing and tabletop games with her friends, and helping out her husband with Apocrypha Comics Studio.

Website: www.margueritelabbe.com
Twitter: @MargueriteLabbe
Facebook: www.facebook.com/marguerite.labbe.3
E-mail: margueritelabbe@gmail.com

DEADWORLD
This Is
How It Ends
NICK WILGUS
DEADWORLD

Deadworld: Book One

High school juniors Billy Gunn and Rory Wilder return from a weekend camping trip to find a mysterious plague has wiped out their small town of Port Moss, Mississippi. The question of why is only the beginning—especially when the dead refuse to stay dead.

Figuring out what happened is job one for Billy and Rory. But complications quickly set in. Not only do the dead rise, but a freak storm threatens torrential downpours as winter looms. And enormous ships appear in the sky, bringing with them alien visitors with technology never seen before.

Left without electricity and modern conveniences, Billy and Rory must figure out a way to navigate horrific zombies, advanced alien life forms, and apocalyptic storms, as well as deal with their growing love for each other in a world gone mad.

www.dsppublications.com

www.ingramcontent.com/pod-product-compliance
Lightning Source LLC
Chambersburg PA
CBHW070505120726
47910CB00003B/1129

9 781635 333534